FLASHPOINT

A Frank Marsh Novel

FLASHPOINT

✦ ✦ ✦

CHARLIE SPILLERS

For Ella Kate Spillers

PART ONE

CHAPTER 1

Frank Marsh was hurt and exhausted. In the night's impenetrable darkness, he staggered blindly through the jungle, desperate to elude pursuers. His energy was depleted, and only adrenaline had kept him going. But now that was gone, and he was crashing. His legs felt heavy, and his mind wandered, unable to focus. On the verge of collapsing, he needed to hide for the night. He vaguely realized it would be best to hide in thick underbrush where noise would give away anyone approaching. He stumbled into a thicket, knelt, and crawled until it became too dense to go further. Lying on his side, he rested his head on an arm. Frank's mind clouded, and everything went black.

Sometime during the night, he woke to the sounds of rustling brush and men moving nearby. He raised his head and strained to hear. They were close and coming closer. He froze as the sounds of movement stopped just a few feet away. Frank heard a man's heavy breathing in the silence, an animal on the hunt. He tried to still his own breath. Then he heard a sharp clink of metal against metal. Frank cringed, waiting for an explosion of gunfire. Long moments hung in silence. A shiver raced up his spine, and his heart pounded.

Events leading to his predicament began months earlier, on an idyllic day in Washington, D.C. Early spring brought brilliant blue skies, graceful white sails on the Potomac, and budding trees promising green landscapes and fragrant pink blossoms. The air was fresh, filled with renewing life and rising optimism.

Bill Nelson, an assistant FBI director, didn't give a damn about the seasonal change. Oblivious to the enchanting backdrop outside his office, he continued reading the President's Daily Brief (PDB), a summary of high-level intelligence on national security matters produced for the president. Nelson's brow furrowed as he delved deeper into the briefing and began gnawing at his lips with mounting concern.

While sanitized versions of the PDB were shared daily with select national security officials, including Nelson, his unease stemmed from his dual role as the head of FBI Legal Attaches, or "Legats," stationed in foreign countries. One particular Top Secret/SCI passage troubled him.

"According to Britain's MI-6, a source had been contacted last month by Middle Eastern terrorists in Europe who wanted to acquire a Stinger anti-aircraft missile to bring down a commercial aircraft. However, the terrorists recently indicated their plans are on hold because it could interfere with 'something bigger.' The source has lost contact with the terrorists. Despite these developments, CIA assesses the probability of a significant terror attack in the near future as minimal."

Nelson recalled vague intelligence reports that Hamas had recently asked Iran for a years-long period free of terror attacks because it was planning something big in Gaza in two or three years and wanted to lull the Israelis into a false sense of security. Launching a terror attack now would interfere with those long-term Hamas plans.

And although the CIA's reasoning in dismissing this specific MI-6 warning was logical—based on a single source, unknown reliability, and lack of corroborating indications—Bill Nelson couldn't shake his gut feeling that something was brewing. But what? And when and where? He made a mental note to alert FBI Legats stationed in Europe.

Nelson wondered if Marwan, the notorious leader of Iran's Quds Force Assassination and Sabotage Unit 400, might be planning something again. The thought of Marwan triggered memories of Frank Marsh, an FBI agent assigned to the CIA-FBI joint counterterror unit, and Kathy Foster, a White House National Security Council staffer. Six months earlier, Marwan had lured the couple to Greece and tortured Foster to discover what they knew about a suspected high-level Iranian source within the American government. Marsh had rescued Foster and wounded Marwan in the process. An incoming call interrupted Nelson. But if the CIA is not worried, maybe I shouldn't be either, he thought as he picked up the phone.

While Nelson was worrying about the potential losses in a mass terror attack, Frank Marsh was thinking about one loss. On that peaceful morning, Frank Marsh knelt on a knee at one of the 400,000 white marble gravestones in Arlington National Cemetery. He made it a point each year to visit the grave of each Marine he had lost in Iraq years before when he led young men as a Marine officer.

This grave was special. It was Lance Corporal Smith, USMC. "Smitty," his cheerful, nineteen-year-old radio man. Frank spent more life-changing time in Iraq with Smitty than with anyone else. He was with Frank nearly every moment, good and bad, until Smitty jerked back and fell from a bullet, the radio receiver clutched in his dying hand. Frank frantically tried to stop the flow of blood, but Smitty's lifeblood ebbed out until he was sightless. Desperately needing to call for air support, Frank worked the radio off Smitty's body and pried the receiver out of his lifeless hand. Frank would have to grieve later.

Even years later, some memories are too dreadful to touch. Revisited, they sear the mind like a hand touching a hot stove. Frank tried to keep them distant, but they always flooded back at Arlington. He touched Smitty's headstone and whispered, "Smitty." Frank rose and wiped his eyes.

The following week, Marwan was on Frank Marsh's mind as he maneuvered through heavy D.C. traffic and across Key Bridge to a sprawling four-story building surrounded by acres of manicured lawns. It looked like a typical corporate headquarters near Mclean, Virginia, except it was isolated and hidden from the street by dense cordons of evergreen trees. Any curious onlooker venturing down the long, winding driveway would discover that the building was protected by a high-security perimeter fence and a guarded gate. Everyone inside had security clearances.

After parking and going through security, Frank went up to the third floor and his office within the joint CIA-FBI terrorism unit. He signed on to his computer and searched for the latest intelligence report mentioning Marwan. He discovered one dated several days earlier.

TOP SECRET/SCI/BLG616

Through voice recognition with an 82% probability, the NSA identified a call involving MARWAN, the head of Iran's Quds Force Unit 400, responsible for sabotage and assassinations. A limited intercept made a more certain probability unattainable.

Marwan received a call in Tehran from an unidentified subject who called from Angola, Africa. Only portions were intercepted. Translation follows.

UNSUB: I had to use this phone because the other phone (Unintelligible (UI)).

MARWAN: You fool! You (UI) call on a (UI).

UNSUB: (UI) couldn't wait. The next shipment is ready. One of my men died (UI) need to move the (UI) quickly (UI) a ship (UI).

MARWAN: (UI) materials on the way. After they are processed, ship everything (UI) and then abandon the camp (UI).

UNSUB: (UI)

END CALL

TOP SECRET/SCI/BLG616

Frank took the report to the deputy unit chief, Tom Dawson. "This needs to be followed up," Frank said, sitting across the desk while Dawson read. When he finished, Dawson looked at Frank and sighed.

"Frank, I know you have a personal interest in Marwan, but we get hundreds of leads like this daily. And a voice probability of 82% means it may not have even been Marwan on the call." Frank started to speak, but Dawson plunged ahead. "Plus, the Iranians, Russians, and others gin up deceptive SIGINT to overwhelm us so we can't find the real stuff. Only the most promising leads can be followed up—and this isn't one of them. Hell, you *know* that, Frank."

"But anything that could involve Marwan and Unit 400 is bad news. They must have something going on in Africa. Think about what they said on the call: a camp, someone died, a shipment, and a ship. Whatever it is, it may be completed soon. I thought if you asked for it to be..."

"No, Frank, no way," Dawson said, shaking his head. "This is too flimsy. Just conjecture. They won't do anything. And this is not enough for me to call in favors. I'm sorry."

A week later, Frank was again reminded about Marwan, this time in the middle of the night. Muffled sobs woke him. It took him a few moments to realize Kathy had cried out in her sleep from another nightmare. He snuggled against her back and put his arm around her. Frank gently kissed the back of her neck, careful not to wake her. "It's alright, baby," he whispered. "I'm here. You're safe."

"Frank," she whimpered, half-waking. Frank continued reassuring her in a calming voice, lulling her into a peaceful sleep. With his chest pressed against her back, he could feel the slow, steady rhythm of her breathing. To make her relax even more, Frank took a deep breath and sighed; moments later, he felt her sigh deeply, an automatic response to his body. Our bodies are in an intimate rhythm, he thought.

Despite their efforts to maintain normalcy, Marwan loomed in the background of their daily lives. Kathy's blue eyes still welled with tears at the sight of the scars on her body, and she felt self-conscious about a faint scar on her cheek. Although the scar was barely noticeable, she had let her blonde hair grow out, hoping to hide it. On the surface, Frank appeared unchanged. He looked like his old self, a lean and athletic six-footer with dark brown hair flopped in a short curl over his forehead. But his lively blue eyes would cringe whenever he thought about Kathy's ordeal.

As Kathy slept, Frank thought about her suffering and difficult recovery—painful skin grafts and troublesome infections. He recalled his own grueling road to recovery after being wounded in Iraq. Parts of his body had been ripped, torn, and swollen. For months, his leg and shoulder throbbed incessantly with excruciating pain. Day and night, his face tightened, his jaw clenched, and, at times, tears welled up in his eyes. He winced, cringed, and focused on making it from one moment to the next without crying out. Frank would grunt and force himself not to complain. But throughout each night, he moaned or quietly whimpered like a hurt animal. "I'm not a victim," he repeatedly reminded himself. "I'm a warrior."

The pain was merciless, he reflected. It didn't matter how strong or clever you were, how young or old, how caring or kind. It didn't let up because you loved or were loved. Severe, grinding pain hammered him relentlessly. Pain meds didn't help, and sleepless nights wore him down. But after days, weeks, and months, a day arrived when the pain finally stopped, and it felt so good not to hurt. Looking back, Frank realized the ordeal had seared a lesson into his soul. No matter how bad things become, you can endure.

A week later, Kathy cried out in her sleep again. Lifting his head from the pillow, Frank saw her curled on her right side, moaning. He snuggled against her back and put his arm around her. He softly kissed the back of her neck, careful not to wake her. "It's alright, baby," he whispered. "I've got you. I'm here."

"Frank," she whimpered, half-waking. Frank kissed the back of her neck again, reassuring her in a calming voice, finally lulling her back to sleep.

The next morning, Frank turned off the alarm before it sounded and let Kathy sleep late. He made breakfast and then woke her with a soft kiss. "Come on, Beautiful," he said, sitting on the edge of the bed. "Breakfast is ready."

Kathy's eyes flickered open. "What? What time is it?" She glanced at the clock beside the bed and quickly started rising. "Oh, no. I'll be late for work. I've got to..."

"Hold on," Frank said, holding her shoulder. "Slow down. The most important thing you have to do is to get well. Okay? Remember, you have a doctor's appointment this morning. You'll go in late at work because of that."

"But Frank, I..."

"Look, they understand what you've been through. It's okay if you're occasionally late. You have to let the grafts heal. And that means you need to get plenty of rest and my TLC. Right?"

Kathy smiled and pulled his head down for a lingering kiss.

"You keep that up," Frank said, smiling, "and I'm going to be late for work too."

After her medical appointment, Kathy arrived late for work at the National Security Council offices in the Old Executive Building near the White House. She felt cool looks as she made her way to her office.

Sitting at her desk, Kathy stared at her computer and felt overwhelmed. And guilty. I'm missing too much work because of the skin grafts and trauma counseling, she thought. It's hard to keep up with the workload, and some days, I'm in a stupor from nightmares and lack of sleep. People resent me for being unable to work full-time and coming in late. I'm losing control of my life, she thought with despair.

Seeing the scars every time she looked in a mirror brought back the horror and pain of being tortured by Marwan. She was helpless and in hell. The memories kept sparking nightmares. And when Frank touched her, she occasionally jumped or cringed from his touch. She did it much less now, but it still happened. Frank had been understanding, but she knew it was hard on him—especially when she was depressed and withdrawn. Maybe if... The intercom buzzed. "Ms. Smith wants to see you in her office," Kathy took a deep breath to clear her head and walked to Smith's office, feeling dread. It was never good when Smith summoned someone. Smith seemed intent on abusing the staff and finding minor reasons to discipline people.

Seated at her desk, Linda Smith peered over her glasses. "Shut the door and have a seat, Foster," she said curtly. Smith's deputy, Mark Yates, was seated to the right of the desk with a notepad in his lap and a pen poised over it. As she sat down, Kathy nodded at Yates and received an uncomfortable look in return. Kathy knew Yates was as unhappy as everyone else with how Smith treated people.

Smith was brought into the NSC by the new White House administration, which had come into office a few months earlier. A former university administrator, Smith was a political appointee. She distrusted career employees no matter how knowledgeable they were. She resisted national security assessments that didn't conform to her own views of the world.

Smith cleared her throat. "Foster, because of your health, we have tried to tolerate your unexpected absences and frequent tardiness for work."

"Yes, Ma'am. And I appreciate that," Kathy said with a knot in her stomach. "I always try to make it up by not taking breaks, working through lunch, and doing work at home."

"All we have is your word for that," Smith said coldly. Kathy's face reddened, and she felt as if she had been slapped. "I think you are taking advantage of our leniency, Foster. And..."

"But, but I'm still having skin grafts," Kathy stammered, shaking her head. "I don't have any control over..."

Smith held up a hand. "That's enough," she snapped. "I didn't bring you in here to argue. This is your official notice of unsatisfactory performance. It will be documented in your performance evaluation report," she declared with a sideways nod toward Yates, who was writing on a pad.

"But, I..."

"That's all, Foster." Smith nodded toward the door. "Get back to your work."

* * *

"What's wrong?" Frank said to her that night.

"Nothing," Kathy said, bending down to put dishes in the dishwasher.

"Something's wrong," Frank said, pulling her up and in his arms, facing him. Their eyes met. "Tell me. What is it? Flashbacks again?"

Biting her bottom lip, she shook her head and looked down.

"No, something's wrong. Tell me," Frank said, holding Kathy's chin and tilting her upward to look at him. "Tell me. Please."

After a long pause and a deep breath, she told him about Smith accusing her of taking advantage of her injuries and giving her an official reprimand. She confessed to Frank about feeling overwhelmed at work because she missed so much time for skin grafts and medical appointments. Kathy buried her head in his shoulder, and between sobs, she told him about feeling guilty because she still occasionally cringed when he touched her.

"You try to cover it up, Frank," she cried, her voice choking, "but I can see the hurt in your eyes when I pull away from you." Her body shook as she cried. He held her tight and stroked the back of her head. When her tears finally subsided, he ran her a hot bath and then put her to bed, softly kissing and caressing her until she fell into a deep sleep.

After Kathy was asleep, Frank quietly got out of bed, careful not to wake her. Putting on a robe, he went into the living room, turned on a lamp, and poured a drink. He stood at the window staring in the distance, frustrated he couldn't relieve her worries. But perhaps I can take care of one worry, Frank thought. His face hardened. When he went to bed, he was unable to sleep. Surges of anger kept him awake.

Two days later, when Kathy arrived at work, Mark Yates, the deputy unit supervisor, called a rare meeting of everyone in the office. They gathered in the conference room, filled seats around the long polished oak table, and the seats ringing the wall. A few had to stand. Yates stood at the head of the table. Smith was nowhere to be seen.

"Thank you all for coming," Yates said when the room hushed. "I have something important to say." All eyes were fastened on him, everyone expectant, wondering. "Ms. Smith is no longer with us. She's been transferred to the Commerce Department. I'll be the acting unit supervisor for the time being." The people crowded in the room greeted the announcement with palpable relief, murmurs, and smiles.

Yates paused until the room was quiet again. "Kathy Foster, would you please come here," Yates said, motioning for her to stand beside him. Kathy hesitantly rose and walked to Yates' side. He greeted her with a nod.

"Most of you may not know of Ms. Foster's background," Yates declared, "and why she has to work part-time and sometimes has come in later than usual. And you may not know that she was kidnapped and tortured while serving our nation." Yates looked around the room at each face and then at Kathy standing beside him. Yates smiled at her and then addressed the room again. "You may not know what a true hero this woman is. Well, I'm going to tell you."

Kathy's eyes glistened as Yates talked. "What I'm about to tell you is classified. You may not repeat it to anyone. Last year, Kathy Foster and FBI agent Frank Marsh disrupted the terrorist bombing of a casino, saving hundreds and probably thousands of lives. They discovered that a high-level traitor in the US government was tipping off the Iranian unit behind the casino bombing. Ms Foster and Marsh were getting close to identifying the traitor, a man code-named 'Magician.' The Iranians lured the couple to Greece to find out what they knew and then kill them. Kathy Foster was kidnapped and tortured, suffering burns on much of her body. Marsh rescued her. While torturing her, the Iranians revealed the identity of the traitor. Later, when Marsh confronted him, Magician committed suicide. Ms Foster continues to undergo painful skin grafts and trauma counseling. That's why Ms Foster works part-time, and that's why she sometimes has to come in late to work."

When Yates finished, the room was still and hushed except for a few sniffles and low sobs. He looked at Kathy and motioned toward her. The group burst into applause.

Late that night, Frank lay in bed in the dark with Kathy snuggled against him. She was sleeping soundly. One of her legs was thrown across his thighs, her head nestled on his shoulder, and an arm rested on his chest. Her hair lay soft against his skin. Frank savored the feel of her breast pressed against the side of his chest and the rising and falling of her steady breathing. He resisted the urge to turn toward her and slide down and take her breast in his mouth. She needs comfort and tender care right now, Frank thought.

He smiled, thinking about seeing her come home from work. She was excitedly telling him about Yates calling everyone together and explaining Kathy's injuries and her ordeal at the hands of terrorists. "Oh, Frank," she said, smiling and looking into his eyes, "it feels like a heavy load has been lifted." Still beaming, she sighed deeply. "What a relief."

Frank hugged her close and kissed her. "Tell me all about it," Frank said. "I want to hear every detail. Twice." He knew she needed to talk. Sometimes, talking is the best medicine.

Just before falling asleep, Frank thought about Kathy coming home from work a few days before, distraught about being accused of taking advantage of health issues to miss work. Kathy's ordeal at the seaside villa outside Athens had been classified. Although her fellow staffers with the National Security Council had the proper security clearances, they didn't have the required "need to know" and thus knew only that she was undergoing skin grafts for burns.

The day after Kathy had come home crying, Frank rushed into a whirlwind of urgent meetings and memo writing. He accomplished in a few days what would usually have taken a month or more. The FBI, CIA, and the White House had approved designating Kathy Foster's supervisor and fellow NSC staffers as having a "need to know" the details of Kathy being held captive and tortured by Marwan and his men. Frank argued that disclosure was necessary to avoid a setback in Kathy's recovery and "maintain and improve the work efficiency" of her office, which were magic words for bureaucrats. Frank smiled again, thinking about how happy and relieved Kathy had been while telling him about everything. He fell asleep smiling.

He shouldn't have.

CHAPTER 2

THE JAROOD RIVER, TEHRAN, IRAN

It was rare for the head of Iran's Quds Force sabotage and assassination unit to personally conduct an interrogation. But Marwan was impatient while awaiting word from Nazar. He needed a distraction.

"Mama! Mama!" the six-year-old boy screamed, his eyes frantic. His thin arms were tied behind his tiny, writhing body, and his feet were bound. Two men balanced the boy on the railing of a bridge perched high over dark, swirling waters far below. "Mama!" he shrieked over and over, tears streaming down his face. Finally, the men looked at Marwan, who stood beside a bound and gagged woman. Because of her annoying screams, he had ordered her to be silenced. Her face contorted as she shook her head violently, crying and begging, her pleas muffled by the gag: "No, no, no! Don't! No!"

Marwan glanced coldly at the woman. Her pleas were tiresome. "Say goodbye to your son." He looked at the men and nodded. They shoved the small boy off the railing, and he plunged toward the river. His howls stopped when he hit the water, his final scream—"Mamaaa!"—echoing as he drowned.

The woman collapsed into a fetal position, her body wracked with wild sobbing. Marwan lit a cigarette, inhaled, and blew the smoke out slowly. He looked down and nudged her with his foot. "Now, when I take your gag off, I will ask you again where your husband is. If you don't tell me, we will return here with your other son, the little one."

He finished his cigarette. The dead boy is her fault, Marwan thought. She should have told me where her husband is or have done more to convince me she doesn't know. Time to take the gag off and ask her one more time.

After finishing with the woman, Marwan was driven back to Quds Force headquarters in a large, black SUV. Bodyguards in two other SUVs traveled ahead and behind. Marwan's skin still prickled from the blast furnace heat, and the SUV's air-conditioner felt good. He called his office on a secure phone. "Any word from Nazar? Any news?"

"No, sir. Not yet."

After the call, Marwan stared irritably out the window at passing buildings. He was notorious for his impatience and temper. But he was also calculating. As he thought about the dead child, a smirk creased his face. The demonstration with the child and woman at the bridge was as much for his own men as for obtaining information. The cruel act would reinforce his reputation for ruthlessness—a man to be feared in an organization of brutal men.

RIYADH, SAUDI ARABIA

It was another hot and dry day in Riyadh, Saudi Arabia, a city of four million. By late morning, temperatures were climbing toward the usual highs of around 115 degrees. Three men surrounded a young boy in a vacant room above an empty carpet shop. The leader, Nazar, a stocky man in his 40s, wore glasses and looked like an overbearing teacher, which he once was. He was intent on his work. "Be still so I can tighten it," Nazar said.

The boy, Babu, stopped moving and stood still. Even standing straight, the young teenager looked small and frail. He gave Nazar a nervous smile. Nazar tightened the straps on the front of a tan canvas vest wrapped tightly around Babu's narrow chest. Rows of filled pouches lined the back and the front of the vest. Finished, Nazar stepped back and scrutinized his work. After a moment, he said, "Alright. Put on your shirt."

Babu pulled a shirt on over the vest. It was too large and hung loosely outside his trousers. After buttoning the shirt, Babu looked at Nazar for more instructions. "Hold out your arms to the sides," Nazar said, motioning with his arms. "Straight out to the sides, like this. That's right. Hold it." After a moment, he said, "Turn around so I can see the back. Keep your arms out." Babu turned and stopped with his back to Nazar. After a pause, "Put your arms down now. Back to your sides."

Nazar had Babu turn and face him and then twist his body from side to side at the waist. After the movements, Babu stood still. Nazar pursed his lips as he assessed the shirt's appearance. Then, satisfied, he nodded. "It looks good. It will work."

"Now, remember everything you are supposed to do," Nazar said, looking directly at Babu. "Walk to the bus stop three blocks from here. Get off at the apartment complex. Then take a bus to the market. Once you get there, act natural. Don't make eye contact with security guards. Look like you're shopping. The biggest crowd will be at the main shops. Work your way into the crowd. When you are in the middle of the crowd, press the trigger button for the vest."

Babu shot an anxious look. "But..."

"No," Nazar snapped, shaking his head. "It's not armed. I told you—nothing is in the vest but dummy packs. Like I told you, this is just a dry run to test security for the real thing."

"I just wanted to make sure that..."

"I know you don't want to be a martyr," Nazar said. "Don't worry. There is no danger in this. None," he said, holding Babu's eyes. "None. Do you understand me?"

After a moment, Babu nodded. "Yes," he said hesitantly. "I just wanted to..."

"I know. It's natural to be anxious when making a test run. We've all done it," Nazar said, glancing at the two men to his side, who each nodded at Babu. "See," Nazar said soothingly, holding his arms out with his palms up. "There is no danger," he said, shaking his head. "No danger." He paused before continuing. "But there is a risk, Babu," he said gravely. "If you are discovered making a test run, they will beat you and put you in prison. So, this is a test in two ways. First, I want to see if the real thing will work later. Second, I want to test your courage so you can join us in doing important work. Is that something you want, Babu?" he said, almost pleading. "Do you want to prove yourself worthy? Do you want to be one of us?"

"Yes," Babu said, nodding. "Yes, I do," he said more firmly. "I do."

Nazar smiled warmly and clamped his hand on Babu's shoulder.

After Babu left, Nazar tracked his movements by cell phone. An hour later, as Babu mingled in a large crowd at the market, Nazar punched in numbers on a cell phone. The phone signal reached its destination milliseconds later. Babu's vest detonated in a blinding explosion. The blast shredded and mangled dozens of men, women, and children. Thirty were killed, and many others lay injured, bloody and moaning. By chance, Babu's older sister was at the market and among the dead.

Miles away, Nazar heard and felt the earth-jarring boom. Shock waves rocked the city, shook buildings, broke windows, and knocked pictures off walls. A large plume of dark gray smoke began curling above the town. Sirens frantically wailed.

Nazar smiled. A job well done. And then he thought about his next target, the biggest one yet, according to Marwan, and wondered what it would be. He was proud Marwan had selected him. "After the bombing, your next big mission will change history," Marwan had declared without giving him details. "It will be felt in many countries."

Nazar's thoughts were interrupted by one of his men, Adid. "I thought this was just going to be a test run," Adid protested, his brow furrowed. A sudden movement. "What…"

Nazar pointed a silenced pistol at Adid's face. Nazar's face hardened, his eyes fierce. "You didn't know because Marwan says you talk too much." Nazar pulled the trigger. The muffled shot sounded like a cat sneeze. The bullet punched a neat hole in Adid's forehead, and his body dropped, arms splayed awkwardly, lifeless eyes staring toward the ceiling. Blood began spreading on the floor from underneath his head. "Pig," Nazar scowled. He fired two more bullets into the body. Two more cat sneezes.

Marwan would be pleased to learn that Nazar had accomplished both missions: the bombing and executing one of their own who had been talking too loosely.

WASHINGTON, D.C. CIA ANNEX

The day after the suicide bombing, FBI agent Frank Marsh sat at his desk reading an initial intelligence summary of the attack. A curl of dark brown hair hung over his forehead, just above his right eyebrow, and dark blue eyes. As he read, Frank absentmindedly rubbed his chin. He froze when he came to one portion of the top secret report. His eyes narrowed, and his body tensed. Frank reread it.

"At this early stage, we assess with moderate confidence that the Iranian Revolutionary Guards Corps (IRGC) Quds Force Unit 400, responsible for Sabotage and Assassination, was involved in organizing and directing the suicide bombing. The bombing was executed by Iranian proxies. Quds Force Unit 400 is led by Colonel Marwan."

Frank's jaw clenched. "Marwan," he muttered. Restless, he rose from his desk and walked down the hallway to cool off. In Tehran, Marwan smiled as he savored the success of the suicide bombing. Then he realized he was absentmindedly rubbing the thigh of the leg that had been amputated because of Frank Marsh. His jaws clenched. Soon, he thought fervently, I will make Marsh pay. Pushing the thought aside, Marwan began visualizing his next operation—one that could change the course of history. Hamas wanted a long period of peace so that they could launch a big surprise attack from Gaza, but Marwan considered Hamas too weak. He would forge ahead with his own plan.

ONE WEEK LATER: TEHRAN, IRAN

While being driven to his office at the Iranian Quds Force headquarters in Tehran, Marwan stirred in the back seat of a sleek gray Mercedes and stared out the window at buildings gliding by in the early morning sun. He had been busy. Each long day was packed with briefings, meetings, intelligence reports, and operational plans. The daily rides to and from his home were quiet times when he could think. Everything was finally set for operation FURY. And now he could think about other things. He winced as the prosthesis fitted to his leg suddenly felt uncomfortable. His lips tightened as his mind flashed with the memory of Frank Marsh firing at him during their ferocious struggle on the boat off the Greek coast.

At the Quds Force compound, guards waved the Mercedes through and sharply saluted. When the car stopped at the main building entrance, another guard opened the rear door and snapped to attention. Marwan strode up the broad steps where his aide waited at the top. An imposing figure, Marwan was tall and muscular, with a shaved head and thick black eyebrows framing piercing eyes. A short, graying goatee and mustache failed to soften a harsh, granite-like face. He wore a bespoke Brioni suit and a crisp white shirt with the collar open at the base of his powerful neck.

As soon as he sat at his desk, Marwan buzzed his assistant to get him the most recent report mentioning Marsh. Within minutes, Marwan was reading it. The report, which was several weeks old, contained information from COMET, a U.S. government official, an ultra-secret source whose information required special handling. One part of the report mentioned Marsh.

HIGHLY CONFIDENTIAL

COMET reports that Katherine FOSTER resumed work with the National Security Council Staff. She is believed to be assigned to European affairs. FBI agent

Frank MARSH is working in the D.C. area. COMET has not been able to determine their current address.

HIGHLY CONFIDENTIAL

Marwan summoned Reza, a Major and section commander in the assassination unit. "I have a mission for you," Marwan said.

"Yes, sir. I am at your service." A burly man with black hair and a close-cut beard, Reza leaned forward in his chair before Marwan's desk.

"It's about the two Americans," Marwan said. "Frank Marsh, the FBI agent, and Katherine Foster, who is on the American National Security Council staff." He paused and absently rubbed his thigh. His amputated leg was fitted with a prosthesis, which enabled him to walk and even jog. An image flashed in his mind of Marsh shooting him in the leg during their confrontation in Greece. He remembered the excruciating pain. After a long moment, Marwan bit his lip and looked at Reza.

"You will go to Washington, D.C., and kill Marsh," Marwan said. "If the Foster woman is with him, then kill her too."

Reza hesitated briefly, knowing the assassination wouldn't be easy. But incurring Marwan's wrath would be worse. "Yes, sir. We will take care of it."

"If possible," Marwan continued, "I want pictures of their bodies."

Two Quds Force intelligence officers visited the Turkish Embassy in Tehran several days later. The Iranians carried a small overnight bag into the embassy and left an hour later without it. The bag's contents were taken in a diplomatic pouch from the Turkish embassy in Tehran to the Turkish Ministry of Foreign Affairs in Ankara, Turkey. Operatives with Turkey's National Intelligence Organization, MIT, took the bag to MIT headquarters at KALE, known as The Castle, in Etimesgut, Ankara. They later returned the bag to the Foreign Ministry, which was then sent out by diplomatic pouch to the Turkish embassy in Washington, D.C.

The following week, Reza and three members of his assassination team filtered into the D.C. area. For high-profile assassinations, he operated with large teams of up to 40 men to conduct extensive surveillance. However, in the U.S., the team had to be kept small because the FBI would likely detect large numbers.

During the week, a locked metal container arrived by diplomatic pouch at the Embassy of Turkey in Washington. Located at 2525 Massachusetts Avenue Northwest, in the Embassy Row neighborhood, the Turkish embassy's three-story brick buildings sit behind low brick walls topped by a high iron fence. Inside a secure vault on the third floor of the main building, Demir, a Turkish intelligence officer stationed with the embassy under the guise of an economic advisor, opened the container and removed two handguns and silencers. The box also contained additional false identity documents for the Iranian hit team.

Using an encrypted app, Demir called Reza and left a coded message. In a small apartment several miles from the embassy, Reza listened to the message, "The books have arrived. Pick them up at the store."

An FBI counterintelligence agent received a tip from a source in the visa section of the Turkish Embassy. The agent filed a report. "Source reports a container destined for unidentified Iranians in the U.S. arrived by diplomatic pouch at the Turkish embassy. The contents of the pouch were unknown." A lead was sent requesting agents with Iranian sources to ask about any unusual activity, but nothing developed from the inquiries.

TEHRAN, IRAN

The next day, the Quds Force cyber warfare unit in Tehran sent messages to the U.S. informing Reza, the leader of the Iranian assassination team, of several possible addresses for Frank and Kathy in the Washington,

D.C. area. Reza's operatives began checking the addresses to spot Frank Marsh coming or going. They could quickly find out if Marsh and Foster lived in any of the apartment buildings. Marwan's men were closing in.

ISRAEL

During her overnight shift, Sergeant Shelly Danon, a cyber warfare specialist with Israeli Military Intelligence Unit 8200, known as 'eight-two hundred,' analyzed Iranian electronic data. Unit 8200 was the Israeli equivalent of the U.S. National Security Agency, NSA. It had secretly penetrated portions of the Quds Force computer systems and internet communications. Danon was assigned to probe Quds Force cyber activities. That night, she filed a routine report on data retrieved during her shift. One portion of her report stated:

CLASSIFIED

"IRGC ACTIVITIES DIRECTED AT USG:

In the past 24 hours, the IRGC cyber unit conducted name searches of USG and US CIV databases and communications for FRANK MARSH, identified as an FBI Special Agent in Washington, D.C., USA, and KATHERINE FOSTER, who works for or did work for the National Security Council in Washington, D.C., USA. The IRGC located several residential and work addresses that might be associated with them, either past or current addresses.

ASSESSMENT: The searches appear to be routine probes of USG national security personnel."

END REPORT

The following day, Danon's report was shared with the cyber war room of the C4I Directorate based at the Israeli Defense Force (IDF) Kirya military headquarters. It was also shared with Mossad, Israel's intelligence agency, and Shin Bet, Israel's internal counterespionage and counterterrorist agency. Later that afternoon, Mossad sent a cable to its intelligence unit at the Israeli embassy in Washington, D.C.

"ACTION REQUIRED: Alert FBI liaisons that 'a reliable source' of the Mossad reported that Iran's IRGC Quds Force is attempting to obtain information concerning FBI Special Agent FRANK MARSH and U.S. National Security Council staffer KATHERINE FOSTER, including their residence addresses. The reasons for Quds Force efforts are unknown, but it appears to be routine probing for information on USG national security personnel.

URGENCY: ROUTINE"

A Mossad intelligence officer at the Israeli embassy eventually passed the information to the FBI. An FBI analyst made a note to forward the information to Agent Frank Marsh and to the NSC where Foster worked, but the analyst's unit supervisor was on vacation, and the acting supervisor didn't see any urgency in passing on the information.

WASHINGTON, D.C.

The following day, one of Reza's men scouted an apartment complex listed as one of the possible addresses for Marsh. He discreetly placed three small devices around the building, each the size of a small matchbox. The devices were motion-activated cameras that would photograph everyone using the front doors of the apartment complex and every vehicle entering and leaving its underground parking lot. The operative would retrieve the devices later, download the contents, and review the photographs for anyone resembling Marsh. Another man placed surveillance devices at a second location that was identified as a possible residence for the couple.

It won't take long to check the four possible locations, Reza thought, but we need to hurry. He had already received a message from Marwan demanding to know why it was taking so long to locate and kill Marsh and Foster.

CHAPTER 3

Frank was reading the latest intelligence summaries at his desk at the CIA-FBI Joint Counter-terrorism Unit in the CIA Annex. Suddenly, he stopped and stared at an NSA report. He took a copy to the office of the deputy unit chief, Tom Dawson.

Seated at his desk, Dawson looked up over the top of his glasses as Frank walked in. "What you got?"

"This," said Frank, putting it on the desk. It was classified as *Top Secret SCI*, Sensitive Compartmented Information, restricted to those cleared for a particular operation or sensitive sources. "This is one of the recent intercepts by NSA," Frank explained. "I highlighted the important part." Dawson adjusted his glasses and began reading.

NSA REPORT

"Summary of an intercept of a mobile phone call from a number associated with **Jean Paul SAVALLE** *in Equatorial Guinea, Africa, to a mobile phone located in the vicinity of Bordeaux, France, recipient unidentified.*

Savalle said he had rescued a man who had escaped from a **secret site in the mountains** *operated by Middle Eastern personnel, perhaps* **Hezbollah or Iranians, and a Russian.** *The site may be guarded by Cuban ex-military personnel.*

When the subject in Bordeaux suggested Savalle pass on the information to security services, Savalle said, "I can't take the chance," but did not explain.

No other significant references to the numbers, names, or locations in NSA databases."

A follow-up by a CIA analyst added:

*"JEAN PAUL SAVALLE is a former sergeant in the **French Foreign Legion** who served with distinction in the Second Foreign Parachute Regiment, e2REP, in Africa, Iraq, and Afghanistan. Following service in the FFL, Savalle established residence in Equatorial Guinea in 2012, where he opened a bar named 'THE LEGION' and an import-export company doing business as 'JPS INTERNATIONAL LIMITED,' which Savalle uses as a front for small-time arms smuggling. He is believed fluent in French, Spanish, English, and German."*

Background: In past decades, Cuba sent thousands of soldiers to Africa to support revolutionary governments and groups. Those forces have been withdrawn, although a few small detachments remain in some countries as advisors or trainers. In addition, some former Cuban soldiers remained as residents, some of whom work as armed mercenaries or bodyguards for mining operations, fringe political groups, and criminal organizations."

With a finger, Dawson pulled his glasses down slightly and peered over the top at Frank. "So?"

"I know *him*," Frank said. He had more to add but waited. He knew what he had to say would have more impact if it was in response to questions rather than volunteered.

"You know him? This, uh..." Dawson glanced down at the document, searching with his finger. " Jean Paul Savalle?" He looked at Frank.

"I do."

"Hmm," Dawson said, his mouth scrunched up in one corner. He looked down and began rereading the report. When he finished, Dawson sat back and took off his glasses. "Well, this could be important," he said thoughtfully and paused before continuing, "or it could just be *bullshit*. What do you think, Frank?"

"Tom, if the Iranians and Russians are working together in Africa, then whatever they're doing is important—and bad for us."

Dawson rubbed his chin and let a few moments pass before he spoke. "Well, it's pretty vague and comes from only one phone call."

"True," Frank said, "but remember, there was a previous intercept of a call between Marwan in Iran and someone in Africa. They talked about the need to move some kind of 'shipment.' It could be connected to the secret mountain camp Savalle talked about."

Dawson squinted at Frank. "Well, it says this Savalle, the former Legionnaire fellow, is an arms smuggler and is wary of security services. You say you know him? How?"

"From Iraq. When I fought in Iraq with Marine Recon, Jean Paul was attached to our unit as liaison from a Legion parachute unit in our area. I saved his life. Or at least he thinks I did."

"*Saved his life?*" Dawson hunched forward on his desk. "What happened?"

"We were on a foot patrol in Ramadi and got hit by an ambush. Small arms fire. Automatic weapons and RPGs. We were outnumbered. Several were wounded. Rather than pull back, I led my men in a counter-attack. Jean Paul believed that saved the whole unit, including him. He thinks I saved his life just because I put a tourniquet on his leg when he was hit."

Dawson stared at Frank and then shook his head slowly. "Damn." He looked back down at the document. Frank saw he wasn't doing it to read but to think. Dawson rubbed his chin and then looked up.

"Frank, you think Savalle will talk to you about this guy he rescued? The one who escaped from the mountain site, Hezbollah, Iranians, or whoever? Assuming the guy really did. Escape from them, that is."

"Tom, if Jean Paul Savalle is willing to talk to anyone about this, he'll talk to me. And maybe he can arrange for the guy he rescued to talk to me. We can find out if this secret mountain camp exists. If there's nothing to it, then we can drop it. But if it's true, it will be worth checking further." Frank paused to let that sink in and then continued. "Look, how about I make a quick, low-profile trip to Africa, talk with Jean Paul, get the details, and come right back?"

The men fell silent. Dawson leaned forward and crossed his arms on the desktop. "Look, Frank," he said frowning, "the Iranians having a secret mountain compound in Africa doesn't make any sense. It's implausible. Crazy. I think you know that, but you're obsessed with Marwan, and that's affecting your judgment."

"I know it's a long shot," Frank admitted, holding his palms upward. "But Savalle may have a lead on something important. It's worth a quick trip to find out." He paused. Sensing Dawson wasn't persuaded, Frank continued. "And remember what the boss said in the meeting last week: in intelligence, the greatest danger is what we don't know. And when the next major terror attack occurs, the American people aren't going to want to hear that we have limited resources; they will want to know if we did everything possible to uncover plots." He cocked an eyebrow, giving Dawson a questioning look.

After a long moment, Dawson sighed and nodded. "Okay," he said. "This is crazy, but your instincts are usually good. Let me see if I can get authorization. Draft a proposal; outline the logistics, communications, security, and costs. Include a risk assessment and the need for urgency." Frank rose to leave. "But I doubt they will approve the trip," Dawson added.

Frank worked quickly and had it done in several hours. After submitting the proposal, he went to FBI headquarters to make a friend in the FBI International Division aware of it. As he came out of an elevator, Frank heard a deep, bass voice call his name. He turned to see Assistant FBI Director Bill Nelson, a big bear of a man, stopped in the hallway, accompanied by two officials. Nelson reminded him of actor Fred Thompson; they had the same looks and mannerisms. "Marsh, you in trouble again?"

Frank shook his head. "No, sir. At least, not that I know of."

"What the hell are you doing here? Last I heard, you were with the CT group at the annex."

Frank walked closer and lowered his voice. "I'm following up on a proposal about a mission to Africa." Nelson cocked an eyebrow, so

Frank gave him a one-minute rundown of his proposed trip. Nelson pursed his lips, nodded for a moment, and then continued on his way.

Frank stood motionless for a long moment, remembering how the Bureau was on the verge of firing him after he and Kathy had disrupted a terrorist bombing plot. The bombing had been prevented only because Frank had been insubordinate and continued investigating after being suspended and ordered to stop. After that, the Bureau didn't know whether to fire Frank or give him a medal. Frank didn't get a medal, but Nelson, an old-school agent and former street cop, had intervened to keep Frank from being fired. At the end of Frank's disciplinary hearing, Nelson cleared FBI lawyers and Human Resource bureaucrats out of the room, leaving the two of them alone. Frank was surprised when Nelson smiled, held out his hand, and unofficially congratulated Frank on a job well done. After the tense hearing and worry about his career, Frank felt overwhelmed by Nelson's gesture and approval.

* * *

Less than a week after submitting the Africa proposal, Frank was surprised when Dawson informed him the trip to Equatorial Guinea to see Jean Paul Savalle had been approved in record time. "Assistant Director Nelson got wind of it, and he put in a word for you. That's amazing," Dawson said, shaking his head. "And I just got off the phone with him. He said to tell you not to break anything and to come back in one piece." Frank broke into a broad smile.

"There's already some pushback on this, though," Dawson added. "So if you're going, you better leave fast before the approval is countermanded."

The proposed mission had been presented as a low-key, routine matter: Frank Marsh was authorized to make a quick roundtrip to Africa to interview Jean Paul Savalle to assess his information for possible follow-up by the CIA or SOCOM. He was not to do anything else. He would be met in Africa by the nearest Legat, Legal Attaché, an FBI agent stationed in Dakar, Senegal. The Dakar Legat covered 12 African nations, including Equatorial Guinea.

He would travel as 'Frank Mitchell,' a travel agent with Universal Worldwide Travel scouting locations in Africa for vacation packages. Universal was one of dozens of cover companies maintained by the FBI for covert operations.

To coordinate the trip, Frank called Sims, the FBI Legat in Africa, responsible for several countries, including Equatorial Guinea. After discussing Frank's itinerary, Sims' tone changed, and his voice became grave. "You need to be aware of three things," Sims said. "First, corruption is endemic in EQ. The police and government officials can't be trusted."

"I was briefed on that," Frank replied.

"Good. I try not to go there unless I have to. Second, crime is a major problem, and I've heard that the town where you're going is controlled by local crime bosses. You'll have to be very careful, Frank. You'll be in hostile territory. It's best to get in, do what you gotta do, and get out. Understand?"

"Got it. You said there were three things I needed to know. What's the third?"

"Watch out for the CIA. Our relationship is frosty at best. They'll cut your throat if they can. They don't want us here. Best to keep a low profile. Watch out for an agency man named Matthews. Hopefully, you won't cross paths, but if you do, good luck. And it would be best to get out fast."

"That doesn't sound good," Frank said.

"It ain't good. I want to make sure you know what you will be dealing with here, Frank. As I said, EQ is hostile territory. Watch yourself."

The next day, an agent named Jake Reynolds showed up at Frank's office and asked to talk over coffee in the building cafeteria. After glancing around, he leaned forward over the table and said in a low voice.

"This is off the record." He looked to each side and over his shoulder before continuing. "Sims said to tell you there's a problem with John Paul Savalle, the subject you're going to meet," he said. "Sims did some checking with his sources and found out that Savalle is wanted in Nigeria for killing a man in a bar."

Frank's brows furrowed. "There's a warrant? Has he been charged? When?"

Jake nodded. "A warrant was issued a year ago. He's wanted, but EQ officials haven't moved on the warrant. They may not know about it. Savalle is involved in arms smuggling and may have the locals in his pocket. I don't know. But it's a problem for you. It means you shouldn't meet with Savalle, but if you do, you have a strict duty to turn him in."

They fell silent. Frank frowned and rubbed his chin. After a few moments, he looked up. "What about Sims? Is he going to stop my trip? Keep me from meeting with Savalle?"

Jake made a quick head shake. "Sims says to come on if you still want. But to remember that you have to turn in Savalle to the locals on the murder warrant."

Back at his desk, Frank grimaced as he thought about having to report Savalle to the local authorities in EQ after meeting with him. Should he call off the trip? Maybe, but a secret compound that could be used by Iran to store WMD materials was too important. Having someone else do it wouldn't work because no one believed in the possibility like he did. Plus, Jean Paul Savalle likely wouldn't cooperate with anyone but Frank, his war-time buddy. And then, there's a possible link to Marwan. His mind roiled with conflicts, and dampened his desire to pursue the Africa mission.

Later that day, Frank looked up as his boss stepped into his office. Frank gave him a questioning look. "Frank, I know you want to go to Africa because something there may be connected to Marwan. But remember this. Marwan probably wants you dead. If you do go and if you get the slightest inkling that he's there, drop everything and get out fast. Understand?"

Frank sighed and gave a small smile. "Hey, 'stay safe' is my middle name. You don't have to worry about me."

Frank's boss bit the side of his mouth and shook his head. "Damn, Frank," he said hopelessly.

"What's wrong?" Kathy said that night. It was the middle of the night, and they had been asleep for several hours. "You've been tossing and turning."

Frank expelled a deep, restless breath. "Nothing. Just keyed up thinking about the trip to Africa. Wanting everything to go well." It was a sleepless night thinking about Savalle being wanted for murder, corrupt EQ police and officials, local crime bosses, and Marwan. A simple mission to talk with his friend Savalle had become complicated.

A few days later, the trip was abruptly set. Frank called Kathy at the National Security Council offices to let her know he was leaving. "I'm going to the apartment to pack a bag, but my flight leaves before you get off. Will you be okay for a few days?"

"Sure, I'll be fine. I'll try to take off to see you before you leave. But you go ahead. I'm fine. Just take care of yourself, okay?"

On his way to the apartment, Frank made a call. After the call, he punched Kathy's number. "Hey baby," Frank said, "I just wanted to let you know I talked to my old Marine Recon sergeant, Tyrone Williams. Remember him? The one who has a private investigation company?"

"Oh gosh, yes, Frank. He helped watch over us when you were worried about the Iranians trying to get to us. Before we went to France and Athens."

"I just wanted to let you know that while I'm away, Tyrone and his nephew, Stick, the one called Crazy Man, will be looking after you again. So don't worry."

Kathy laughed. "Oh my, Frank. Stick, the skinny man with the dreadlocks and gold tooth?"

"Yeah, that's him."

"Sorry. I had to laugh, Frank. I remember that time we were talking to them, and Stick looked at me and said, 'Doan worry, we gonna be looking after yo ass.'"

Frank joined in her laughter. "I remember. He's a good guy; we were lucky to have him on our side. Something I may not have mentioned to you at the time. There was a guy who *was* following us then. Stick spotted him and sent the guy to the emergency room with gunshots in both legs."

"Oh my God, Frank."

"Yeah, Stick has a habit of shooting a guy in the leg and then saying, 'Just to show you that ain't no accident,' and then he shoots the guy in the other leg. Between Tyrone and Stick, I'm sure you'll be all right while I'm gone."

As Frank drove home to pack, Hamid, a member of Reza's hit team, walked to the ramp leading down to an underground parking garage at Frank's apartment building. A waist-high brick wall topped by low shrubbery lined the right edge of the ramp as it descended toward the parking garage. Hamid stood near the street entrance to the ramp and leaned with his back against the wall. He lit a cigarette. Hamid looked like a resident who had stepped outside for a smoke break. While leaning against the wall, he reached back and retrieved a small video camera hidden in the shrubs and replaced it with another camera.

He would download video and examine images of vehicles leaving the garage that morning for anyone resembling Frank Marsh. He didn't have a photo of Katherine Foster, so he could only watch for Marsh.

Just as Hamid finished switching cameras, a charcoal gray Toyota Land Cruiser SUV turned onto the top of the ramp from the street and drove slowly past Hamid and down into the garage. His hand halfway to his lips with a cigarette, Hamid stopped and stared as Frank drove past, within a few feet. He threw the cigarette down, reached under his jacket, and gripped the gun at his waist to ensure it was ready.

Hamid strode down the ramp after the Land Cruiser. At the bottom of the ramp, a guard booth and a metal arm across the driveway blocked access to the parking area. The metal arm was lowering behind Frank's passing vehicle. The guard eyed Hamid and stepped from the booth. As Hamid walked around the metal arm, the guard moved toward him. Hamid saw Frank's brake lights glow red as he parked near an elevator on the far side of the garage. Hamid walked faster and veered around the guard.

"Hey," the guard called out behind him. "Hey you," he called louder. "Stop!"

After parking, Frank walked to the elevator and pushed the button. Hamid was closing in.

"Stop," the guard yelled.

The doors opened, and Frank stepped inside and pushed a button for his floor. He stood staring distantly, preoccupied with the upcoming trip and oblivious to his surroundings.

Hamid hurried, almost trotting. "HEY!" the guard called out to him. Hamid moved faster, reached under his coat, his hand gripped the butt of his pistol, ready to whip it out and fire, his eyes focused like a laser on Frank. Hamid knew he would shoot Frank in the head and heart and then spin around and kill the guard.

The elevator doors began closing from each side toward the center. Hamid realized he was still too far away, so he broke into a run. The doors were closing. Hearing a message ding, Frank looked down at a text on his cell phone. As he closed in on Frank, Hamid got ready to pull his gun out and fire. The yells of the guard brought Frank back to the present. His eyes focused on his surroundings. He suddenly saw a man running toward the elevator, his hand under his coat. Their eyes met. The doors were closing; then they closed and clicked shut. The elevator began moving up. Frank didn't register the close call. His mind was still on Jean Paul Savalle, his French Foreign Legionnaire friend, and the possible Iranian and Russian secret site in Africa.

Hamid pulled up, panting. He shook his head. I almost had him, he thought, shoving his gun back into his waistband. He turned and glared at the guard as he walked past, up the ramp, and to the street. On the street, Hamid pulled out his cell phone and called for help. He took a position across the street from the apartment building and waited.

Kathy arrived at the apartment just as Frank came out of the bedroom carrying an overnight bag slung over his shoulder. He set it down and held her shoulders with both hands.

"Are you going to be all right while I'm gone?" Frank said, their eyes locked. His look was questioning and concerned.

Kathy nodded. She touched his cheek and held his eyes. "I'll be fine. Just make sure you come back," she said softly, her face anxious. "Because I am not me without *you*."

His eyes watered, and he pulled her into his arms. "I love you," he whispered in her ear, his throat tight. Frank was overwhelmed by how completely Kathy had expressed the depth of their love in six words: "I am not me without you." He held her tighter, and their lips met in a lingering kiss.

After Frank left, the apartment was suddenly too still and quiet, and the air was heavy. With a lump in her throat, Kathy pressed her lips tight, holding back tears. Her eyes were still moist when she walked into the bedroom. Then she saw it on a nightstand beside the bed. A single red rose with a note card. She picked it up and read.

"It was always you," F. Scott Fitzgerald.

"Kathy, I can't say it any better than that. I say it from my heart to yours. It was always YOU. My One and Only True Love. YOU."

Kathy stared at the note and sighed. Then she realized she was smiling. She wiped her eyes with the back of a finger.

Frank walked out of the front doors of the apartment building and slipped into a taxi for the ride to Dulles Airport. Hamid saw him duck into the cab with an overnight bag, but it was too late to follow him. He called Reza. "Our friend just left. He's going on a trip, but I don't know where."

A short time later, Frank sent a text message to Kathy just before his flight took off.

"B out of cell service for few days so don't worry if U don't hear fm me. Miss U already! I love U!!"

Reza joined Hamid across the street from Frank and Kathy's apartment building outside.

CHAPTER 4

WASHINGTON, D.C.

Tyrone Williams, Frank's former platoon sergeant in the Marines, had several new jobs for his private investigation business. He would be stretched thin trying to spot-check on Kathy Foster while Frank was out of the country. He thought about calling his nephew Stick to help out. Tyrone cringed at the thought of Stick turned loose on D.C. again.

THE MISSISSIPPI DELTA

Flat delta farmland stretched to the horizon, an ocean of brown earth etched with long, green rows of soybeans. A yellow crop-dusting plane roared at a tree line in the distance and suddenly shot straight up from a field, barely avoiding trees. The plane wheeled in a tight circle as it rose and dove for another ground-hugging sprint over the field, this time in the opposite direction. Leveling off and spraying, the plane skimmed eight or ten feet above the ground. Racing at 150 mph above soybean rows, the yellow plane seemed certain to crash into another tree line at the end of the field. At the last moment, it zoomed up, barely clearing treetops. The pilot swung the plane in a tight circle and swooped down for another low-level run. The cropduster looked like a giant yellow bird repeatedly circling and diving.

Standing in a cemetery on the edge of a small crowd, Stick watched the plane, fascinated by the death-defying show and precision flying. He loved watching cropdusters and wished he could fly free like a plane. The distant buzzing and occasional roaring of the cropduster was accompanied by the drone of the pastor's voice rising and falling as the service ended and the casket was lowered into the grave. A grandfather Stick had never really known.

Walking away at the end of the service, he heard his uncle Deron come up beside him. "Hey, Stick, ain't you got no love for your favorite uncle?" he said tauntingly.

Without changing stride, Stick cast him an accusing, sideways look. "What you want now?"

"Why you want to be that way, Stick? I see how you flush every now and then. You should share with your kin. You feel me?" Stick ignored him. After a moment, Deron continued, his voice lower. "Look here, man, I got something good going and you can get in on it. I hear you been going to Chicago and to D.C. I got people buying at gun stores and pawnshops all over the delta. All you gotta do is take guns up there and sell them to the gangsters. They pay top dollar. I was using Chico, but he got revoked. You can... What's the matter?"

Stick had stopped and turned to Deron. "The last time you had me do something with a gun it didn't work out so muthafucking well," he said bitterly.

"Shit, you still crying about that. You oughta thank me. It made you a muthafucking man. That wasn't ..."

"Naw, man. You lucky I don't bust a cap up your ass," Stick said, glaring. "Stay outta my way." Stick turned and walked away, his jaws clenched. As he neared his ride, he wondered why a sheriff's SUV was parked beside it. The Sheriff's department had provided vehicle escorts for the funeral procession from the church to the cemetery, but they always left when a procession reached a graveyard. "Hey, Stick," the Sheriff called out from the open driver's window. "Got a minute?"

A commanding presence, Sheriff Andrews was a large and powerfully built Black man with a shaved head and a deep voice. He was beloved by many, hated by a few, but respected by all. Always nervous around the law, Stick stopped at the SUV's driver's door and gave Andrews a questioning look. "You need to talk with me, Sheriff? Something wrong?"

"I saw Deron talking to you. What he want?"

Stick shrugged. "Ain't nothing. He just be talking."

"Well, Deron's bad news. And you don't need to be catching any charges. You hear me?"

Stick held out his open palms and smiled. "You don't have to worry about me. I ain't doing shit."

"Just like you weren't doing shit when you were caught with that stolen pistol when you were 16," Andrews said sarcastically. "Hell, Stick, you were doing good until then. You were going to be the starting quarterback. You had talent. You were skinny as hell, like you are now, but man, what an arm you had. Small colleges would have recruited you. But you sure as hell screwed all that up," Andrews said, shaking his head. "Screwed it up good."

"Oh well, ain't no big thing," Stick said dismissively, but his face was somber.

Andrews stared silently at Stick as if trying to make up his mind. Finally, he said, "I got a story to tell you. I hope it means something to you." Stick cocked an eye. "There was this man on death row. When they strapped him in the electric chair, they asked if he had any last words he wanted to say. The man said, 'Sho do. This sho been a lesson to me!'"

Stick squinted, and after a moment, he said, "That true?"

"Hell, I don't know," the Sheriff said with a shrug. "But I do know there's a good lesson in that."

"Yeah? What's that?"

"Well, some people finally learn a lesson only after it's too late." He paused and held Stick's eyes. "I don't want it to be too late for you. You can still make something of yourself. Think about it." He nodded at Stick and drove away. Stick stood motionless and watched the SUV until it was out of sight.

Driving away moments later, Stick glanced in the rearview mirror and saw his eyes staring back at him, filled with guilt, anger, and bitterness. He remembered the night he got caught with the stolen gun. Until that night, he was going to be the next star quarterback for the high school. He was skinny but had a good arm. As the Sheriff said, small colleges probably would have recruited him, beefed him up, and trained him. He had a future. But then that night happened.

Dusk was falling, and he was walking home from football practice when he saw Uncle Deron and flagged him down for a ride. Deron had been drinking and was driving erratically. Suddenly, blue lights began flashing at the car's rear, almost on the rear bumper. As Deron slowed to stop, he pulled a pistol out from under his shirt and shoved it at Stick. "Here, hide this under your seat. Hurry!" Stick shoved it under the seat. "I'm an ex-con. If they find it, they'll send me up again." The car stopped. An officer was getting out of his vehicle, and another police car with flashing blue lights was pulling up.

Deron grabbed Stick by the arm, gripping him tight. His eyes were glassy and wild. "If they find it, tell them it's *yours*," he said hurriedly. "You got that? It's yours! Don't worry, they won't do anything to you. You're just a kid."

The police did find the gun, and Stick claimed it. Deron forgot to tell him it was stolen. Through everything, including the arrest and the hearings, Stick kept hoping Deron would come forward and take the blame. But he never did. Stick's future was gone, and reform school set him on another path. He had never told another soul what had happened.

Stick glanced up at the rearview mirror again. Why is it always so hard to be the man I want to be, he wondered.

He cleared his mind and headed to his favorite juke joint, the Amnesia Club. The sign outside set the tone, "Amnesia Club. Open from 9am til Damage." Stick settled on a barstool and ordered a whiskey. After pouring the drink, the bartender, Eddie, a large man with short, gray hair, ambled away to take care of another customer.

Stick was well known around the area—an occasional coke dealer who was renowned for having shot a man in both legs for welching on a drug debt. He also stood out. Dreadlocks hung to his shoulders, and a black Pittsburg Steelers ball cap with a flat brim sat just above his eyebrows, with the brim turned towards the left front. In his mid-20s, Stick was lean but looked even leaner in the black silk shirt and trousers he had worn to the funeral that afternoon. His most distinguishing feature was a gold-plated upper tooth. It was especially noticeable when he grinned. A flashy gold tooth was an outdated style, but no one was fool enough to say anything about it.

When Eddie returned from serving another customer, he plopped his elbows on the bar top across from Stick and cocked an eye. "What kinda shit you in now, Stick?"

Stick frowned. "What you mean, man?"

"Two fellas dropped by here this afternoon asking about you, wanting to know if anyone seen you around. Said they was friends of yours. But they didn't look like they friends with *nobody*. Ain't never seen them before." He held Stick's eyes. "They look like some heavy hitters."

"Shit, a mutherfucka don't have to *look* for me," Stick declared, thumping his chest with a thumb. "Everybody knows where to find me. And they ain't gonna be heavy hitters with my 9mm up *they ass.*"

"Well, I'm jus saying, Stick. Somebody's looking for yo ass."

Stick cocked an eyebrow. "See what they be driving?"

"Yeah, when they left, I took a look. They in a black Escalade with black windows, and an Illinois tag." Eddie frowned and shook his head. "I know trouble when I see it. And they *trouble*, man."

Stick froze. Illinois. Chicago. Damn! It's Big Al. He sent them. Mutherfucka! Stick downed his drink and drove off in a hurry, watching for the Escalade and casting repeated glances at his rearview mirror. It looked clear. He drove to another town and checked into a motel after dark under another name. He had driver's licenses with different names, forgeries that might not be good enough for a highway patrol check but good enough for motels and careless police.

The dilapidated motel was faded green with peeling paint. It was a single-story building with a small office, ten grungy rooms on the front side, and a dozen rooms on the back. Only five or six rooms were occupied, mostly by crackheads. Stick took a room on the back side so his car would be hidden from the street, and he was careful to park away from his room.

He drew the curtains, locked the door, and propped a chair against the bottom of the doorknob. After checking out the parking lot at the edge of the curtain, he turned on the lamp on the nightstand and plopped down in a chair. He checked his 9mm to make sure it had a full magazine and a round in the chamber. Then he turned off the light and began sipping whisky in the dark with the gun in his lap.

He had turned off the rattling air conditioner below the window so he could hear noises from outside. Temperatures rose quickly, and beads of sweat formed on his forehead and ran down his face. The Mississippi Delta's heat and humidity made life miserable even at night.

By two in the morning, crackheads in other rooms had quietened down, and Stick climbed on the bed and slept off and on. Suddenly, he heard a cough near the door. Stick pushed off the bed and sprang to the window with the 9mm. He crouched at one side of the window and peered out. He could see part of the dimly lit parking lot through a narrow opening at the edge of the dingy curtain. He slowly edged the curtain another fraction of an inch. He could see his car parked in front of a room near the far end of the building. Everything looked normal, and he didn't see anyone. After five minutes, nothing had moved, and Stick began feeling relieved.

He glanced back at the bottle of whiskey on the nightstand. I'll give it five more minutes, he thought, and if nothing moves, I'll relax and have a sip. It's probably nothing and... A shadow outside flickered in the corner of his eye, and he jerked back against the wall. He heard a car door open and shut with a thud. His heart racing, he gripped the gun tighter.

He carefully edged the curtain back and scanned the parking lot. Stick didn't see anyone, but he could see only part of the parking area. He moved away from the wall, went to the other side of the curtain, and carefully peered out. He saw two empty cars parked in front of the rooms but couldn't see the rest of the parking area. Using a fingertip, he moved the curtain back a fraction of an inch. He took a sharp breath when he saw it—a black Cadillac Escalade SUV with black windows. It was parked near a tree line on the far back end of the lot and was backed in facing the rooms.

It's them, he thought, feeling his chest tighten. That's the ride Eddie saw at the Amnesia Club. He cringed. Of all the people to have after him, Big Al was one of the worst. A big time Chicago drug supplier, crime boss, killer. Mutherfucka, shit. Stick bit his bottom lip and stared at the SUV.

Stick couldn't tell if anyone was in the Escalade because of the blackened windows. They must have spotted my car, he thought. Damn lucky I parked it in front of another room. I got to get away, but I can't get to the car without being seen. They probably in the Escalade watching my car. Or they're in a room where they can watch it. Damn, I need to think.

Stick backed away from the window and sat on the edge of the bed in the dark. He laid the 9 mm on the nightstand and poured whiskey in a plastic cup. It bit as he took a slug. As the burn faded, he felt the warmth spread. Got to think. How to get out of this damn fix. A plan began forming in his mind. He thought it would work best at daylight when others might be stirring.

When daylight broke, Stick picked up the room phone and dialed every room in the motel. If anyone answered, he would whisper urgently, "Hey, somebody's breaking into cars in the parking lot. They in a black Escalade." He then called in the same anonymous report to the police department. At the window, Stick watched as people ventured out of rooms and checked their cars. Soon, two police cars sped into the lot and blocked the Escalade; police officers jumped out and approached it with guns drawn. Several people stood outside their rooms watching. During the commotion, Stick hurried to his car and quickly drove away, constantly checking the rearview mirror.

After leaving the city limits, Stick breathed a sigh of relief and cruised north toward Chicago. He had no idea what to do when he got there except that he would confront Big Al. Stick tensed, thinking about what could happen. His mind raced as he drove.

Life ain't fair, he thought. It's full of choices, but the only choices I get to make are always between two bad decisions. He frowned and shook his head slowly. Damn, I shouldn't have taken Big Al's money to kill that guy. But I had no choice because Al had me over a barrel on the coke I ripped off from him. And then after I took Al's money to make the hit, I shoulda gone ahead and done it. But I couldn't cause it turned out my cousin was stuck on the guy and gonna have his baby. By then, I couldn't give Big Al his money back for the hit because it was all gone.

What the hell did I do with the money? Stick wondered. It went fast. He rubbed his chin. Yeah, that's right, I spent most of it on gambling, whiskey, and women. And just wasted the rest. I shouldna lost so much at the casino, but I just knew I was gonna win big. "Damn those dice," Stick muttered out loud and shook his head. "They ain't got no conscience. Shit, shit, shit. Muthafucka." Now, Big Al is after my ass. I'm a damn fool, but life ain't fair.

After driving for an hour, Stick pulled off the road and stopped at a Waffle House next to the highway for breakfast, careful to park his car where it would be hidden from the highway. He was almost finished when he saw the black Escalade zoom by, heading north. They probably think I'm way ahead of 'em, he thought. It might be good to stay overnight instead of getting right back on the highway and taking a chance to run into them up the road. After finishing breakfast, he found a cheap motel and got a bottle.

As night fell, Stick huddled in a grubby motel room with a bottle of Wild Turkey. The carpet was worn thin and stained with large dark spots. Tattered curtains hung above a rattling air conditioning unit. Cigarette burns scarred the nightstand and small bathroom sink. The bottom of the sink was rusted yellowish brown, and a cockroach crawled up the wall above the tub. The air smelled stale and moldy. The bedding was stained and threadbare. An ancient 19-inch television was ready for the trash heap.

During the night, Stick leaned back in a creaky chair with a plastic cup of whiskey in his hand. His bloodshot eyes were glazed under drooping eyelids, and a lopsided grin creased his face. "Shit," he mumbled, "those muthafuckers don't want none of *me*. I'll stomp *they ass*." He took another drink. The last thing Stick remembered was looking at the bottle and thinking it was almost empty.

Lying flat on his back, Stick woke in an alcoholic haze with bright light burning through closed eyelids. The mattress felt stiff, like concrete. Damn, I must be on the floor, he thought. He hated to open his eyes, but the floor was uncomfortable. Need to get up and get on the bed. Stick slowly opened his eyes and let out a sharp cry. From overhead, brilliant sunlight blazed down from a blue sky and pierced the backs of his eyeballs with stabbing pain. Squinting at the sky, he suddenly realized he was outside. But where? He turned his head to one side and then the other and saw high concrete walls on each side. He pushed himself to a sitting position. Suddenly, he realized he was lying at the bottom of an empty concrete pool. He frowned, and his forehead furrowed. Damn, he thought, how did I get in the bottom of a pool! Shit. The left side of his head throbbed, and his elbows were skinned up.

Then Stick realized he was naked and wearing only his red underwear except for white tennis shoes on his feet. His mouth dropped open, and he stared at the tennis shoes, the white shoes a curious sight at the ends of his skinny legs. He squinted and shook his head slowly. "Tennis shoes," he muttered. "*Tennis shoes*! I don't never wear no tennis shoes. I ain't even got no tennis shoes!" After a long moment, he uttered, "*Muthafucka!*"

Two hours later, Stick was back on the road with a throbbing hangover, driving toward Chicago. He couldn't remember how he wound up at the bottom of the pool or why he was wearing tennis shoes. And whenever he thought about it, he shook his head and muttered, "Tennis shoes. *Muthafucka.*"

His cell phone rang, and he saw that the call was from his uncle Tyrone Williams in D.C., a retired Marine First Sergeant who now owned a private investigations company.

"Yo, it's me."

"Say, what you got going, Stick?"

"Just a little sightseeing trip," He glanced at the rearview mirror. No black Escalade. Still clear, for now. "Why? What you got?"

"I need your help on a job for Frank."

"Frank?"

"Captain Marsh. Frank Marsh. You remember him, my captain in the Marines, but he's now with the FBI? We watched his woman, Kathy Foster, for him a while back. Remember? And there was some trouble."

"Oh, yeah," Stick said, nodding and smiling. He remembered the high-quality pistol and silencer he had taken from an Iranian hitman who had been stalking Foster. Stick had shot the Iranian in both legs. It was becoming his trademark.

"Here's the deal. Frank's out of the country and needs us to spot-check on her again, but I'm stretched thin on some other jobs and need your help. When can you be here?"

"I can head that way now, but I'm gonna need some pocket money."

"When you get here, I'll give you $300 and $150 a day. You can stay in that one-bedroom safe house I keep downtown; it won't cost you anything."

With Chicago gangsters after him, Stick thought a change of scenery would be good. He changed direction and began heading east toward D.C.

CHAPTER 5

PORT TOWN ON THE COAST OF WEST AFRICA

Frank arrived at a small port town in Equatorial Guinea as the early evening light dipped toward the horizon. The sleepy village featured a hotel built by the French in the 1930s. The graceful white building was once elegant and beautiful, but now the paint was faded and peeling. It looked tired and worn. After his long journey from the States, Frank felt the same way. He checked in and took a refreshing shower. Brownish water splashed on his head and body in the cramped shower stall while pipes rattled and water gushed fitfully.

After showering, Frank donned a short-sleeved sports shirt and slacks and headed out. The balmy evening air was freshened by a sea breeze, and Frank could smell the salty tang of the ocean. He inhaled deeply and set out for Jean Paul Savalle's Legion Bar, a few blocks from the hotel. The bar occupied the bottom floor of a two-story, cream-colored building dating from colonial times. A porch ran the length of the front, and above it was an equally long balcony. A series of louvered French doors opened to the balcony, giving the place an inviting, airy feel.

As Frank reached the porch, a man staggered out of the bar, stumbled down the steps, and bent over, retching. He skirted the man and stepped inside. Crossing the threshold, Frank stood, taking in the crowded, churning scene: two men in a heated argument at a nearby table, customers weaving among tables, and the din of dozens of alcohol-infused conversations, shouts, and laughter. The Legion Bar pulsated with raw energy.

The bar stretched along the back wall, backed by a long mirror. Animated patrons perched on barstools, each with their own story. To the right of the bar, stairs led to the second floor. Above the bar, bras and sheer panties hung from the ceiling, a rainbow of lacy reds, blacks, lavenders, and pinks. It reminded him of Charlie's Bar in Aruba, located in a port town that was once a boisterous hangout for merchant seamen, where dozens of panties and bras hung from the ceiling. Probably not surprising to see it here, Frank thought, as The Legion Bar was also in a port town, and many customers looked like merchant seamen.

Booths lined the walls on Frank's left and right, and filled tables crowded the center of the room. Large louvered shutters stood open along the side walls, catching ocean breezes. The walls were decorated with graffiti in several languages, displaying the names of seamen, merchant ships, and tributes to women. The lights were dim, and candlelight danced inside red globes on the tables, casting soft, flickering illumination on lively faces. From an ancient record player at one end of the bar, Edith Piaf, "The Sparrow," sang French love songs on a scratchy 33 rpm vinyl record, her trembling voice an emotional background to the rowdy din. Four ceiling fans circled lazily overhead, dispersing hints of spilled beer and clouds of cigarette smoke. I'm back in an old classic movie, Frank thought, and everything should be in black and white instead of color.

As his eyes adjusted to the dim light and the haze of cigarette smoke, Frank spotted Jean Paul Savalle sitting at a table with a striking woman. Another couple stood bent over the table, talking with them. Jean Paul still had a short, thick beard, but his black hair was thicker and longer now, reaching the back of his collar. With his rugged, handsome looks, athlete's body, and poised self-confidence, Jean Paul looked like the dashing legionnaire of their wartime days in Iraq.

As he glanced in Frank's direction, Savalle stopped mid-word, did a double-take, and stared with widened eyes. Those at the table followed Savalle's gaze toward Frank.

"Frank!" Savalle sprang to his feet and bounded forward. "It is! It's you!" Grinning, the two men grabbed each other by the shoulders and bear-hugged. With an irrepressible smile, Savalle ushered Frank to a chair at the table and introduced his companion. "This is my woman, Nicole," Savalle said proudly, wrapping his arm around her shoulders. She reminded Frank of actress Penelope Cruz. A native of Spain, Nicole had golden caramel skin, lively dark eyes, high cheekbones, and full pouty lips. Luxurious black hair fell over her shoulders. Melon breasts and erect nipples strained against a flimsy white cotton blouse. Her voice sounded husky and sensual, as if she just had sex. Which she may have, thought Frank. Jean Paul certainly looked relaxed and happy.

Nodding sideways toward Frank, Jean Paul said, "Nicole, this is my friend Frank, a U.S. Marine. We fought together in Iraq. He saved my life. When I was wounded, he rushed forward under fire and kept me from bleeding to death," Jean Paul said exuberantly. "We are brothers." But what are you doing here?" he said to Frank. How are you? What have you been doing? I'm so glad to see you. You and me, we no longer have short, military haircuts. You look good. How did you find me? How do you like my place?" he said, waving around the room. "Me and Nicole, we live upstairs above the bar. You stay here with us."

Frank cast a questioning look at Nicole, who met his gaze with a nod and a warm smile. She leaned in, her voice sultry. "We have a spare bedroom. You and Jean Paul must have a lot to talk about. About the war. And I want to ask you about the bar fights. He says they weren't over women," she said skeptically, glancing at Savalle. "But I don't know if he says the truth," she added, shaking her head.

"See, Frank," Savalle said hastily. "We want you here. I know you were wounded bad later. How are you?"

"We'll talk later, Jean Paul, but I want to catch up on you right now. When did you leave the Legion, and how did you get here?"

Later that evening, they were deep in their reunion when Savalle froze in mid-sentence and stared toward the entrance, his face tight. Frank followed his gaze and saw a large, burly man with a bushy mustache and a scarred face just inside the open doorway. With a scowl, the man was scrutinizing Frank. Savalle began rising, and as he did, the man turned and swaggered out of the bar. Patrons coming in veered out of his way. Savalle remained standing, watching the entrance for a few moments before resuming his seat, his face flushed with disgust and anger as he sat.

Frank realized that something serious had just passed. Turning toward Savalle, he nodded toward the door. "Who was *that*?"

Savalle leaned close, his voice low and grave. "That was Tabor, a bad one," he said, frowning. "Watch out for him, Frank. He is handy with a knife. Me and him, we got into it when I first got here." Savalle rolled up his left sleeve, revealing a long scar on his forearm. "But after we fought, Tabor is the one they carried out of here." Rolling down his sleeve, he continued. "Tabor is the enforcer for the big crime boss here, a man called Kruger."

"Kruger? A German?"

Savalle nodded. "There are several Germans here. Kruger came here a few years before I did. He had trouble in Europe but operates freely here. He probably heard that an American is in town and sent Tabor to find out if we are connected." Savalle raised his eyebrows and said solemnly, "You will be an enemy to them now. Be careful. Kruger and Tabor, they have their hands in everything here, including the police. Some people pay Kruger every month just to stay in business. But not me," he said, with a shrug, and then added, "Kruger and me, we don't get along."

Frank gave Savalle a questioning look, and he continued. "Kruger uses underage girls to turn tricks. Very young girls. He buys them from poor families in the countryside or kidnaps them and then hooks them on drugs. He keeps the girls in rooms above his bar and makes them turn tricks for men from the ships. I won't let his girls in my place, so he stays angry at me. It is a dirty business, what Kruger does," Savalle added, slowly shaking his head. "A dirty business."

Nicole reached and clasped Savalle's hand on the table. The couple exchanged looks, and Frank realized something meaningful had passed between them.

"Remember Teresa?" she said to Savalle. He nodded and looked at Frank.

"One of the young girls, Teresa, she got away and came here for help," Savalle explained. "Kruger showed up with Tabor and another man to get her back."

"Jean Paul and his friend Rafe ran them off," Nicole said proudly. "And then Jean Paul got her back to her family."

"The police?" Frank said. "What about the police?"

Savalle shook his head. "The police, they won't do anything. Kruger pays them. This whole country, it is like that."

Frank thought about getting the regional FBI Legal Attaché to pressure the government of Equatorial Guinea to do something. But he dismissed the idea when he remembered that EQ was notorious as one of the most corrupt countries in the world. He dismissed the idea but decided that when he returned to DC, he would ensure Kruger went into FBI and Interpol databases as a human sex trafficker, and maybe... His thoughts were interrupted by Nicole.

"Frank," Nicole said slowly in her husky voice, holding his eyes, "you must tell me more about how you saved Jean Paul's life."

Late that night, in Jean Paul's living quarters on the second floor above the bar, Frank and Jean Paul Savalle sat at a table, drinking whisky and talking about old times and the men they served with in Iraq.

"What about that little short Marine," Savalle said, "the one called Little Bit?

"Johnson? Oh yeah, 'Litte Bit,'" Frank said, laughing.

"He always looked overloaded with gear." Savalle grinned. "And that time, he threw a grenade and started crawling in the window before it exploded."

"You grabbed him just in time, Jean Paul. The blast knocked both of you back, and until the dust cleared, I was afraid you were both hit. Damn, that was *close*."

"Little Bit's timing, it was off, I think." They roared with laughter until tears rolled down their cheeks. Wiping his eyes, Frank realized this was the first time he had fully relaxed in a long time. The tension of the last few weeks and worry about how he would deal with Savalle was gone. For now.

Savalle took a deep breath and continued in a more serious voice. "What about your other radio man, the one who replaced Smitty?"

Frank bit his lips and shook his head. "He lost a leg and a hand," he said grimly. "But he was lucky to be alive. Last I heard, he was going to college and doing well."

They fell silent. Not wanting to talk about others—those they lost. Frank thought about Gonzales whimpering and crying for his mama as Frank held the dying Marine's head. Gonzales cried for his mama, thought Frank, but my face was the last one he saw.

Savalle refilled their glasses, and they sipped quietly. After a while, Frank noticed Savalle was staring at him with pursed lips as if trying to figure out something. A question on his face. "What?" Frank said, putting down his glass. "What is it?"

Savalle shook his head slowly and crunched his lips on one side. "We last saw each other in Iraq. And after all these years, you walk into my bar. Here in Africa." He paused. "This, it doesn't make sense to me."

Frank took a deep breath. This was the moment he had been dreading. How to approach Savalle? How would Savalle react? What he would have to do about Savalle being wanted for a killing. Despite worrying about it for days, Frank didn't have a plan. Even if he could get Savalle to help on the mountain compound, Frank would have to urge the EQ police to arrest him. A war buddy. A friend. Frank felt trapped. He had no idea what he would do, what he would say, what he *should* say to Savalle.

Frank downed the last of his whisky. Setting down his glass, he looked Savalle in the eye. "The terrorists we fought in Iraq may be here," he said deliberately. "They may have weapons of mass destruction, WMDs, on a mountain in Angola." He let that hang in the air before continuing. "I need your help."

Puzzled, Savalle asked, "But you're not in the Marines now? Are you? I don't understand."

Frank couldn't avoid it any longer. "I'm with the FBI. I'm an agent."

Savalle's eyebrows shot up, and then he frowned. "You are FBI," he said, puzzled. "FBI? Why are you here? Is it because of some trouble I had?" His eyes were intense, locked on Frank, watching closely. "Because I..."

"No," Frank said quickly, shaking his head. "No. I don't want to hear about any trouble you had. I'm not here about that."

Savalle leaned back in the chair and crossed his arms on his chest. He cocked his head to one side, and his eyes narrowed. "Then why are you here?"

"Like I said. The terrorists you and I fought against may have WMDs here. On a mountain. We're trying to talk with anyone who may have heard about it. Someone reported that you may have heard about it, so I asked to come and talk with you. About anything you may know." Frank held out open palms. "That's all."

His lips tight, Savalle scrutinized Frank. After long moments, Savalle's face relaxed. He uncrossed his arms and leaned forward, arms resting on the table. "You saved my life, Frank. I can help you, my friend," he said, nodding. Savalle told Frank about finding the man who had escaped from the mountain compound. When Frank asked about talking to the man, Savalle promised to arrange a meeting for the next night.

Frank still didn't know when or how he would turn in Savalle. A war buddy. A friend. A wanted man. For a killing.

Hours later, the bottle of Four Roses whiskey on the table was nearly empty, and Frank and Jean Paul were slurring their words. They were talking about the real reason for Frank's trip. "Like I say, Frank," Jean Paul said thickly, "the man, his name is Miguel, and he's a mixture of Portuguese, Guinea, and who knows what. Just like everybody else in this place. His tale about the secret mountain camp, it is strange. It makes no sense."

"Vel, what do you tank?" Frank said, slurring. His lips and mouth felt numb. He had to concentrate on pronouncing words.

"I tank, this Miguel, he believe it. Dat's wat I tank," Jean Paul said.

"Otay," said Frank. He took another drink. He was going to ask another question about Miguel, but his mind wondered. "Hey, wat about the panties over the bar? Are they your trophies?"

"Trophies? Oh, no, no." Jean Paul said, shaking his head. "Not trophies. It's how you say, uh, tributes. *Tributes* to my special women. Zey women, they put them up there. Oh, ze love-making." Jean Paul said with a loopy grin and a dreamy look. "After the first one did it, the next woman was jealous and put hers up. And then the next. But no more," he said, shaking his head. "Since Nicole, no more. But I tank she is proud all zey women; they like her man," Jean Paul said with a flourish, just before they both passed out.

The next day, Frank and Jean Paul sat at a table in the bar with hangovers and bleary eyes, nursing their drinks. Nicole was serving drinks to seamen from a newly docked ship. She came to the table with fresh drinks and warned Jean Paul that Kruger, the crime lord, and his henchman Tabor had come by earlier, looked around, and left. Jean Paul's face tightened. "It is never good news when those two show up," he said to Frank.

Before returning to the bar, Nicole leaned down and kissed Jean Paul on the cheek. A low-cut blouse exposed her breasts as she bent over, and she flashed Frank a big smile before straightening up. Frank and Jean Paul watched her sashay back to the bar, her swaying bottom holding them spellbound. "What a woman," Jean Paul said with an admiring smile. Turning to Frank, he raised his glass, and the two men toasted her.

After setting his glass down, Frank asked, "Do you do enough bar business in this small town to make a living?"

"There aren't enough customers from the village itself," said Jean Paul, "but small freighters dock here, and the seamen come to my bar. So, it is good." Lowering his voice, he added, "And I make money with arms dealing on the side."

Frank's eyes widened. "Arms dealing? Is that legal?"

"Oh, no, no. Not legal," Savalle said, shaking his head. "But it's nothing big," he said dismissively, "Just AK-47s, FLNs, and a few light machineguns. AKs and FLNs, they are always in demand." After a long moment, Jean Paul narrowed his eyes and cocked his head sideways. "Wait, should I be telling this to you?"

Frank smiled. "Relax, Jean Paul. I'm not here about that," he said, holding his palms up. "It's between you and the law here. I'm just here to talk to Miguel."

Jean Paul returned his smile and nodded. "Good. I thought so, Frank. We meet Miguel tonight."

"Just out of curiosity," said Frank, "how do you get them? The arms, I mean."

Jean Paul nodded toward the ocean. "They are smuggled in on freighters that dock here. Usually, just a few boxes at a time, manifested as tools or equipment. Very easy. I pay small bribes to ship captains and to the customs man here. It works well, Frank. A friend from the Legion lives in France, and he takes care of getting them on the ships. We are partners."

Jean Paul's eyes suddenly lit up, and his face brightened. "Wait, Frank, just a moment. I have something for you."

He left the table and went upstairs, returning with a gold-colored button. Jean Paul placed it on the table and proudly declared, "This is for you."

Frank picked up the button and said to Jean Paul. "A button?"

"It's a Legion button for our dress uniform. The gold Legion button is a famous tradition. French law says only the Legion can have this button," Jean Paul explained, his expression and voice reverent.

Frank looked closely and saw the words "Légion étrangère" on the button. He realized Jean Paul was doing him an honor. "This is special," Frank said, looking up and meeting Jean Paul's eyes. "Thank you for honoring me with it, my friend."

"Wait, I'm not finished," said Jean Paul. He handed Frank a tattered business card for Marc Rousseau, an Import-Export Agent, with a phone number and address in Bordeaux, France. "I wrote Marc's mobile number on the back for you."

Frank gave him a questioning look.

"Marc is the partner I told you about. He handles the shipments to me," Jean Paul explained. "If you ever need anything, *anything* at all, in France or the rest of Europe, go to Marc, and he will help you. If he cannot help you himself, then he will find others who can. Former Legionnaires live in every country of the world. Just tell Marc you are my friend, tell him AK 47, and show him the Legion button."

Jean Paul was pleased with himself. Smiling broadly, he raised his glass and said, "Semper Fi, U.S. Marine."

"Honneur et Fidélité, Legionnaire," replied Frank, reciting the Legion motto and returning the smile. They emptied their glasses. As Jean Paul refilled the glasses, Frank thought about their special bond, fighting in Iraq, experiencing hardships and sacrifices that only fellow warriors could understand.

As evening approached, Frank's thoughts turned to Miguel. He was anxious to learn what Miguel could tell them about a secret camp in the mountains. He wondered if Miguel had made up the story or exaggerated it. Was there really a hidden compound? And if so, was Miguel mistaken about who was running it? Having read up on Africa, Frank knew mining camps were active in the region and would naturally be guarded. Some camps were abandoned, and others were being illegally mined. Perhaps that's what Miguel discovered, Frank wondered. Am I on a fool's errand? Did the remote possibility that Marwan may be involved cause me to overreact? As the meeting with Miguel approached, Frank was besieged with doubts.

In Washington, D.C., Reza and his men were watching Frank and Kathy's apartment building. In Tehran, Marwan was impatient for word that Frank Marsh and Kathy Foster had been killed.

CHAPTER 6

After dark, Frank and Jean Paul met with Miguel in Frank's second-floor hotel room. Two lamps cast pools of warm yellow light as a slight breeze stirred thin cotton curtains at two open windows. A ceiling fan hummed overhead, its blades lazily circling, producing a soothing drone. The three men sat at a small table near a window. Frank sat across from Miguel, who smoked a cigarette, his eyes darting around the room. He bit his bottom lip, nervous but trying not to show it. Wiry, with a brown leathery face and mustache, Miguel looked in his mid-thirties but could have easily been years older. He had the wary look and watchful eyes of a survivor.

After Frank asked a few preliminary questions to relax him, Miguel began describing his experience with the mountain camp. He was halting at first, but then the story started flowing, a rushing stream of vivid memories. It started one night, Miguel said, when someone hired him to use his truck, a small box truck, to haul freight from the docks on an overnight trip. They needed a last-minute replacement for a truck and driver, but they wouldn't tell him what the cargo was or where it would go. He was to show up at the docks late that night.

"I drove to the dock at midnight," Miguel said. "The streetlights at the dock were out, except for one at the gate. Two men at the gate motioned for me to stop. They had submachine guns. One of the men opened the passenger door and climbed in. He told me to turn off the headlights and drive to a small freighter at the dock. As I drive, the man, he talk on a two-way radio."

"What language did he use?"

"At the gate, they talked to me in Spanish, but when the man used the radio, he spoke in a foreign language. What it was, I do not know," Miguel shook his head. "Maybe German or Russian or something like that, I think so."

"You drove to the dock, then what?"

"I saw the dark shape of a ship. It was a small freighter, but look like a big black beast rising out of the night." Miguel frowned at the memory. "No lights were on," he continued. "A ramp slanted down from the ship to the dock. A dark shadow, a man, stood at the bottom of the ramp. The man in the truck with me, he say, 'back up to the ramp.' After I back up, the man told me to wait in truck. He got out and went to the back. Then I heard a racket when he slid the rear door up. In the truck mirror beside my door, I saw shadows move down the ramp from the ship like black ghosts. They carried crates and rolled barrels."

"My window was down, and I tried to listen, but they moved quietly. The ocean lapped against the side of the ship and the pilings. Mooring lines and ship riggings squeaked and clanged in the breeze. I heard low sounds as the shadows reached the back of the truck, but I could not make out what they say."

"Then there were loud thumps and scraping sounds in the back of my truck. I heard the rear door slide down and shut. The man climbed back up into the cab with me. 'Start motor', he tell me, 'but no lights.' He talk on his radio, and then he told me to drive."

"After we drive through the gate, he tell me, 'Turn on headlights.' Headlights came on behind me. A big SUV was following us."

Miguel paused and lit another cigarette. Looking at the cigarette, his eyes widened. "Oh yeah," he said, looking up, "when we were at the dock, the man, he told me not to smoke."

"Did you smell anything at the dock? Any odors?"

Miguel shook his head. "No, not then."

As Miguel resumed his tale, he stared into the distance, reliving the experience. "We drive all night to Ambriz. There, we sleep in truck, and at dark, we begin traveling again. From Ambriz, we took the road going east to the mountains. Nobody else on the road. Once, a small animal run across the road in front of my truck, and I swerved and ran off the road. The man with me was thrown against the side of the cab. He swore and glared at me, 'You fool!' he say. 'You almost kill us because of animal. If you do that again, I kill you.' Me, I'm already scared."

"After driving hours at night, we turn off the main road to a road on the right, drive south, and then turn left on a narrow dirt road. Soon, we start climbing upward, winding up the side of a mountain. We travel slow because of sharp turns. The SUV was following behind."

"We climbed higher, against the side of the mountain, and the outer edge of the road fell off very steep. We crawled up slow, with the motor straining in low gears. We keep going up for maybe one hour until finally, we turned left on a small, narrow track to the left. Trees and bushes rubbed against the sides of the truck."

"After driving slow on the track for a few minutes, I saw in the headlights a pile of clothes lying on the left side. But when we got close, I saw it was a body." Miguel stared, unseeing, reliving. His face tightened. "I slow down to stop, but the man told me to keep going. When we go around the next turn, the headlights lit a gate across the road and two armed men. I stop at gate. The man in the truck cab, he talk to them and then told me to go on."

"A guard climb on the truck's running board and ride with us. We drive into a compound. It was surrounded by coils of barbed wire lit by lights. The guard on the running board pointed to a small warehouse. I back up to it, and the doors slid open. That's when I could smell it."

"Smell what?"

"A smell like a doctor's office or a hospital."

"What did you see inside the warehouse?"

"A row of black drums with yellow markings, stacked two high. Men motioned for me to get out of truck. They looked like Cubans.

The Cuban army was here years ago, but some soldiers, they stayed after the army left."

"What about the SUV that followed you from the dock?"

"Some men got out of it and were going into the warehouse as I was led away from the truck. One man stood out. He was maybe in his 40s, with a mustache and a pockmarked face. The men, they act like he is a big boss. He gave orders in Spanish, and the men hurried to the back of my truck." Miguel paused and looked directly at Frank. "But him and another man, they spoke Arabic to each other."

"*Arabic?*" Frank said, leaning closer. "How do you know? Do you speak Arabic?"

Miguel shook his head. "No, but people from the Middle East live here, and this man who was a boss, he said something in Arabic like, 'As Aslam alkem.' And the other man greeted him the same way. They said more in Arabic to each other, but I don't know the words."

Miguel paused a moment, lost in thought. "One more thing about this man, his eyes." He looked up at Frank. "When he looked at you, his eyes burned into you. He look at me, and I felt a cold chill. This man, him, I never forget," he said to Frank.

"Go on," Frank said.

Miguel took a deep breath and continued. "A guard led me to a small wood building. It was an office with bare walls, except for a Cuban flag inside hanging on a wall. A bearded man in a tan uniform was sitting at a small desk. He look like an officer. His black hair was messed up, and he looked sleepy, like he just woke up. He rubbed his face with one hand while pouring rum in a glass. He looked up at me as I come in with guard. He grunted and nodded to chair in front of his desk. I sit down as he finished pouring his drink. He held the glass of rum up and slowly swished it around the glass. He drink it down and then looked me over. His eyes, they are glassy from drink or no sleep. 'You know where you are?' he say in Spanish. 'You know why you are here?'

I shake my head.

'Good.' He poured another drink. 'You do not need to know.' This officer, he thought for a moment and then said, 'Well, I guess it does not matter. You sit there and be quiet.'

"The man who had ridden with me in the truck came in and whispered in the officer's ear. While listening, the officer nodded and looked at me. I know they talk about me. I thought about the body outside the compound, and I began to panic. I felt trapped. When the man finished speaking in the officer's ear, he straightened up and looked at me. The officer leaned forward. 'Now,' the officer say, looking at me and tilting his chin toward the door behind me. 'You go with the guard.'

"As I stood up, the man with fierce eyes who spoke Arabic came in. The officer frowned and stood up. The guard led me out but stopped a few meters from the building, and we waited in the dark. The guard wanted to listen. I could see the two men through the screen door and hear them. Their voices carried in the night air. They spoke in Spanish. The officer called the man Abu Farek. Farek called the officer Captain Morales. Morales said something would be ready soon; I could not hear everything they say. I heard the words 'three weeks' and 'ship' or 'shipment.'

"They argued and talked loud. Morales said something about being a 'soldier,' not someone who kills children. Farek shouted that Morales must follow orders. Farek stabbed a finger in Morales's chest, and Morales swatted his hand away."

"Did they mention any names or places," Frank asked.

"One name," Miguel said. "The men say the name Marwal or Marul. Something like that."

A jolt of electricity shot through Frank. "*Marwal? Marwan? Marwan,*" Frank said excitedly, his voice rising. Could the name have been Marwan?"

Miguel pursed his lips and thought for a moment. Finally, he nodded. "Yes, I think that's it, maybe. I think so, maybe."

"You heard them say *Marwan,*" Frank repeated slowly, his mind racing. He realized that the main reason he had made the trip to Africa was the remote possibility that the secret compound might be connected to Marwan. "What did they say about him? Marwan?"

Miguel shook his head. "I could not hear what they say, only that they say that name—Marwan." Miguel paused a moment and continued when there were no more questions. "My guard, he was watching them argue, and he moved closer to the building. He forgot about me. I started backing away, quiet and quick. As I backed away, my heart beat loud in my ears, and sweat was running down my face. I turned and ran and ducked behind a truck. Then I ran behind the warehouse."

"A generator was running, and the noise covered sounds I made. I ran to the edge of the compound and started clawing through the coils of barbed wire. It was tearing my skin and clothes. Suddenly, I heard shouts. Flashlights waved in the darkness. A shout went up close by, and a spotlight blinded me. More shouts. I tore through the wire and ran for the forest. My legs felt very heavy, like cement, and moving them took all my effort as I ran. It felt like I was moving in slow motion. The lights chased me as I raced for the tree line. I heard guns shooting. I was almost in the trees. Bullets buzzed by my head. I hit the tree line, and branches hit my face as I crashed into the black forest and ran deeper."

"I ran, tripping and falling. It was so dark I could only see a few feet. My lungs hurt, and my heart felt like it would bust, but I kept running. I heard shouts behind me. I ran faster. After I ran for a while, the ground suddenly dropped out from underneath me, and I pitched forward and fell straight down. I flipped over in the air and slammed into the ground on my back. The fall knocked my breath out, and I must have blacked out."

"When I woke, a bright sun was overhead. I was on my back with broken branches and leaves covering me. The side of a ravine rose straight up from where I lay, with the top maybe 25 feet above me. I lifted my head and looked around. I was on a narrow ledge on the side of a ravine, and it dropped down another twelve or fifteen feet below me."

"At the top of the ravine above me, a two-way radio crackled with static. Then, a soldier appeared at the edge above. I could see his head and shoulders. He was talking on a radio. He was staring down at me while he talked. I froze. After a few moments, he turned and walked out of sight, still talking. He didn't see me because of the brush."

"I heard a dog barking in the distance. Voices came from somewhere below me in the ravine. The sound of a barking dog was louder and moving closer. I had to move quickly. I crawled over the ledge I was on, hung by my arms, and dropped to the ground. I kept quiet and moved into the undergrowth. I heard thrashing sounds and voices moving closer. I hurried through the ravine, and soon the voices were falling behind me."

"I knew the dog would be on my trail and kept running through the brush. Then, all of a sudden, I crashed hard into a soldier, knocking us both to the ground. The soldier was knocked on his back with the wind knocked out of him. He was gasping for air. I scrambled to my feet and ran tearing through brush."

"I heard shouts and dogs barking behind me. They were getting closer, but I couldn't run any faster. My heart hammered, my lungs were hurting, and my legs were burning and getting heavier. Then, all of a sudden, I plunged into a river with vines wrapped around me. I was underwater with water roaring in my ears, and everything was black. I tore at the vines and fought my way to the surface. When I broke the surface of the water, I gulped air down. The river was deep but narrow, with trees hanging out over it on both sides, the limbs almost touching over the water. The dogs were louder, getting close."

"I reached the other bank, pulled myself up, and ran through the jungle. After that, everything became a blur. I lose track of time. Maybe it was the next day, but I don't know, I stumble onto a narrow dirt road. I walk a long time. Then I lay down next to the road and fell asleep or passed out. When I woke up, I was in the back of a truck bouncing on a road, and I went out again." Miguel stopped. He had returned to the present. He took a deep breath, exhaled, and then looked at Jean Paul.

Jean Paul said to Frank. "I came upon him on the road while returning from a side business trip. Miguel was banged up. I put him in the back of my truck and got him to some friends in town here, and they've been looking after him. He's afraid they will come looking for him. I keep my gun handy now."

"What about the authorities, Jean Paul? Have you reported it to anyone?"

Jean Paul shook his head. "Making a report could put Miguel in more danger. Years ago, the Cuban military had 25,000 soldiers in Angola and didn't leave until around 1990, so there is a big community of Cuban ex-pats there and in neighboring countries, including this one. The Cubans have influence in many towns and with some governments. Suppose Cubans are involved in the mountain camp, as Miguel says. In that case, it may even be secretly sanctioned by the government. Miguel and anyone who helps him may be in great danger if they discover where he is."

"How many know he's here?"

"Only a few, but this port town is a small village, only 30,000 people, and when it finally gets around that he's here, then word will get to the government."

Frank looked at Miguel. "Would you be willing to go with me and show me the route you took to the mountain camp?" Miguel's eyes widened. Frank quickly added, "We would just go part way, not all the way to it." Frank glanced at Jean Paul.

"Yes," Jean Paul said, looking at Frank and then Miguel, "we would just go a little way, Miguel." Frank cocked an eye at Jean Paul, relieved he was volunteering to help.

Frank went back over several points with Miguel, testing his memory and truthfulness. He was careful not to take notes, knowing it was distracting to interview subjects and made them hesitant to talk. Following his usual procedure, Frank asked the easy questions first and saved the difficult ones for last—the type of questions that make people hesitant to be entirely forthcoming. "Why did they ask you to be a driver," Frank finally said.

Miguel shrugged and crossed his arms across his chest. "I have a truck."

"That's true," Frank said. "But others have trucks," he persisted. "Why did they come to you? Why *you*?"

"Well," Miguel said, glancing at Jean Paul and then back at Frank. I'm known."

"*Known*?"

Miguel took a deep breath and exhaled. "People, they know me. Me, I don't always follow the law," he said with a shrug. He looked at Frank and cocked an eyebrow. Frank nodded.

That night, Frank slept fitfully, besieged by doubts and worry. He was filled with dread over his duty to turn in Jean Paul and worried about when and how to do it. He pushed it out of his mind. I'll deal with it later. But he couldn't put off thinking about his strict orders. He was authorized to interview Jean Paul, but he could only interview Miguel to obtain identifying information and nothing else. "You are NOT authorized to conduct any other interviews or take any actions." I've already exceeded those authorizations, Frank thought. With his career in jeopardy, he worried whether he should try to find the mountain compound.

He thought about the cell phone intercepts of Marwan talking about a last shipment occurring soon. Finding the camp is urgent. But if I ask for permission to look for it, they would never approve until I return to the U.S. and go through weeks of reports and meetings. If I stay and search for it, I may lose my job. Maybe I'm overreacting about it being important and urgent. The possibility of Marwan's connection could be warping my judgment. And what if we can't find it or there's no camp? Just looking for it may ruin my career. What should I do? A shipment soon... Marwan... my career. He tossed and turned. When Frank woke, he knew what he was going to do.

That morning, they would set off in Jean Paul's battered Land Rover on the long journey to Ambriz. From there, Miguel would try to retrace the route to the secret camp in the mountain. Frank focused on the mission. He felt anxious but would plunge ahead, uncertain of what lay ahead in the search for the mountain compound and the future of his career.

CHAPTER 7

It had been two days since Reza's men had seen Frank Marsh leave his apartment building carrying an overnight bag. There had been no sign of him since then, and Reza was impatient. He sent a message to Marwan.

"We located Marsh's apartment building. It is the Bridgeport Towers in Washington, D.C. He left on a trip two days ago. We are watching the building. Can the cyber unit determine which apartment is his and when he will return? We need current photo of Katherine Foster."

After reading it, Marwan picked up the phone, and within minutes, the cyber unit was trying to hack into the apartment management's computer system. The unit also began searching social media and U.S. government systems for Frank Marsh's whereabouts and a current photo of Kathy Foster. While those searches were going on, Hashem, commander of the cyber unit, received a call from Marwan. "Why aren't you tracking Marsh's mobile phone?" Marwan demanded.

"But sir, the last mobile number we had for him is no longer in service, and we do not have a current number," he pleaded. There was silence on Marwan's end, and Hashem cringed, aware of Marwan's volcanic temper and notorious impatience.

"*You,*" Marwan hissed through clenched teeth. "You will find his number and track it. Report to my office in one hour." He slammed the phone down.

"Well?" Marwan demanded when Hashem stood nervously in front of his desk.

"By checking calls on Foster's phone and calls by others connected to Frank Marsh, we identified a possible number for Marsh. Then we—"

"Where is he?" Marwan snapped.

"The last known location was in Washington, D.C., two days ago."

Marwan's eyes flashed, and his mouth tightened. "Where is he *now*?"

"The phone went dead two days ago, sir. He must have changed phones. We don't know. But we're checking everything," Hashem hastily added. He started to say more but was stopped by Marwan's glare.

After Hashem left, Marwan raged with frustration, incensed that Marsh couldn't be located immediately. Word quickly spread in the building that Marwan's fierce temper was flaring worse than usual. He was barking orders and snarling; it was best to try to avoid him.

Seething in his office, Marwan recalled a proverb, "Go and wake up your luck." But how? He knew the Russian GRU had hacked into American government computer systems, including some that were highly classified. The Americans had not discovered the penetrations. The Russians should be able to pinpoint Marsh's location, he thought. Elated by the prospect, Marwan reached for the secure phone to call his GRU counterpart, Dimitri, but then hesitated. The Russians always demand a lot in return. His hand hovered over the phone.

ISRAEL

Sergeant Shelly Danon, a petite brunette with Israeli cyber Unit eight-two hundred, the Israeli equivalent of the U.S. National Security Agency, filed a report during her shift. The report included the following passage:

"IRGC Quds Force again querying the names Frank MARSH and Katherine FOSTER in US databases, social media, and communications."

The Mossad sent the report to the Israeli embassy in Washington. But Iranians checking on Marsh and Foster again seemed routine, and the Mossad officer at the Israeli embassy didn't see any urgency in passing it on to the FBI. Besides, they had recently passed info to the FBI about the Iranians searching for information on the couple. The Mossad didn't know that the FBI had never acted on the previous tip.

WASHINGTON, D.C

The next morning, Kathy Foster walked out of the front doors of her apartment building for the subway several blocks away. Walking among dozens leaving the building, she passed within a few feet of Hamid, a member of Reza's hit team. Hamid wondered if she was the Foster woman, but he wondered the same thing about other women who emerged from the building. If he only had a photograph of her. Hamid noticed a barely visible scar on her cheek. He thought of asking Reza if the Foster woman had a scar, but surely they would have mentioned it.

Later that day, Marwan was handed a message from Reza. "Does the Foster woman have a scar on her face?" Irritated, Marwan wrote a curt response, "No scar," and handed it to his aide. Moments later, a phone buzzed on the desk of Marwan's assistant as the aide walked past. "Yes, sir," the assistant said into the phone. "Wait!" the assistant called hurriedly to the aide. "Go back in. He wants to see you." Marwan remembered he had burned Foster on the cheek with liquid nitrogen when she was his captive at the seaside villa in Greece. Shortly, Marwan sent a response to Reza. "Affirmative. Foster should have a scar on her cheek."

WASHINGTON, D.C.

After reading the reply from Marwan, Reza called Hamid. "The Foster woman does have a scar," Reza declared. "Describe the woman you saw."

"She looked to be in her early or mid-30s," Hamid recalled, "with blonde hair, about 5'4" and she has a trim figure. She is attractive. Except for the scar," he added. Reza briefed other members of the hit team on the description. Surely, they would be able to intercept her when she was returning or leaving for work.

That afternoon, Kathy emerged from the subway and walked toward the apartment building among a crowd of pedestrians. Floor-to-ceiling plate glass windows lined the lobby of the apartment building, along with three sets of double plate glass doors. Hamid spotted Kathy as she neared the entrance. He hurried to catch up. The automatic glass doors slid open, and Kathy walked inside the lobby with dozens of others and waited at a bank of four elevators. Hamid rushed to the lobby and walked quickly toward the elevators. As he closed on Kathy, he pulled out a cell phone and punched Reza's number.

"Yes," Reza answered.

"I'm at the elevators," Hassan said, "with our friend and ..." Elevator doors opened. Kathy and others crowded in. Hassan moved to the elevator, but there wasn't any more room. He stared helplessly with the cell phone at his ear as the doors slid closed.

"What? What?" Reza demanded.

"I will call back," Hamid replied. He watched the progress of the elevator. Above the closed doors, numbers lit as the elevator stopped on different floors. Hamid left the building and called Reza for instructions.

Reza rubbed his chin, realizing he needed to make a decision about Foster. He had been thinking about what would likely happen if they killed Foster instead of waiting on Marsh. They would probably miss an opportunity to kill Frank Marsh, the main target, because of the ensuing uproar over Foster's death. It would cause Marsh to return immediately from his trip but might lead to increased security.

"Just watch her for now," Reza said. "But if Marsh shows up, kill him, and if she's with him, kill them both." Kathy Foster was unaware she had just been given a temporary reprieve, but one good only until Frank returned or Reza changed his mind about waiting on Frank.

CHAPTER 8

AFRICA

The sun was rising over Equatorial Guinea when Frank, Jean Paul Savalle, and Miguel set off in Jean Paul's battered green Land Rover for the seaport at Ambriz, Angola. From Ambriz, they would try to retrace Miguel's route to the secret camp in the mountains. The trip to Ambriz turned into a grueling two-day journey through the coastal region stretching south from EG through Gabon, the Republic of the Congo, the Democratic Republic of the Congo, and finally, Angola. They took circuitous routes to enter at border control stations where bribes would produce instant visas.

At first, they traveled along narrow roads, passing through sparsely inhabited areas and small shanty towns with no electricity. There was little traffic, and noisy motorbikes dominated dusty villages. They spent an uncomfortable night in the Land Rover in Ndende, a small town with dirt roads and weatherworn shanties. The three men set out again the next day. They traveled along the P2 road, crossing a narrow strip of the Democratic Republic of the Congo, and finally arrived at Landana on the coast. From there, they followed the coast south to Angola. The air conditioner in the Land Rover stopped working, and stifling heat and humidity made the journey torturous. Finally, they arrived in Ambriz, hot, sweaty, and exhausted.

They stayed overnight at a small hotel in Ambriz and set out the next day on the final leg of their journey. The men traveled inland toward a distant belt of green hills backed by mountains. Soon, the Land Rover was the only vehicle on the road. Flat lands and brush changed into sharply rising hills and dense green forests as they approached the mountains. "There," Miguel said excitedly from the back seat, pointing to a narrow road to the right. "Turn there. We took that road."

Jean Paul turned and maneuvered the Land Rover along a dirt road snaking through the jungle toward mountains rising ahead. Around a bend, the skeleton of a tall dead tree loomed next to the road, its bony limbs spread wide in long, slender claws. A row of black vultures perching on a dead limb stared sullenly as the men drove past. An invisible creature screeched nearby. Frank wondered if this was a warning about what lay ahead.

After a short distance, they stopped and refueled from gas cans stored in the rear. From underneath the rear compartment, Jean Paul took out an AK-47 assault rifle with a folding stock. "Here," he said, handing it to Frank. "I think it's good to keep this handy from now on." The rifle with its 30-round magazine felt heavy and solid to Frank. More reassuring than the .40 caliber handguns each man carried under their brown bush jackets. They resumed the journey with the rifle tucked beside Frank's seat. Miguel leaned forward from the back seat. "Why you have gun?" he said anxiously. "You said you no go to the camp."

"Don't worry," Frank said over his shoulder. "We're not taking you all the way to the camp. We just want to make sure we can protect you—and us."

As they reached the mountains, the road turned into a steep and winding climb. The slow, torturous drive wound around hairpin turns, and the engine complained and whined in low gears. The road twisted through dense forest. Just to their right, through breaks in the foliage, they caught glimpses of the mountainside falling off steeply. Frank put the AK47 across his lap. "Keep alert," he said, glancing at Jean Paul. "If they're still using the camp, we might run into someone on the road." The men strained to watch each approaching turn, anxious that vehicles with armed men might suddenly appear. Finally, Miguel leaned forward between the two front seats and pointed ahead at a slight break in the foliage on the left.

"There," he said. "I think we turned there to go to the camp."

Jean Paul stopped at the junction, and they could see a barely visible narrow track running to the left. High weeds stood between rutted tire tracks, and dense forest crowded each side of the overgrown path. "How far is the camp?" Frank asked.

"We drive slow. It took maybe twenty minutes to get to it from here." Miguel sat back. "But please. Do not go to it," he said, shaking his head vigorously, his voice quivering. "Please. We will be killed."

Jean Paul and Frank exchanged looks. Miguel picked up on it and looked from one to the other. "Please. You said we no go to the camp. Please, no go," he pleaded.

No one said anything. Finally, Frank opened his door and climbed out. "Just drop me off here, Jean Paul," he said.

"But..."

"No, it's okay. Take Miguel back to Ambriz and drop him off. You can come back tomorrow and pick me up. I'll scout the area and do a recon for the camp." Miguel's shoulders slumped with relief, and he audibly exhaled. Jean Paul climbed out and gave Frank a canteen of water and two small pouches of dried food.

"What about a net or a blanket?" Frank said. "Do you have anything like that?"

"Ah," Jean Paul said, "You want to make a ghillie suit, yes?"

Frank had learned to make a ghillie suit in Marine Scout Sniper School. A cloak of hanging cloth strips helped a sniper blend into vegetation and remain hidden. Jean Paul rummaged in the Land Rover and came up with an old fishing net and a faded brown bush shirt. They agreed to meet the next day at five in the afternoon.

"When I come back," Jean Paul said, "I can pull off the road so the Land Rover will be out of sight. Behind us, there's an opening maybe 200 meters below this junction where I can pull off."

"I'll find you," Frank said. "If I'm not there at five, then wait on me for one hour. No longer. After an hour, leave if I haven't shown up."

Frank watched the Land Rover disappear around a bend as it headed down the mountain. Engine sounds grew fainter and then vanished. Suddenly, it was still and quiet. Dead silence hung heavy in the air, and Frank felt isolated as if he were the only human on earth. He remembered the same feeling in Iraq: noisy helicopter assaults, rushing out and taking up positions. Then the helicopters left, their thumping growing fainter until it was suddenly quiet. A menacing silence would hover like a deadly monster ready to pounce.

Shaking off the feeling, Frank cut the bush shirt into long, narrow strips and tied them to the fishing net, creating a hooded grass poncho that would blend in with the dense forest. He draped it on and pushed the hood off his head so he could see and hear better.

Before setting out on the rutted track toward the camp, Frank hesitated. He took a last look at the winding mountain road. The road led to safety, while the path ahead led to danger. He took a deep breath and then carefully picked his way along the tire ruts. Waist-high weeds stood between the ruts, and dense forest crowded the sides. The track wound through the woods with sharp turns every 40 or 50 yards. Frank paused short of each turn, knelt on a knee, and listened before moving again. He was especially alert as he rose and edged around each one.

As dusk began to fall, Frank couched near a bend and listened. The top of his head was even with high weeds. He was about to get up when he heard it. A metal clang from just beyond the bend. It was the sound of a rifle's metal sling fastener bumping against the rifle stock. Suddenly, he heard another clang, louder and closer, and he knew someone would emerge from around the bend at any moment. Ducking low and pulling the hood of the ghillie cloak over his head, Frank scrambled toward the forest to his left. Breathing heavily, he reached the forest's edge and backed into it, watching the track. Frank couldn't move further without making noise. He lowered himself flat on the ground, gripped his pistol, and watched the bend. Above the tops of weeds, a head suddenly bobbed into view and was joined by two more. Catching glimpses between the weeds, Frank saw three men in tan uniforms emerge with AK47 rifles slung across their chests.

As they neared, one glanced in Frank's direction and squinted. He stopped and stared. Frank's heart raced, and he was panting in shallow breaths. A shiver up his back. The other men stopped and said something to the staring man. Time froze. Frank gripped his pistol tighter, and sweat dripped off his brow. After a long moment, the man looked at the other two and shrugged. "Hah," responded one with a laugh. They resumed walking, moving past Frank, their heads finally disappearing from sight. After a long silence, Frank eased up on a knee and looked. They had disappeared around the far bend. He inhaled deeply and blew it out heavily,

Frank had taken a chance walking along the lane, but creeping quietly through the dense forest would be slow going. Now, he had no choice. Frank began moving parallel to the lane, catching glimpses of it through breaks in foliage. He pulled the hood of the ghillie suit off his head. It was getting darker and more difficult to keep sight of the lane.

He thought the three men would be returning to the camp soon, so he stopped every few minutes to listen before moving on. During one of these stops, he heard indistinct sounds of men talking, the sounds coming from behind and growing louder. He stood motionless, listening intently. The men were chatting and no longer alert; they had already swept the area. Dusk had fallen, and a flashlight beam jiggled ahead, lighting the way. After they walked past him, Frank eased onto the track and trailed behind. Darkness and the noise the men made covered his movements. The three black figures were outlined by the flashlight shining ahead of them. As he moved forward in their wake, closer to the camp, Frank was uncertain and anxious about what awaited him. He thought about Kathy and wondered if he would ever see her again.

TEHRAN, IRAN

Marwan was impatient, and Yassin, his intelligence chief, knew it. "Send a message to our source COMET for more information about the two Americans, Marsh and the Foster woman," Marwan demanded. "I want to know where Marsh is and when he will return to Washington."

Marwan needed to decide soon about Reza's hit team in D.C. They couldn't stay much longer without being discovered. Risk waiting a few more days to see if Frank Marsh returns? Or have them kill Kathy Foster now and leave? He needed to decide.

WASHINGTON, D.C.

At lunchtime, Kathy Foster was eating in the building cafeteria with a co-worker who asked about Frank. "He's overseas on a trip," Kathy said, "and I'll be glad when he gets back. He couldn't tell me exactly where or when he would be back. More secret business," she sighed. "When I asked Frank if it was dangerous, he said, '*Dangerous!* Heck, if it was dangerous, *I* wouldn't be going.' And then I said, '*Frank*,' and he said, 'No. *Really*. I wouldn't be going if it was dangerous.'" Kathy shook her head. "What are you going to do with a man like *that*."

Although her comments were lighthearted, she was worried. What if Frank never comes back? What if... Her thoughts were interrupted by a stab of pain from the last skin graft. Her mouth tightened until the pain subsided after a few moments.

Worrying about Frank while dealing with work and the lingering pain of skin grafts was wearing on her. Time for a reminder, Kathy thought. After lunch, she retrieved a small notecard from her purse. Frank had given it to her months before when she was beaten down and depressed from trying to deal with the most agonizing period of medical treatments and trauma. She read again the quotation Frank had written on the card.

"Courage doesn't always roar.
Sometimes courage is the quiet voice
at the end of the day saying,
'I will try again tomorrow.'"
—Anonymous

Frank had added, "Kathy, your courage inspires me to be worthy of you and your love. Frank."

Kathy sighed deeply and smiled.

CHAPTER 9

Thankful for an ink-black night, Frank lay flat on the ground and watched the compound some 50 yards away through binoculars. After carefully following the three-man patrol to the compound, he had eased into position. Situated in an old mining camp bordered by thick forest, the small rectangular encampment rested on hard-packed dirt stripped bare of trees and vegetation. Chest-high coils of barbed wire encircled the perimeter. Pole-mounted floodlights, spaced at intervals along the barbed wire, cast small pools of dim yellow light. An area 40–50 yards wide had been cleared outside the barbed wire to the forest. It was sparsely covered with ankle-high vegetation.

Frank lay in the forest at the edge of the cleared area and slowly swept his binoculars from right to left. The narrow dirt lane he had followed entered at a floodlit gate on the right and led inside to a line of four small wooden buildings. The first appeared to be the warehouse Miguel had described, where barrels from the ship had been unloaded. A dozen yards to the left of the warehouse was a small, one-story wood building, the camp commander's office where Miguel had been taken. Lights were on inside, and through the windows, Frank could see a man moving about.

To the left of the office was a tin-roof, rectangular building resting on supports a couple of feet off the ground, with steps leading to the door and screened windows lining the walls to let in breezes. Several men moved about inside, and it appeared to be a barracks. The night air carried distant voices to Frank in faint murmurs. About 40 yards beyond the barracks was a small structure resembling a shower house and latrine.

Two large diesel generators hummed in a steady low rumble, and Frank smelled diesel fuel, a sulfuric, rotten egg odor. A mosquito whined in his ear, unbearable high-pitched drilling. He swatted it away and resumed his survey. The floodlights were dim but enough to spot an intruder. One man with an AK47 guarded the entrance, and another man stood watch in a guard tower in the center of the camp. The guard tower was about a dozen feet high. Another guard roved just inside the barbed wire perimeter. Two Land Rovers, two pickup trucks, and a military truck were parked near the guard tower.

Frank wondered if he could slip inside the compound to check the warehouse's contents. He would have to elude the guard in the tower, the sentry at the gate, and the roving guard. The front of the warehouse was in the open, but if he could get by the guards, perhaps he could get inside the warehouse through a back door.

Did the warehouse have a rear door, and would it be unlocked if it did? He needed to move to the opposite side of the perimeter to see the back side of the warehouse. Frank eased back into the forest, stood up, and stretched. Mosquitos whined in his ear and feasted on his face and neck. He kept slapping them away and running his hand over his face. He regretted forgetting insect repellent. Before moving out, Frank ate dried food from a pouch and drank water from the canteen. Then he began picking his way inside the forest's edge, circling the compound.

Hours later, he reached a position in the forest directly to the rear of the warehouse. Peering at the compound, he could just make out what appeared to be the frame of a door on the rear wall of the warehouse. The door was on the far right of the back wall, close to the corner of the building.

To Frank's front, a cleared area about 50 yards wide stretched between the edge of the forest and the barbed wire. Floodlights lit the barbed wire and half of the cleared area beyond it. Behind the floodlights, the interior of the compound and buildings were cloaked in darkness. About 20 yards inside the barbed wire, the warehouse loomed as a large black shadow.

To get to the warehouse, Frank thought, I'll have to move undetected across the cleared ground and through the lit area at the barbed wire. The cleared area was clustered with weeds and brush one to two feet high, maybe enough to cover low-crawling to the barbed wire. The biggest problem would be getting through the lit area and barbed wire without being seen.

Frank didn't have to be concerned about being seen by the tower guard. The warehouse blocked the view from the guard tower of the area behind the warehouse. To the far left of the warehouse and Frank's left front, the gate guard sat in a waist-high sandbag enclosure next to the compound's entrance, facing outward toward the lane running to the compound. If the guard didn't turn around or look over his shoulder, he wouldn't see the cleared area or the wire Frank would have to cross. But he might spot Frank if he turned or looked over his shoulder. The roving guard presented the biggest problem. Strolling with an AK slung across his chest, he roved randomly inside the compound while staying out of the lit area along the wire.

Flying insects hit Frank's face, and mosquitos incessantly whined in his ears. He could swat insects away now, but once he got into the cleared area, he would have to endure the agony. Leaving his canteen and binoculars behind, Frank eased down on his hands and knees and began crawling toward the compound. As he crawled, he watched for the roving guard and the guard at the entrance. Crawling across the first part of the cleared area was in darkness, but the final 20 yards were lit by dim floodlights, and he would have to low crawl and be much more careful.

When he reached the edge of the lighted area, Frank eased down flat on his stomach and began slowly low crawling. After moving a few yards, he carefully lifted his head to look. Suddenly, he saw movement from the corner of his eye to the right front. The dark shape of the roving sentry was moving toward the back of the warehouse. Frank froze. The sentry came abreast of the rear wall of the warehouse, stopped, and looked in Frank's direction. The guard flashed a beam of light toward the cleared area, and the beam swept the ground several yards to Frank's right.

Frank eased his head down and pressed the side of his face against the ground. The beam of light danced around. Time slowed. A mosquito whined in his left ear, nearly unbearable high-pitched power drilling deep inside his ear. A bug crawled down the back of his neck.

The flashlight went out. Frank slowly raised his head, ignoring whining mosquitoes. A flame flared as the sentry lit a cigarette. He stood smoking. Frank eased his head back down and pressed his face against the dirt. The mosquitos whining in his ears and bugs crawling down the back of his neck were driving him crazy. He was sweating heavily. Suddenly, someone grabbed the back of his right leg. He drew a sharp breath and felt something heavy slithering over the back of his right leg—and now both legs. A snake. Frank stifled a grunt, his jaw clenched, and his heart hammered.

The flashlight beam suddenly came on again and swept over Frank's back. He wondered if he had cried out or moved without realizing it. The snake was still slithering across his legs. The flashlight beam hovered and lingered on Frank's back. A few moments later, the beam moved away, sweeping toward Frank's left. Frank was breathing in short pants, willing himself not to panic. The snake cleared his right leg, but he could still feel its weight moving across his left leg. Finally, the flashlight beam went out. The snake slithered off his leg and was finally gone but still close. Frank took a deep breath and sighed. He was drenched in sweat.

Why am I doing this? Frank wondered. I'll never make it inside the warehouse without being seen. And even if I do, who knows what I'll find. It could be empty or just filled with supplies for the compound. This is crazy. The risks are too great and probably all for nothing. No one expects me to do this. Kathy's waiting for me. I may never see her again. If I can back out of this cleared area, I'll go back to the U.S., and then we'll send the special ops guys to scope it out.

Even as these doubts roiled his mind, Frank knew he was not stopping. He reminded himself that you can always find a reason to do the wrong thing or to quit. He had learned in the Marines that to 'take the hill,' to succeed, you had to disregard those negative voices in your head and keep going no matter how hard it was. Never stop, never quit, and keep going. I'm getting into that warehouse, Frank thought, no matter what. If it's possible, I'm getting inside.

Moments later, the sentry began moving. He walked past the warehouse toward the guard in the sandbag emplacement at the compound entrance. When the roving sentry reached the entrance, he and the gate guard smoked and talked in low voices. While they were occupied, Frank moved quickly in a low crawl to the barbed wire. He was now under the floodlight, blinded by its glare and vulnerable if either guard glanced in his direction.

He rose into a crouch at the barbed wire and began picking his way through the coils. The two guards were still talking and facing away. He needed to hurry before either one looked his way. Long seconds seemed to drag endlessly. Frank finally worked through the wire, stepped out of the light, and then rushed to the rear door of the warehouse.

He was panting from the desperate effort to get through the wire unseen. Catching his breath, he gripped the doorknob and pleaded it would be unlocked. He held his breath and tried to turn the knob. It wouldn't turn. He tensed and tried again. Finally, the knob turned, and Frank slipped inside, feeling a rush of relief. Closing the door carefully behind him, he stood in impenetrable blackness. Frank lifted his hand before his face but couldn't see it. He stood still and listened. No sounds inside. He had a tiny LED light bulb on a string around his neck. He took it from under his shirt and pressed it on. The miniature bulb cast a faint glow, lighting a palm-size area less than one foot away.

Moving carefully in the dark, Frank came upon rows of black steel barrels stacked two high and several rows deep. He held the light up to barrels and looked for markings. Finally, Frank found a barrel with white stenciled markings turned toward him. When he read the markings, his heart raced, and he realized why they were so important. The barrels were marked: "Deuterium Oxide, 2H2O." Now he understood why Iranians were using and guarding the compound. The barrels contained heavy water, Deuterium Oxide. Used for putting plutonium into atomic bombs utilizing a heavy-water reactor suited for weapons-grade plutonium production.

He needed to get away and get the information back to the CIA and Defense Department as quickly as possible. The agency would want to know not only the contents of the barrels but also the quantity. Using the small LED light, Frank began counting the rows of barrels. Along one wall of the warehouse, the barrels were in two rows of ten barrels each, and the barrels in each row were stacked two high, 40 barrels of Deuterium Oxide.

Frank moved to the front of the warehouse to ensure he had not missed anything. He almost fell over metal cylinders standing upright on a wood pallet to the right of the sliding double doors. Each cylinder was about four feet high and two feet in diameter, with a thick locking mechanism sealing the top. Using the dim LED light, he saw there were dozens of cylinders. Frank bent down and examined one with his tiny light. He found yellow and red markings that read: "DANGER" "Isopropyl Methylphosphonofluoridate." He drew a sharp breath, jerked upright, and stepped back. Sarin nerve gas.

He remembered seeing images of its use. In March 1988, Iraqi warplanes attacked the Kurdish city of Halabja in northern Iraq with chemical weapons, including Sarin, and killed 5,000 people. Newspapers worldwide carried shocking pictures of dead mothers holding lifeless babies in the streets. In 1995, Sarin was used in a subway attack in Japan, killing 13 and sending over 5,000 for medical help. If a purer form of Sarin had been used, the death toll would have been much higher. In 2013, the Syrian government used Sarin in the Ghouta region, killing hundreds of people. Hospital videos showed panicked children with contorted faces, desperately struggling to breathe, and their horrible deaths prompted a world outcry. The outrage led to an agreement by Syria to give up its chemical weapons, although it never fully complied.

Next to the canisters of Sarin, he bumped into boxes packed with kilogram bricks of plastic explosives. Perhaps a total of several hundred pounds.

Frank needed to rush. It was urgent to get the warning out about Sarin at the compound. He checked his watch. Dawn would be coming soon, and he needed to get out of the compound before daylight. Getting away unseen would be difficult because he had no idea where the roving guard was. He couldn't take a chance on the guard spotting him going through the barbed wire or in the cleared area beyond. The best option was to watch at the back door until he saw the guard walk past, and after the guard was out of sight, Frank would move quickly to get through the wire.

Frank crept to the rear door and eased it slightly open, just enough to peer out with one eye. Daybreak was coming sooner than he thought. The sky had lightened from the deepest black to shades of gray. The camp would be coming to life. He couldn't wait. He would be caught in daylight with men stirring about if he didn't get out now.

Opening the door further, he suddenly saw the back of the roving guard a few feet away. Frank jerked his head back and eased the door almost closed. The guard stood smoking and looking across the barbed wire toward the cleared field. The rear of the warehouse was apparently a favorite place to take a break on his rounds because he couldn't be seen from the rest of the camp. It was getting lighter outside as each moment passed, but Frank would have to wait for the guard to move on before he could try to escape. Loud metal scraping and an extended roar erupted from the front of the warehouse. Whipping his head around, Frank saw the double doors at the front sliding open. He shut the back door and ducked behind the rows of barrels that ended a few feet away.

Overhead lights flipped on, bathing the warehouse in a harsh white glare. Frank heard the sounds of men coming inside, their voices sounding unnaturally loud inside the warehouse. He pulled out his Glock and held it ready. If anyone went to the back door or the end of the rows of barrels, they would discover him.

He backed against the wall and saw that the rows of barrels next to him, stacked two high, sat a foot or so away from the wall, creating a narrow space. With his legs bent, he squeezed sideways into the opening, his back against the wall and his chest pressed against a barrel. It was a tight fit. Frank couldn't move his arm across his body to use his gun. Stressed joints and overextended ligaments shot jolts of excruciating pain through his body. He took quick, short breaths, almost panting. He wouldn't be able to stay in the cramped space much longer. He was trapped. What to do? Stay hidden but helpless if discovered? Or crouch at the end of the rows of drums, where there was a greater chance of discovery, but at least he could fight back for a few moments.

More scraping sounds came from the front of the warehouse. It sounded like the men were wheeling barrels out. His circulation was cut off, and his limbs were going numb. He squeezed out of the compartment and felt blood flowing back to his limbs. Inhaling and blowing out a deep breath of relief, Frank crouched at the end of the rows of barrels with his gun ready.

He eased to the front row of barrels and peeked at an angle, just enough to see the left side of the opening at the front of the warehouse. Through the open doors, he saw it was almost daybreak but still dim and gray with thin wisps of mist curling up from the ground. While the men are busy with the barrels, maybe I can quickly slip through the back door without being noticed. If the roving guard is gone, then once I'm outside, I'll try to get through the barbed wire and low crawl through the cleared area beyond. He realized getting away would be a long shot and felt desperate.

For a backup plan, if I'm discovered, I'll rush toward the entrance to the compound, shooting at the guard there, and take my chances running for the jungle with the tower guard and others shooting at me. Or, I can stay here and hope no one comes to this end of the warehouse, and then try to sneak out tonight. I'm trapped. It was crazy, he thought again, to sneak into the warehouse.

He peeked further around the rows of barrels toward the front. If no one was in sight, he would try to get out the back door, and... A noise erupted behind him—the back door was opening, and then a shout. He jerked around and swung his gun toward the door. A guard at the open door rushed at him. Frank saw a blur coming upward toward his head from the left and ducked as the butt of an AK-47 rifle hit the left side of his head with a glancing blow. He saw a blinding white light and felt a sharp stab of pain in his head as he was knocked back against the barrels, stunned. Frank fired; an explosion erupted, and the guard dropped. The back door stood open, and Frank staggered through it and outside.

Taking a deep breath, he put his hand on the left side of his head and felt warm, sticky blood running through his fingers. Shouts came from behind him, inside the warehouse. The barbed wire was only a few yards away, but with the camp stirred up, he would never make it through. The warehouse blocked him from the view of the guard in the tower. About 40 yards to his right, the guard in the sandbag enclosure at the gate gripped his rifle across his chest and stared toward the center of the camp and the sounds of commotion following the gunshot. He had not noticed Frank.

The gate's my only chance, Frank thought, and if the guard sees me out of the corner of his eye, he may initially think I'm the roving guard. Frank took off, walking fast toward the gate, cringing at what might happen if the guard saw him too soon. The guard's AK47 would outgun Frank's pistol at this distance, but the odds would even out if he could get close enough before being noticed. Frank was two dozen yards away when the guard turned and saw him. The guard gave a quizzical look, then his eyes widened. Frank broke into a run, closing the distance fast. The guard swung his rifle toward Frank and fired a burst from the hip but swung too far, and the bullets went wide. Frank fired twice on the run, and the guard jerked backward and dropped.

Frank sprinted through the open gate and down the rutted track, his legs pumping furiously and his lungs straining. A burst of AK-47 rounds cracked by his head like a string of exploding firecrackers. The tree line was still 30 yards away and seemed like a mile. Dirt kicked up around his feet and ahead of him. His legs felt heavy, his leg muscles burned, and his lungs felt like they were about to burst. His foot hit a rut, and he pitched forward and sprawled in the dirt. His face hit the ground, and he saw grasshoppers kicking up grains of dirt a few inches from his head. Then he realized it was the impact of bullets. He scrambled up and ran. Ten more yards to go to the tree line, then five. He crashed into the forest and kept running. From behind, he heard sharp pops and then the stutter of automatic weapons as guards sprayed the tree line. Bullets smacked into a tree beside him, and bark exploded in splinters. More bullets snapped by his head, a vicious swarm of angry hornets. He tore through the dense brush; branches smacked his face, and tangled vines grabbed for him, trying to slow and trip him. The forest would soon be swarming with men trying to kill him.

The firing stopped. Frank was desperate to distance himself as quickly as possible from his pursuers, to get beyond their hearing as he ran and thrashed through the forest. He would have to stop running and try to pick his way quietly if they were too close. But then they would quickly overtake him. He had only a few more seconds to get enough distance into the forest before they reached the tree line. If only... it was too late. He heard men thrashing through the underbrush behind him. If he could hear them, then they could hear him running. He dove to the ground, panting and near panic.

The silence was suddenly shattered by bursts of automatic weapons spraying the forest; the pursuers were blindly firing. Frank realized the noise of the gunfire could cover his movements. Chancing being hit, he rose and ran through brush as random bullets slapped around him. A bullet tore through the sleeve of his shirt. The ground abruptly sloped downward, and he was finally out of the line of direct fire and far enough away that the sounds of his movement wouldn't give away his location. He stopped and bent over with his hands on his knees, panting and catching his breath. Then, after a moment, he moved out in a steady jog, dodging trees and weaving through the brush.

Somehow, he needed to get his bearings and circle back to the mountain road he and Savalle had traveled. After dropping Frank off the day before, Savalle had driven back down the mountain to take Miguel to safety. Savalle was to return, and they had arranged to meet next to the road just below the turn-off toward the compound. But if Frank's pursuers were searching or watching the road, they would discover Savalle. He needed to head Savalle off if it wasn't already too late.

"Search the road," the camp commandant barked at guards who had returned from pursuing Frank. "Whoever it was, he had to get up here by the road, and he has to come out on it. So, search the road for him. Don't stop looking until you find him." Three vehicles soon rushed out of the camp toward the road.

Several hours later, Savalle shifted the Land Rover to a lower gear as it climbed the winding mountain road. The motor whined in alternating low and high-pitched noises. When I'm about a half-mile below the turn-off to the camp, Savalle thought, I'll pull off the road and into the forest to hide the Land Rover. Then I'll wait and watch for Frank to show up and find me. He's probably already there waiting. Savalle glanced at the items on the passenger seat and smiled. Frank will be surprised when he sees I've brought food and cognac.

After eluding his pursuers, Frank quietly worked his way westward toward the road. He hoped he would come out on the road a few hundred yards below the turn-off to the camp. Once I hit the road, Frank thought, I'll move down to intercept Savalle before he runs into the men looking for me. Frank suddenly felt sluggish. His legs became heavy, and his mind filled with cobwebs. His throbbing forehead bloody from the guard's rifle butt, he struggled to move and think. Rest, he thought; I better rest a little and then move on.

Frank stopped and flopped down with his back against a tree. He crossed his arms on his knees and rested his head on his arms. He felt thirsty, starved, and drained. He realized he had not eaten since yesterday and hadn't slept since the night before last. He dimly realized the adrenaline was wearing off, plunging him into total exhaustion. He lay down on his side with his head resting on his arm and closed his eyes. Just rest a few moments, he thought, then get up and find Savalle before ... A gray cloud flooded his mind, and then came darkness.

CHAPTER 10

Lying on the ground, Frank heard a woodpecker hammering, dat, dat, dat. His eyes blinked open, and he dully remembered where he was. He heard the woodpecker again and realized it was an AK-47 firing in the far distance—dat, dat, dat. It stopped. Frank pushed himself to a sitting position and rubbed his face with both hands. His head was still hurting. Checking his watch, he saw it was already afternoon and remembered he and Savalle had agreed to meet. The firing had come from the west toward the road where Savalle would be traveling. Frank felt a sense of dread. Was it too late to head off Savalle? He rose stiffly and began moving west. More than an hour later, he reached the twisting mountain road. Standing just inside the jungle, he listened for several minutes, hearing only jungle sounds. The dirt-packed road sloped uphill to his left and downhill to his right, disappearing around bends in both directions. On the far side of the road, the mountain dropped off sharply.

Holding his pistol ready, Frank stepped onto the road. Moving uphill, he crept along the edge of the road, eyes and ears straining for signs of danger. As Frank moved around a curve, he saw Savalle's Land Rover, about 50 yards ahead on the left, pulled into the jungle, its rear protruding from the brush. He felt a flush of relief but then remembered the gunfire he had heard could have come from this part of the road. He stopped in mid-step and listened, straining to detect any manmade noises ahead.

His mind raced with possibilities. Was Savalle waiting for him at the Land Rover? Or had he been captured or killed? If they're watching the Land Rover, I'll be walking into a trap. He felt a rising urge to back away and put as much distance as possible between himself and the Land Rover. But what if they've already spotted me. I could be in the sights of AK47s right now with eager fingers on the triggers. Sweat dripped off his brow. After long moments of silence and indecision, Frank took a breath and began moving cautiously toward the Land Rover. With each step, he braced for an eruption of gunfire, the danger growing the closer he got.

Nerves on edge, Frank reached the back of the vehicle and saw the driver's door standing open. He dreaded what he might find and imagined seeing Savalle's body slumped over. Taking a tight breath, Frank moved to the door and saw the vehicle was empty. The front windshield was punctured with bullet holes, and dark blood splotches stained the driver's seatback. He checked the underbrush and was relieved not to find a body. If Savalle is still alive, he'll be held at the compound, Frank thought. Now, it became urgent to get off the mountain to get help and return.

The Land Rover sat wrecked; three tires shot flat, and its radiator pierced. He would try to use it anyway. But fatigue gnawed at him, leaving him weak, famished, and parched. On the floorboard, he found a can of sardines and a water bottle with a few sips left. He gulped down water and devoured the food. He felt restored but anxious. Night pressed in around him, adding to his sense of unease. Settling behind the steering wheel, Frank turned the key in the ignition. The engine stuttered and protested, its strained rumble echoing in the darkness. He feared the sounds would carry back to the camp in the clear night air.

Frank backed out and maneuvered the vehicle slowly downhill. He fought the steering wheel as the vehicle pulled to one side on flat tires. The Land Rover jerked up and down, rolling with flapping tire rubber slapping against the road. The headlights had been shot out, but a solitary fog light still worked, piercing darkness a few feet ahead. Hunched over the steering wheel, Frank strained to see the road. After he rounded the first curve, the radiator hissed and began spewing steam.

The engine sputtered to a stop and quit. Silence fell, punctuated only by the fading hiss of steam. Frank climbed out and stood in the quiet night, a wave of fatigue washing over him again. He was ready to sink to the ground and sleep but heard an ominous hum.

Suddenly, the rumble of approaching vehicles shattered the stillness, the sounds coming from up the mountain behind him and quickly becoming louder. The bend in the road about 40 paces behind him was abruptly lit by headlights. Bright beams emerged, sweeping toward him as the lead vehicle negotiated the turn. Frank turned to run but was suddenly blinded by a white glare. Gunfire erupted. He dashed into the jungle and was swallowed in the black night. He ran blindly in the dark, tearing through dense foliage and clutching vines. Branches slapped at his head and body.

Bursts of AK 47 gunfire sprayed the jungle around him, but Frank knew he would die if he stopped and tried to hide. Run, he told himself, run. Suddenly, he ran headfirst into a thick tree branch, and the jarring blow slammed him flat on his back. The impact knocked his breath out and flung the gun out of his hand. He opened his eyes and realized he must have blacked out a few moments. Frank pushed himself up to a sitting position. His face and head throbbed. He felt around for the gun, but pursuers searching with flashlights were getting close, and he couldn't wait. He struggled to his feet.

Stunned by the blow, Frank ran, staggering and stumbling in the dark. His forehead was gashed and sticky with blood. It compounded the earlier blow to his head by the guard's rifle butt at the warehouse. His head throbbed, and a concussion kept him from focusing. He knew he had to get away but couldn't remember why.

Lack of sleep and fatigue weighed him down, made his legs heavy and his mind sluggish. He began hallucinating and imagining groups of men rushing toward him. A bridge appeared in front of him but disappeared as he approached it. With his mind confused and body giving out, Frank realized he desperately needed to stop and sleep.

From his years as a Recon Marine, he vaguely recalled it would be best to hide for the night in thick underbrush where noise would give away anyone coming close. He stumbled into a thicket, knelt, and crawled until it became too dense to go further.

He lay on his side with his head resting on an arm. Frank's mind clouded, and everything went black. Sometime during the night, he woke to the sounds of rustling brush and men moving nearby. He raised his head and strained to hear. They were close and coming closer. He froze as the sounds of movement stopped a few feet away. In the silence, Frank heard a man's heavy breathing, an animal on the hunt. He tried to still his own breath. Had they heard him sleeping? Did he mutter out loud?

Then he heard a sharp clink of metal against metal. Frank cringed, waiting for an explosion of gunfire. A shiver raced up his spine, and his heart pounded. Long moments hung in silence. The brush rustled, and Frank flinched. Seconds later, he heard the man again; he was moving away, and the sounds became fainter. When Frank could no longer hear movements, he breathed a deep sigh of relief. He lowered his head on his arm and blacked out again. Later during the night, he was dimly aware of other sounds and of men calling out to each other, but exhaustion had numbed him to danger, and he was unable to open his eyes and fully wake.

As daylight broke, Frank woke with insects biting his neck and face. He lifted his head and rested on his elbow. He dimly recalled men had hunted him in the night. He strained his ears for any signs of their presence. All he heard was the forest's natural symphony. He crawled out of the thicket, struggled upright, and took in his surroundings. Mahogany, ebony, and sapelli trees soared more than 200 feet, blocking sunlight and creating an evergreen canopy over tangled undergrowth of leafy plants and vines. It was dark, gloomy, hot, and humid, typical of tropical rainforests. Frank heard screeching monkeys, chimpanzees, and mandrills. Birds were fluttering and bickering. Their riotous chattering was almost deafening. He smelled damp, earthy loam, rotting vegetation, and the moldy odors of green moss.

Frank felt stiff and sore. His face was swollen on one side, and his head throbbed with a fierce headache. Stabbing pain made it hard to think clearly. He gingerly touched his forehead and felt a deep gash and thick blood—a sticky, red molasses oozing from the wound. Jumbled thoughts flooded his mind: find Savelle, escape his pursuers, find a way off the mountain, raise the alarm about the secret mountain camp. Groggy and drained, he was unable to follow a chain of thought. He forced himself to focus on one simple goal: getting off the mountain.

Just keep going downhill, he told himself. He began moving, each step igniting aches and pains. Sometimes, he stumbled or fell but struggled up and kept going. At times, he realized he was moving in circles. Time moved in a hazy, numb blur. By nightfall, he was blindly moving, dragging his feet, and virtually sleepwalking. Dreamlike hallucinations triggered bizarre visions of a cow, a narrow steel bridge, and armed men charging toward him.

The following morning, Frank woke slumped against a tree, exhausted, starving, and thirsty. His lips were cracked, his mouth dry, and his tongue swollen. The gash in his head was festering, and he felt feverish. Waist-high gray fog shrouded the ground, and rainforest rose out of it as if from clouds. A sour smell hung in the air. He heard the cry of a leopard, sounding like a wailing baby. The ground was damp, and his body felt chilled. Frank wanted to sleep forever but knew he needed to keep moving if he wanted to live. Uttering agonizing moans, he struggled to his feet. He bent over with his hands on his knees, took a deep breath, and then began moving downhill. Stumbling and falling, he started mumbling and frequently blacked out for a few seconds while still on his feet. During the afternoon, Frank staggered off the mountain and into the open. Under a harsh, blinding sun, he stumbled upon a deserted road and collapsed.

Sometime later, rough hands lifted Frank and dropped him in the back of a pickup truck. He regained consciousness off and on, and images passed in a fuzzy slow-motion blur. The hot, blazing sun overhead, the truck bumping and jerking. When the truck finally stopped, he felt hands lifting him and carrying him into a building. He was dropped on a hard floor, and his hands were tied behind him. Someone was yelling at him, first in Spanish, then in French. Through half-opened eyes, Frank saw a bearded face inches away.

"You," the man yelled, slapping Frank's face. "You. Who are you? What are you doing here?"

Frank tried to remember what he was doing there, but his mind was too cloudy. If he could just have some water and sleep, then maybe he could— His head snapped to the side as the man slapped him again. Frank tried to talk, but words came in mumbles. He remembered Savalle. I must tell them to save Savalle, but his words were unintelligible when he tried. Another hard slap, and then another.

"Who will pay to get you back alive?" the man demanded. "Ransom? You understand ransom? Who will pay for you alive?"

Savalle, Frank thought. Save Savalle. Then he blacked out again. During the night, he half-woke, his eyes closed, and heard men arguing over whether they should kill him or try to find someone to pay a ransom first. Someone finally gave him water through his dry, cracked lips, and Frank lost consciousness again.

The next day, he heard shouts, followed by gunshots next to the building, then loud explosions of gunfire inside. Half-conscious, Frank was dimly aware his hands were being untied. He was drug by his arms across the floor and thrown into a vehicle. He heard a roaring engine and felt the vehicle moving fast and swerving.

CHAPTER 11

Frank woke in a bed, a hand under the back of his head. Through half-opened eyes, he saw a woman's creamy caramel skin, full lips, and dark hair. He recognized her but couldn't remember who she was.

"Here, drink some more," Nicole said soothingly, holding a cup of water to his lips. "You must drink." Frank gulped water hungrily until she held the cup away. "Not too fast. Now, some more." He drank and fell asleep, mumbling "Kathy" and "Savalle."

The following day, Frank woke feeling refreshed and realized where he was. The French doors and windows of Jean Paul Savalle's living quarters above the Legion Bar were open. Sea breezes stirred thin curtains hanging at the sides of windows. Ceiling fans in the bedroom and living room languidly circled. After a shower, Frank pulled on trousers and stood bare-chested and barefoot before a mirror, getting ready to shave off the beard that had grown since he had left for the mountain. The face staring at him in the mirror looked gaunt, the eyes shadowed and tired. He had dropped ten pounds. Dark circles hung beneath his eyes. A large white bandage covered the wound on his forehead. After a moment, he raised the razor to his face.

"Why don't you leave it on?" Nicole called from the balcony as she set a coffee pot and two cups on a small table. "It looks good on you." Then, after a moment, "Come and have coffee with me."

Frank put down the razor and rubbed his beard, cocking an eye at the mirror. Maybe shave it off later. He pulled on a short-sleeved shirt, leaving it unbuttoned, and joined her at the table. She poured coffee, and they sat quietly overlooking the dusty street below. A block away, an open-air market was lined with vendors and tables of goods in front of small shops. The sky was a cloudless blue. His shirt hung open, and the morning sun and breeze felt good on his chest. He took a deep breath and sighed. Nicole watched him, caught his eyes, and smiled. He smiled back.

"Yes," she said, nodding. "I think you look good with a beard. Mysterious. Like my Jean Paul."

Frank put his coffee down. "My head is clear now. How did I get here?"

A cloud crossed her face. "After Jean Paul left you on the mountain, he spent the night in Ambriz and sent word to me about everything. Jean Paul left the next day to go back and meet you. Before Jean left, he called me and told me that if I didn't hear from him the next day, I was to let his friend Rafe know."

"After a day passed, Rafe got two others, and they set off to find you and Jean. A few days later, they came back with you. You were unconscious and had a head injury. And then—"

"What about Jean Paul?" Frank said. "Did they find him? Is he okay?"

"They found the mountain but ran into armed men when they tried to go up. There was shooting, and Rafe and his men had to retreat. After they came off the mountain, they heard about an American being held for ransom by local gangsters. They thought it might be you or even Jean Paul. They found you but had to shoot their way in and out. They brought you here." She frowned. "You were in bad shape, Frank, with fever and chills. A doctor came and sewed your forehead and gave you shots. You fell in and out of consciousness for two days until you finally woke this morning."

"What about Jean Paul? Has anyone gone back to try to find him?"

"You don't remember the man who talked to you?"

"What man? When?"

"It was yesterday, Frank. A man from the American embassy in one of the other countries showed up looking for you, and he talked to you yesterday during one of your waking spells." Nicole looked at him questioningly. "Do you remember now?"

Frank thought for a long moment and finally shook his head. "No. No, I..." Frank stopped and tried again but still had no memory. "Who was he? What did he say?"

"A man named Matthews. He asked you about going to the mountain. You were still weak, but you told him about going into the camp and being chased. You kept insisting that the Americans go find Jean Paul. We had to calm you down, and then you fell asleep. The man kept trying to wake you, but I made him stop. He was arrogant. A pig," she said scornfully.

"Anything else?"

"I asked him about looking for Jean Paul, and he told me to mind my own business. He warned me not to say anything to anyone about the camp on the mountain, and he wanted to know who I already told about it. He is coming back to see you today," she said, frowning.

In the late afternoon, Matthews showed up and questioned Frank about the mountain camp. He was slim, sharp-faced, with thinning brown hair, perhaps in his 40s. Frank had hoped for an understanding American who realized it was urgent to get the word out about Sarin at the compound and mount a rescue for Savalle. But instead, Matthews was cold and abrupt.

"What else?" Matthews said when they finished. "What haven't you told me?" It was an accusation, not a question.

Frank stared at him. "Who the hell are you?" he said.

"If it's any of your business, I'm with the embassy Political section."

"You're *agency*, aren't you?"

Matthews shot Frank a look but didn't answer. Instead, he took a satellite phone out of a satchel and punched in numbers. Frank heard muffled ringing on the other end. "I'm calling for Mr. Price," Matthews said into the phone. "This is Matthews calling. He's expecting my call." After a few moments, Matthews said, "Matthews here. I'm with Marsh now. More details from him today. They will probably share part of my report with you." A pause and then a glance at Frank. "Yes, he can talk." Another short pause. "All right. Here he is." Matthews handed the phone to Frank. "Here. He wants to talk with you."

It was a conference call with FBI Assistant Director Price and others, including the head of FBI Intelligence. Frank suspected the CIA was also on the call. He was questioned briefly and sharply about what he saw at the compound. The questions were curt and seemed hostile. "You say this, BUT..." "You CLAIM you..." "You say that, BUT..." It was clear that they didn't believe him or thought he had exaggerated. As the call continued, Frank grew frustrated. Finally, Price declared, "I think we've heard enough. That will end the call."

"Wait," Frank said hurriedly. "Hold on. What about Jean Paul Savalle? Has anyone tried to find him? What are you doing to—"

"Your friend is not our problem," Price said coldly.

"But..."

"That's none of your concern. You never should have been in Africa in the first place, Marsh. You are to do nothing. I repeat—*do nothing*. And as soon as you can travel, you are to fly back as soon as possible. We will expect you back here within 72 hours. Do you understand?"

"But, Jean Paul..."

"Is that *clear*?"

"Yes, sir. But we have to find..." The connection went dead.

Matthews took the phone and put it in his satchel. He had been able to hear the discussion. A smirk hovered on his face. "As your people directed, you are to do nothing and fly back as soon as possible." Matthews put a plane ticket on the table and stood. "Your flight leaves from the capitol in two days. I'll arrange transportation for you to the capitol."

Stunned by the call, Frank stared numbly at the ticket. Matthews stood, waiting for a response.

"Well," Matthews demanded.

Frank stood and looked Matthews in the eye. He took a deep breath. "You can take the ticket with you. I'm leaving in the morning to search the mountain for Savalle."

Matthews smirked and shook his head. "No, you're not going to ...."

Frank flushed with anger, and a look stopped Matthews in midsentence. "My friend *is missing*," Frank said fiercely. "No one believes what I've seen, and I'm treated as if I did something wrong. I've been shot at, chased, and taken for ransom. And no one is looking for Savalle." Frank was ready to take his rage out on someone. "Take the ticket," Frank said through clenched teeth, looking Matthews in the eyes, "and get out."

They stared at each other. Then, after a long moment, Matthews picked up the ticket and left.

TEHRAN, IRAN

Marwan re-read two new intelligence reports at his desk in Unit 400 at Quds Force headquarters in Tehran. The first read:

HIGHLY CONFIDENTIAL

"Two intruders discovered the secret storage facility in Africa. One of the intruders, a Frenchman, was caught. Two days later, an American was captured near the mountain by a criminal group and held for ransom, but he was rescued.

END REPORT.

The second report read:

"Source COMET reports that an American agent in Africa may have discovered a covert site where chemical warfare materials may be stored. However, the report is disputed in high levels of the American government and dismissed as not credible."

END REPORT

Marwan stared at the reports and rubbed his chin. Then, after a moment, he looked at the man sitting across from his desk, the head of intelligence, Major Mohsen, a bearded, stocky man in his late 40s.

"Yes, sir?" Mohsen said in response to the look.

"Major, I had your section keeping track of the FBI agent Frank Marsh. Remind me about the most recent information on him."

"Sir, as we reported, we found the apartment in Washington where he lives with the woman, Foster. We believe Marsh recently left America on a trip out of the country, but we don't know where."

Marwan looked down at the reports again. After a long moment, he looked at Mohsen. "Major, could this American in Africa be Marsh? Frank Marsh?"

Mohsen gave Marwan a questioning look. After a moment, he pursed his lips and began nodding. "Yes, sir. Yes. It could be him," Mohsen said thoughtfully.

Marwan suddenly felt restless. His face hardened. "Find out if it could be Marsh, and if so, where he is now. If Marsh is there, I want him found and killed."

"Yes, sir," Mohsen said, and paused a moment. "We have influence with some criminal groups in that area. Should we use them? If we have to," he added quickly.

Mohsen recoiled from Mawan's glare. "I want Marsh dead. I don't care how."

WASHINGTON, D.C. FBI HEADQUARTERS

Sitting at a small conference table, Assistant FBI Director Bill Nelson stared across at Assistant FBI Director Price and Dick Johnson, the head of FBI Intelligence, long-time rivals of Nelson. Nelson was one of five assistant FBI directors, all reporting to the Deputy Director.

"Why wasn't I told about the conference call with Marsh?" Nelson demanded. Price glanced at Dick Johnson before answering. "Bill, we had a narrow window for the call because Gary Wyne at CIA was only available for a brief time. I was told you were out of the office, so we went ahead without you. We didn't realize you were still in the building."

Bill Nelson looked at Dick Johnson, who pretended to study his notepad. Price cleared his throat and said to Nelson, "We're meeting now because the deputy director wants us to brief him on the situation in Africa and what to do about Frank Marsh. We'll only have 20 minutes at most with him. I hope we can agree quickly on the essential facts." Price glanced down at his notes and back up. "Marsh went off to Equatorial Guinea 'unofficially' on some wild goose chase," he said accusingly, "based on flimsy and unsubstantiated raw intelligence."

"That's right," agreed Dick Johnson with a superior look at Bill Nelson. "We all know that Marsh jumps at anything that might involve Marwan, the head of Iran's assassination and sabotage group. He's pursuing a personal vendetta. He hears about a supposedly secret camp on a mountain that allegedly might somehow be connected to the Quds Force. Which is implausible on its face. Marsh has a friend in the area who runs a bar, so Marsh suddenly drops everything and flies off to EQ to join his drinking buddy. The next thing we know, Marsh disappears and then reappears in Africa, banged up and looking like he's been on a week-long drinking binge with his old buddy." Johnson paused a moment and looked at Nelson. "Which I think is what really happened with Marsh—your fair-haired boy, Nelson," he said snidely, chin jutting upward.

Before Bill Nelson could respond, Price said, "Wait, Bill, before you say anything. I know you may have a different view. But Dick has a good point, especially when you consider the past. Remember when Marsh and Kathy Foster were found coming out of the Louisiana swamps? They were clearly intoxicated when they arrived at the small hospital down there. And... Wait, Bill," Price said, holding up his palm. "I know what you're going to say. Yes, Marsh and Foster were recognized as heroes for disrupting the casino bombing in Mississippi, but there's a different take on that. Many have a very different view of Marsh. In our view, Frank Marsh is an insubordinate drunkard who got lucky once and stumbled into a terrorist bombing plot. This business in Africa is just further proof of that. And besides that—"

"Sir," said a secretary, sticking her head in a partially open door. "The Deputy Director had to move his schedule up, and he said all of you could come up right now."

Bill Nelson, Price, and Johnson sat in armchairs facing FBI Deputy Director Walters across his desk. "Thank you all for changing your schedules and coming," Walters said graciously. "As usual, I'm pressed for time. So, let's get to it. Brief me on the Africa situation and our agent in the middle of it. Marsh, his name is, I think."

Price took the lead and presented some of the facts, but with negative connotations, Bill Nelson noticed. In the constant battles of meetings and memos among rivals, Nelson knew this was not just an attack on Marsh but also on him. But more important to Nelson, it was an intra-agency battle that could blind the Bureau to intelligence about possible WMDs.

"And," said Price, removing a sheet of paper from a folder and handing it to Walters, "thinking it would be helpful for you, Mr. Walters, Dick Johnson and I prepared a one-page briefing summary for you. It lists reference documents and reports." Walters put on glasses and began reading. As Walters read, Price glanced smugly at Nelson.

Nelson knew exactly what had happened. Price and Johnson had prepared the briefing paper to blindside Nelson, knowing Nelson wouldn't have a written response with document references.

Walters took off his glasses and looked up from the paper at Price and Johnson. "Anything you can add to this?"

Price spoke up. "As we conclude in the briefing paper, Marsh was probably on a drunken binge. He shouldn't have been there in the first place, and there's no good reason to pursue his claim of WMD being at a secret mountain camp. His wild and unsupported claims are simply too implausible. And as you know, we will catch holy hell from CIA on venturing onto their turf outside the U.S."

Walters chewed his lips and looked silently at Price for a long moment. When Nelson cleared his throat, Walters looked at him questioningly.

"Bill, do you have anything to add? Do you agree with Price and Johnson? I recall this man Marsh is someone you have always been high on. Still, as Price and Johnson wrote," he put on his glasses and glanced at the paper again. "It says in the casino case, Marsh was insubordinate and drunk and just stumbled onto the casino bombing in Mississippi." Walters put the paper down and took off his glasses. "And now Marsh may have just been on another drunken binge in Africa and comes up with this cock and bull story." Walters frowned and paused. "So, what do you say to that, Bill?"

Nelson took a breath. "Like all of us, I've made mistakes during my career and sometimes misjudged people. I thought Frank Marsh was one of our best agents. I always thought he was ingenious, tenacious, and bold—someone who cared more about the mission than his career or self-advancement. As I said, I have sometimes been mistaken in my judgments about people." Price and Johnson allowed themselves satisfied smiles. Nelson paused a moment and added, "But I haven't been mistaken about Frank Marsh."

"What...?" Price said, taken off guard.

"Marsh and Foster disrupted the casino bombing in Mississippi," Nelson declared. "They didn't stumble onto it; they pursued leads and discovered the plot. He was insubordinate only because he wisely kept investigating even after being told to stand down. In the end, his insubordination saved hundreds of lives. And, incidentally, he made the Bureau look good." Nelson knew that would get Walters's attention.

"It's true that Marsh was slightly intoxicated when he arrived at the hospital after coming out of the swamps in Louisiana," Nelson continued. "But it was only because he and Foster hadn't had water for days, and all the man had who picked them up was two cans of warm beer. They drank that on the way to the hospital, and with their empty stomachs, they got loopy on just one beer each." Nelson looked at Price and Johnson. "Marsh is no more of a drunkard than we are."

"Well," demanded Price, "what about going to Africa just to visit an old buddy and pursue a personal vendetta against Marwan. That certainly—"

"No," Nelson said flatly. "Marsh's friend had information about a secret WMD camp in the mountains, and Marsh knew the man would only talk with him. We're fortunate that Marsh had the connection. As to Marwan, he's still a threat to Marsh and Foster; therefore, it's natural for Marsh to be alert for anything concerning him."

"Still," said Deputy Director Walters, "it does seem implausible that a secret WMD camp would be in the mountains in Africa."

"Exactly," said Price, "that doesn't make any sense."

"That's true," Nelson agreed. "It *is* implausible that a WMD site would be there. But, that's exactly *why* it may be there."

Walters gave Nelson a questioning look. "You see," Nelson continued, "the fact that it's implausible that WMD would be hidden in a secret camp in Africa is exactly what makes it plausible for me." Nelson held his palms open. "If you were trying to hide something, wouldn't you try to hide it where people would be least likely to look? Hide it in an *implausible* place."

Walters stared at Bill Nelson, pursed his lips, and finally nodded. "Bill, you make a good point," Walters said with a wry smile. Price started to speak, but Turnow held up a hand. "I think I've got all the facts and arguments on both sides. In this briefing paper, Price and Johnson recommend we bring Marsh back immediately for possible disciplinary action and that we drop anything concerning the mountain camp. What say you, Bill?"

"I think we should recommend that the CIA and Special Ops Command look for the camp and that Marsh remain in Africa for a short time to assist those efforts."

"Bill, I've got the briefing paper from Price and Johnson on this, along with their references to reports and documents, but nothing from you. And they're pretty persuasive." Walters rubbed his chin. "Just how *strongly* do you feel about this, Bill?"

Nelson knew what Walters was asking him—*do you want to go out on a limb on this and put your career on the line? And should I trust your judgment enough to go out on a limb with you?* The two men looked at each other silently for a moment. Then, Nelson took a deep breath. "I feel *very* strongly about it, sir," he said confidently.

Walters nodded, put on his glasses, and looked down at the briefing paper. After a moment, he removed the glasses and looked at the three men. "Here's my decision...."

CIA HEADQUARTERS, LANGLEY, VA

After clearing security, FBI Assistant Director Bill Nelson was escorted into the office of Tom Drake. Drake rose from his desk and greeted him with a warm smile and firm handshake. The two men had worked together for many years on joint matters. Drake waved him to an armchair and sat down again behind his desk.

After small talk about friends and families, Drake's face turned serious. "Bill, I'm sure you know what this is about. All hell is about to break loose because one of your agents went snooping on his own in Africa. That violated every protocol between our agencies and could have screwed up agency operations. And it still may have, for all I know right now. We're still assessing the potential damage." He paused a moment. "I'm letting you know because heads may roll at the Bureau. The CIA Director is going to raise the issue with the AG and the White

House. We go back a long way, and I wanted to give you a heads up so you could protect yourself over there."

Nelson nodded thoughtfully. "I appreciate that, Tom. I do. Look, there are some things you need to know about. I can shed some light on this and maybe help you."

Drake lifted his brows. "I hope you can. This is serious. That prick Semore has gotten involved and is pushing the director to make heads roll at the Bureau. He—"

A knock came at the door, and a tall, broad-shouldered man came in. He gave Nelson a contemptuous glance. "I heard you two were meeting," Semore said to Drake, "and thought I would join you." Semore stopped in front of Nelson and stared down at him.

"I only have a few minutes, Nelson, so I'll come to the point. I'm sure you're here about the Bureau fuckup in Africa. I'm preparing a complaint for our director to send to the Attorney General and the White House. The Bureau can get ready because the shit is going to hit the fucking fan," Semore seethed. "I just dropped by to tell you to keep your damned agents in the U.S. And, *if* you're still working after this, don't even *think* about having your people work outside the country again," Semore snapped. "*Understood*?" He glared at Nelson and turned to leave.

Drake glanced anxiously at Bill Nelson and saw barely suppressed fury.

Nelson stood. "Just a moment, shithead," Nelson said as Semore opened the door to leave. Semore snapped his head around with an incredulous frown. "That's right," Nelson said, chin jutting up. "I said, *shithead*. Semore, you better try to save your own career because it won't be worth much when the White House and NSC learn that the FBI found WMD materials in Africa—WMDs that the CIA knew nothing about."

Semore squinted at Nelson. "WMDs? Who said there were WMDs?" he said weakly.

Nelson turned to Drake. "Tom, I came by to give *you* a heads up. Maybe our agent shouldn't have been there—but the big story is that he found WMDs that the CIA knew nothing about. That's going to take a lot of explaining by your guys."

Nelson strode for the door and stared at Semore, who stood dumbly holding it open. "So long, shithead," he said with a smile.

CHAPTER 12

After Matthews left, Frank and Nicole met with Rafe in the quarters above the Legion Bar and looked over a map spread on the table. The two men decided to leave the next day to go back to the mountain to search for Jean Paul Savalle. "I can lead us to the compound," Frank said. "If we spot Jean Paul, we can come back for help. Or maybe we can even slip in at night and rescue him ourselves. We'll just have to see what the situation is." It was a risky plan and a long shot, but Frank felt driven by a need to do something.

As they talked, Nicole stirred, and Frank could tell she was anxious to say something. He looked at her. "Nicole?"

"I'm going with you," she said, holding his eyes. "To look for Jean Paul."

"I know how you feel," Frank said. "But you would slow us down because we would be trying to look after you. It's too dangerous."

"I can take care of myself," Nicole said defiantly. "Ask Rafe. He knows how I take care of drunks and fights in the bar. Isn't that right?" she said to Rafe.

Rafe raised his eyebrows and spread his hands. "Nicole, you *are* tough, but as Frank says, this is *too* dangerous. It's more dangerous than drunks and bar fights."

After the planning was finished, Nicole and Rafe went downstairs to run the bar for the evening. Frank felt a sudden overpowering exhaustion, a lingering effect of his ordeal. He took off his shirt and lay on his stomach across the bed. A ceiling fan hummed overhead in a soothing rhythm, stirring a caressing breeze. Under the comforting droning, Frank drifted into a deep sleep.

He dreamed he was being chased by murderous devils and cornered with no way to escape. Frank sensed he was calling out in his sleep, but he couldn't wake himself. He was trapped in the nightmare. Later, he was holding Kathy in his arms, but she was being pulled away and crying for him. He struggled to reach her. In the end, he dreamed Kathy was snuggled against him, sleeping. He would wake her with soft kisses and tender caresses.

Frank woke at daylight. He was on his back, and Nicole was snuggled against him. She was asleep on her side, her arm lying across his chest and a leg flung across his thighs. Her head nestled on his shoulder, and long black hair covered part of her face. The end of one strand rested at the corner of her full and slightly parted lips. She wore a light blue camisole and matching panties. The blue accentuated her honey skin and graceful curves. The scent of lavender was in the air. Frank felt Nicole's breasts against him and the slow rhythm of her breathing.

He was puzzled. The last thing Frank remembered was falling asleep alone after meeting with Rafe and Nicole. He had fallen asleep bare-chested and wearing trousers. But now Frank wore only navy blue briefs. Try as he might, he couldn't remember how he and Nicole wound up in bed together. Frank carefully moved his shoulder from under her head and then edged out from under her arm and leg. He quietly got out of bed. With a murmur, Nicole turned over and slept on her other side, with her back to him. After dressing, Frank made coffee and then sat on the balcony sipping the hot brew, still wondering.

"Oh, Frank," Nicole called out. He looked over his shoulder. She was propped up on an elbow in bed, yawning and rubbing her eyes with the back of a hand. She opened her eyes and gave him a dreamy smile. "How long have you been up?" And after a pause, "Oh, you made coffee!"

Minutes later, barefoot and wearing tan cotton pants and the blue camisole, Nicole joined him for coffee. "This is so good," she sighed after taking a sip, her hands cupped around the mug. "You make good coffee, Frank."

"Nicole, about last night. We were together in bed when I woke up. And I, uh, wondered... I mean, I don't remember how we... what we..."

She gave him a sweet smile and a dismissive wave of her hand. "Do not worry, Frank. We just sleep together, that's all. I undressed you when I came to bed." She saw his confused look. "We've been sleeping together every night. You were unconscious the first night and slept nonstop the next nights. I thought it would help you rest better. I like sleeping against you, Frank," she said with a perky smile. "We fit together good in bed. Yes?"

Relieved, Frank returned her smile and nodded.

After coffee, Nicole replaced the white gauze bandage on his forehead with a smaller, flesh-colored one. "I still want to go with you to find Jean Paul," she said as she finished and looked him in the eye.

He shook his head. "No. It's best if you stay here." They argued until she unhappily conceded. Later that morning, Frank and Rafe set off in a dented, four-wheel drive pickup with a shell camper on the back. They carried food and water in the back, along with backpacks. A blanket covered two AK-47 rifles with 30-round magazines and extra ammo. Rafe had given Frank a 9 mm Glock pistol, which was now tucked at Frank's waist under a dark green bush shirt.

Rarely do events unfold in a vacuum. As the dust settled on the outskirts of town, where the men had vanished over the horizon, Matthews, the agency man, received a phone call. "It's me," said Kruger, the local underworld figure. "The American and another man just left town." After obtaining a description of their vehicle, Matthews unfurled a map across his desk, his fingers tracing potential routes.

After calling Matthews, Kruger nodded and murmured with satisfaction, "So the American is gone, and Savalle is still missing." A grim smile spread across his face. "And Nicole is left all alone."

Instead of traveling to Ambriz and then inland, Frank and Rafe took a more direct and dangerous route to the mountain, stopping overnight and sleeping in the truck. By late the next morning, they had passed only a few small villages and rarely encountered other vehicles. The road followed a broad river on the right. On the left, forested hills sloped down to the road's edge. The steady droning of the motor made Frank sleepy, and he dozed off and on. Then, as they rounded a curve, Rafe saw a police roadblock ahead with three vehicles blocking the road. "Oh no!" He shook Frank's shoulder. "Frank. Frank," he said urgently. Frank woke with a start, blinked, and looked ahead.

"What? What...what is it? .. . Police?"

Staring at the police roadblock ahead, Rafe frowned and shook his head slowly. "This is not good, Frank. Not good," he said grimly.

WASHINGTON, D.C. THE WHITE HOUSE

"What the hell is it now?" said Dennis Simpson irritably. It had already been a busy and chaotic morning for the intense White House Chief of Staff, and he didn't like the worried look on the CIA official's face. The President's PDB, the President's Daily Brief, was scheduled to begin in 30 minutes. Simpson and Tom Drake, the President's CIA briefer, usually met just before the briefing so that Drake could alert Simpson about anything critical or controversial before it was presented to the President. The two men would usually discuss how to address the President's potential questions on critical issues in the PDB. The daily barrages of domestic and international matters vying for the President's attention were overwhelming. As the President's gatekeeper, Simpson didn't have time for anything but essential facts. "Well?" Simpson demanded.

"We may have a Flashpoint situation," Drake said with a frown.

"Flashpoint?" Simpson squinted. "Flashpoint? What the hell is that?" he said, raising his voice.

"You and the President have been briefed on Flashpoint, but it's been a while. Flashpoint is the classified designation for possible WMDs. Flashpoint intelligence may only be shared with those specially cleared for Top Secret SCI/FP (Flashpoint). Flashpoint has—"

"Hurry up, dammit, Drake. What the hell does it have to do with the PDB? We've only got a few minutes until we start."

"Right here," Drake said, handing him a copy of the PDB and pointing to a passage.

<u>FLASHPOINT</u>

"[TS/SCI/FP] AFRICA: An FBI agent discovered possible WMD materials being guarded in a secret compound in the mountains of Angola. Personnel at the camp are believed to be Cuban, Iranian, and possibly Russian. Heavy water and containers of Sarin nerve gas were allegedly seen. There is no indication of imminent WMD use, and the agent's report has not been substantiated. The Flashpoint executive committee and the task force will continue to monitor and assess the situation. The existence of WMD is assessed at FLASHPOINT LEVEL ONE until more is developed. [TS/SCI/FP] [END]"

White House Chief of Staff Dennis Simpson scrunched his mouth and looked up from the page. "You've got 60 seconds to tell me what the hell this means, whether the President should be concerned, and whether the White House needs to authorize action."

"Flashpoint level 1 means only a possibility of WMDs, but should be investigated further," Drake said hurriedly. "We want to covertly send CIA and SOCOM teams into Angola to assess the situation. But we can expect pushback from SOCOM. They always demand more time to plan. If WMD materials are found, they will be seized or neutralized. There's a slight possibility there could be U.S. or foreign national casualties. Best case—no WMD materials are found. Worse case—casualties and/or the Angolan government finds out and lodges a diplomatic complaint or a demarche."

Simpson thought a moment. "Neither the Angolan government nor the Iranians would want to make a public stink about it—right?"

Drake nodded. "That's what we think."

"So, for now, we should downplay this with the President?"

"I think so."

"All right, Drake, but this had better not blow up, dammit. I don't want the President raising hell later because we didn't warn him. Next. Quick. What else do I need to know on the PDB?"

When he returned to CIA headquarters at Langley, Drake briefed his boss on the President's reactions to the PDB and the need for agency follow-ups on several questions the President raised. "What about Flashpoint? Did the President have any questions about that?"

Drake shook his head. "None."

"Good. Because we wouldn't have had any good answers at this point."

Whether to designate the information from Frank Marsh as "Flashpoint" had generated heated discussions within the CIA. Some thought the information was too vague and were reluctant to divert resources to follow it up. Intelligence could always be followed up or not, but anything designated Flashpoint had to be investigated further. Flashpoint One, the lowest level, required minimal follow-up. Higher levels required increased national resources, such as automatic authorizations for using the most sensitive satellites and SOCOM assets. The highest level, Flashpoint Five, designated possible imminent use of WMDs. Level Five would trigger emergency responses by all national security agencies and the military.

Just then, Frank Marsh was on the road with Rafe in Africa, encountering a roadblock. He had never heard of Flashpoint, but he was about to be thrust into the middle of a Level One follow-up. If it wasn't already too late.

ANGOLA, AFRICA

Frank did a quick assessment as Rafe began slowing for the roadblock. Forested hills on the left sloped down steeply to the road's edge. On the right, a marshy area ran from the road to the river about 50 yards away. A marked police vehicle, a dented SUV, and a small Toyota pickup truck were parked crossways on the road with a small car behind them. No room to get by on either side. A policeman wearing a ragged and ill-fitting uniform stood in the road in front of the vehicles. He held up his hand, signaling Rafe to stop. Several other men with grim faces and dark sunglasses stood to the sides, clutching assault rifles across their chests. They wore civilian clothes.

"This is not good, Frank," Rafe repeated. "Gangs, they often dress up like police. And the police sometimes rob or kidnap, too."

Rafe slowed to a stop about 40 yards from the roadblock. He was gripping the top of the steering wheel tightly and staring ahead, sweat dripping off his forehead. The uniformed man standing in front of the roadblock began waving vigorously for Rafe to come on. The others started raising their assault rifles. "What do we do, Frank?" Rafe said nervously. "What do we do?"

Frank glanced at him. "Rafe, let's—" Spat! A small hole punched through the windshield, Rafe's head jerked back, and the window behind splattered with blood and brain matter. "Rafe!" Bullets punched more holes in the windshield, some hitting Rafe's chest and others just missing Frank. He dropped down sideways on the bench seat toward Rafe. The pickup was idling in park. Loud metallic dings erupted as bullets exploded against the front of the pickup and punctured the radiator, which began spewing plumes of hissing steam. Leaning over and carefully staying below the top of the dash, Frank reached past the steering wheel, opened the driver's door, and pushed Rafe's sagging body out. As it tumbled onto the road, bullets tattooed holes in the opened door.

Keeping his head and body down, Frank edged under the steering wheel and pulled the driver's door partially shut. He put the truck in reverse, pressed the accelerator, and began backing up blindly. The truck shot backward, and Frank let off on the accelerator to control the steering. He kept the road's edge in sight through the partially open door and maneuvered the truck backward. The truck swerved erratically from side to side as Frank jerked the wheel, trying to stay on the road while backing. Everything was occurring in a blur: bullets hammering the truck, windshield shattering, and the din of vicious metallic dings.

After backing about a hundred yards, Frank spun the steering wheel in a hard turn, swinging the rear of the truck toward the roadblock and the front pointing away from it. He jammed the brakes, shifted from reverse to drive, and stomped the accelerator. The truck jumped forward, and he rose up, just enough to peer over the dashboard. Several bullets punctured the rear of the truck and its camper shell, but most of the gunfire missed.

Frank gripped the steering wheel and peered over the dashboard as the pickup hurtled around a curve, and the roadblock disappeared from view. He sat up, hunched forward, and kept the accelerator floored as the truck careened around onrushing curves. Plumes of hissing steam blew over the hood and through the shattered windshield. The steering wheel was slippery with Rafe's blood. Using the bottom of his shirt, Frank wiped some of it off and glanced up at the cracked rearview mirror. Nothing yet, but he knew pursuing vehicles would soon be in sight and catching up, so he had to get off the road fast. As the truck sped down the road, he desperately searched for an escape.

The road followed the river, which lay about 40 yards to his left, down inclines, but filled with woods and occasional openings of low bushes between the road and the river. On the other side of the road, hills covered with tangled forests crowded against its right edge, making it impossible to escape on that side.

In a few rushed seconds, Frank ran through his options: stop and shoot it out, swerve toward the river at the next bushy area and try to swim across under a hail of gunfire, or stop and try to flee on foot in the forested hills. None were good options, but he needed to do something before the pursuing vehicle came in sight; by then, anything he tried would be hopeless. Frank realized he wouldn't know what he would do until he did it, and it would be a spontaneous decision.

As Frank roared around a curve to the right, he saw a narrow break in the woods coming up on the left. The gap in the woods was filled with weeds and low bushes from the road to the river bank. Frank jammed the brake and jerked the wheel to the left. The pickup fish-tailed and slid sideways, rushing toward trees on the bushy area's far side. It started tilting over toward the passenger side, teetered in the air, hesitated for a long moment, and then slammed back down on its wheels. Frank jammed the accelerator down. The pickup shot off the road and became airborne over the incline toward the river. After flying, it dropped and crashed down hard. When the airborne truck dropped out from under him, Frank's head hit the ceiling, and as it crashed down, he was slammed down on the seat. His hands were jarred loose from the steering wheel. Grabbing the wheel again, he stomped the accelerator. The front of the truck wildly bounced up and down until the front wheels sank in the mud at the river's edge. The pickup came to rest, with the driver's side almost touching trees that lined the low bushes from the road to the river.

Frank glanced over his shoulder up at the road. Nothing yet. Leaning over, he ransacked the glove compartment and found a box of matches. He jumped out of the truck, tore off his shirt, and pushed it into the gas tank opening. He moved and pulled on the shirt until it became soaked with gas, with one end hanging out of the opening.

Suddenly, he heard the screaming roar of speeding engines on the road. The police SUV flashed by, followed by the pickup and the car. After the vehicles flew past the break in the tree line, he heard brakes screeching and tires squealing. They would turn around and would be firing down at him in moments. He struck a match on the matchbox, but it broke. His hands fumbled, trying to get another match out, and some fell to the ground. Quickly striking another match, he lit the gas-soaked shirt, and it burst into flames.

Frank whirled around and dashed into the tree line, running and weaving through tangled woods. He heard screeching brakes, followed moments later by shouts. Suddenly, a string of firecrackers exploded as they fired at the pickup. A deafening whoosh erupted behind him as the pickup burst into a massive fireball. Flames began crackling while the pickup burned furiously. If he was lucky, they would believe he was killed in the fire and wouldn't stay to make sure.

As Frank moved deeper into the woods, dusk descended, the surroundings darkened, and the burning truck became a huge flaming torch. Frank picked his way through the woods until he was sure he was past the last curve he had taken. Then, changing direction, he scaled the wooded incline toward the road. It was completely dark when he emerged at the road, just out of sight of his pursuers. To his left, the road curved to the right, out of sight. His pursuers were just around the bend, watching the fiery inferno. A reddish and yellow glow from leaping flames danced in the upper reaches of trees.

Frank crossed the road, edged into the forest, and then started following the road around the curve. The police SUV was parked on the road with the Toyota pickup behind it, both facing toward him. The third vehicle, an older compact car, was beyond the two vehicles, facing in the opposite direction. When the first two drivers turned around to rush back toward Frank's pickup, the driver of the compact car apparently just backed up and stopped. It was still facing in the direction Frank had been traveling while trying to escape.

Flames leaping skyward from the burning pickup on the river bank illuminated the night and woods. Frank saw dark figures gathered halfway down the incline, silhouetted against the crackling flames. Crouching low and keeping the vehicles between himself and the men, he reached into the open driver windows of the police SUV and the pickup behind it and removed keys from the ignitions. Then he crept to the small car parked further away. Unlike the other vehicles, the driver's side was on the same side of the road as the men watching the burning truck. Keeping low, Frank slowly pulled the passenger door handle and eased the door open. Leaning over the seat, he felt for the key. It was in the ignition.

He crawled inside and slid under the steering wheel, bending down to stay under the window. He peeked above the driver's window sill. The men were still in a group on the incline. Frank tensed. He put his foot on the brake, cringed, and turned the key in the ignition. The motor stuttered, coughed, and then began running. Frank shifted it into drive, sat up, and stomped the accelerator. But the small engine struggled to gain speed, and the car moved slowly. Shouts broke out behind him. Men were running and getting closer, their yells getting louder. The car was only moving about 10 mph, and they were gaining, then it was up to 15, and straining to go faster. Now close to 20 mph.

Gunshots rang out, piercing holes in the rear window. Frank ducked down sideways on the seat, his foot pressing the accelerator. Loud metallic dings erupted as bullets punctured the trunk. Peering over the dash, he steered around a curve as the car got up to 35 mph, now building speed more rapidly. After rounding the bend, he sat up, switched on the headlights, and was soon zipping along at a fast clip.

Breathing a sigh of relief, Frank wiped his forehead with the back of a forearm and tried to clear his thoughts. He felt terror, panic, and anger over everything that had happened. His mind swirled with images of Rafe's violent death and his desperate escape. He pushed those thoughts aside and forced himself to focus on the road ahead.

Later that night, Frank pulled into a wooded area, hiding the car from the road. He spent a restless night, contorted while trying to sleep in the small car. The next day, he parked down the street from Savalle's Legion bar and climbed the outside stairs to Savalle's quarters above the bar. Nicole should be there. Frank found the door unlocked, and his heart sank as he saw Nicole sitting in an armchair, crying. She was hunched over, her head close to her knees, her arms folded across her tiny waist. Her shoulders were shaking with sobs. Frank was flooded with dread. Savalle must be dead, he thought, and Nicole just found out. He rushed to her.

"Nicole," he called out. She looked up, her red-rimmed eyes wide with fear and then with relief. She dropped her head back down. Frank knelt in front of her and held her shoulders. A .45 automatic pistol was in her lap, and the thought jumped in his mind that she was going to commit suicide over Savalle's death. "Nicole, Nicole," he said softly. Then, holding her shoulders, he helped her raise back up. And then he saw it.

Her face. The left side of her face was bruised and swollen. Her left eye was almost swollen shut. Yellowish, red bruising around the eye that would eventually turn bluish-black and then black. Dried blood under her nose and a cut lip.

"Nicole! What happened? Who..." She burst into tears again. Frank held her, and she buried her face in his shoulder. She tried to speak but kept breaking into sobs, and he let her cry it out. Finally, after long minutes, Nicole sat up and wiped tears. When she finally spoke, her voice was shaky.

"I'm okay, Frank," she said in a low voice. "I'm okay now."

"Who did this?"

"It was Kruger and Tabor."

"Kruger?"

"Kruger, an enemy of Jean Paul. And his muscle man, Tabor. Kruger makes young girls turn tricks, and Jean Paul won't let them come into the bar. You saw Tabor in the bar the night you first came here. Remember?" Frank nodded. "This morning, they came and told me that Jean Paul must be dead. And Kruger said, 'the American,' meaning you, Frank. The American, he said, is not coming back. Then he said, 'Now the bar is mine, and you work for me, Nicole.' I told them to get out, but they started hitting me and calling me a bitch. They knocked me down and kicked me. They tore my blouse off and put their hands all over me. Kruger said he would return tonight to get the money when it was closing time. And he said I was going to be his woman now. His 'bitch.'" She shook her head. "Never!" she said angrily, but her voice was weak. "Never."

"The gun," Frank said with a nod toward her lap.

"I'm going to kill them," she said fiercely. Frank lifted the .45 from her lap and removed the magazine. He pulled the slide back, and a .45 bullet ejected onto the floor. She was ready. Kruger and Tabor were close to meeting their Maker, Frank thought.

After doctoring Nicole and giving her pain medication to help her sleep, Frank put her to bed. "Don't worry, Nicole," he said. "I'm going to be right here. No one is going to hurt you." He sat beside the bed as she drifted off to sleep. After Nicole was asleep, he slipped on one of Savalle's shirts over his tee shirt. He reloaded the .45, tucked it in his waistband under the shirt, and left.

With pent-up fury, Frank found Kruger's office in the back of a bar. Two underage girls sat drugged at a table in the bar, some of the young teenagers he forced to work as prostitutes. Tabor was behind the counter, surprised to see Frank, but led him to the office and hovered behind as they stepped inside. Kruger was seated at his desk, leaning back with his feet propped up while talking on a phone. He ended the call and stood up. A large, imposing man with a shaved head and heavy jowls, Kruger looked like a professional fighter. Kruger said something to Tabor, who closed the door and stood against it, blocking Frank's exit.

"The American," Kruger said with a smirk. "You're back. You saved me a trip," he said, reaching down and coming up with a small baseball bat. He tapped the fat end in his hand. Then, he called out to Tabor. Frank looked over his shoulder just as Tabor came at him with a small club. He spun around and caught Tabor's jaw with a crushing roundhouse. Tabor flew back against the door and slid unconscious to the floor.

Frank turned just in time to see Kruger charging with the bat. Kruger swung, Frank ducked, and the bat just missed his skull. The wild swing threw Kruger off balance, and Frank hit Kruger with a crushing upper-cut. Kruger reeled backward, dropping the bat. Regaining his balance, Kruger pulled out a pistol. As he raised it, Frank leaped forward, grabbed his wrist with both hands, and twisted the gun loose. Keeping hold of Kruger's beefy arm, Frank put it in a painful arm lock. With his free fist, Kruger swung and hit Frank in the ribs, the powerful blow almost causing Frank to buckle at the knees. Gasping for air, Frank applied all the pressure he could with the arm lock, and Kruger's arm suddenly broke. Kruger emitted a ferocious roar and clawed at Frank's face with his other hand. Taking a step back and pulling out the .45, Frank swung it and hit Kruger in the face. He staggered backward, his broken arm dangling and his smashed face bloody. Kruger dropped to his knees.

Frank heard movements behind him. Gripping the club, Tabor was getting up on one knee. Frank turned and kicked him in the face, sending him flying backward. Tabor bounced off the wall and fell in a heap. Frank picked up the small club and smashed the backs of Tabor's hands. He wouldn't be able to hurt anyone for a long time.

Panting to catch his breath and wincing at the pain in his ribs, Frank thought about what they had done to Nicole. He looked at Kruger, and his face tightened. Kruger was still on his knees, sitting back on his heels, bloody and moaning. Frank shoved him to the floor and jammed the barrel of the .45 in his mouth. Frank cocked the hammer, his finger on the trigger. Just the slightest pressure and a bullet would blow a large hole in the back of Kruger's head. Frank's eyes narrowed, and his finger tightened on the trigger. Frank saw the terror and panic in Kruger's widened eyes. Finally, he caught himself, took his finger off the trigger, and released a tense breath. He locked eyes with Kruger, the gun still jammed in his mouth.

"Nicole," Frank said through clenched teeth. "Nicole. If you *ever* touch her again, I will put this gun in your mouth and pull the trigger." Frank paused, his jaw clenched, and he thought about killing Kruger anyway. He took a deep breath. "Do you believe me?" Kruger managed a terrified nod.

Frank stood up and found Tabor's small club. "This is just to make sure," Frank said as he went back to Kruger and then to Tabor.

When Nicole woke that night, she found Frank asleep in the chair beside the bed. She sighed and fell back to sleep. The next morning, they sipped coffee together on the balcony. Nicole was sore and developing a black eye but felt better after a night's sleep. "You don't have to worry about Kruger," Frank said offhandedly.

"Frank, Kruger will be back. You don't know what he's like. He's mean, and he will …"

"No, he won't," Frank said confidently. She gave Frank a questioning look. "I paid him a visit yesterday. While you slept. Kruger has a broken arm and two broken hands." Nicole's eyes widened. Frank shrugged. "And a broken nose and broken jaw." He took a sip of coffee. "Also, two broken ankles," he added.

"Frank," she said cocking her head to the side. "You? You did that?"

"It was either that or kill him. To make sure he doesn't bother you again. You won't have to worry about Tabor, either. He's in the same shape. They won't be able to hurt anyone, or even walk or use their hands, for a long, long time." Frank paused and looked directly at Nicole. "I warned them what would happen if they ever touched you again. They understood," Frank said matter-of-factly.

It had been a long time since Frank had exploded in a spasm of unchecked violence. He regretted it. He had gone too far, and he knew it. It was rare, and it would take a lot to trigger it. The last time was when Kathy was tortured at the seaside villa on the Greek coast. Frank was always calm, unfazed, and easygoing. He never let emotions overpower him, except when it came to Kathy. And this time. In dealing with Kruger and Tabor, Frank realized he could be overcome with rage at those who preyed on the weak and vulnerable.

Later that day, Nicole told him that shortly after Frank and Rafe had left to find Savalle, two men had shown up asking for Frank. "They knew your name, Frank. They said, 'Marsh. Where is the American,

Marsh?' I told them I didn't know, and they got angry, but they left. They weren't from here."

Late that afternoon, local police officers arrested Frank and threw him in a small, dingy cell. Frank asked if he was being detained because of Tabor or Kruger, but the police official just shrugged. Later that night, they led him handcuffed from the cell to a small room. Frank was surprised to see Matthews, the CIA man, sitting at a table. Frank looked at him questioningly, and Matthews nodded to a chair on the other side. Frank sat, and they stared at each other silently. Finally, Matthews raised his chin and jabbed a finger at Frank. "Next time I tell you to leave, you leave," Matthews said angrily. "That's right, Marsh. You're here because I made some calls."

"This is crazy, Matthews. You don't understand. There's work to be done, and we need to be searching…"

"No, Marsh," Matthews said, shaking his head slowly. "*You* don't understand. This is my turf, and you're trespassing. Tomorrow, the police will drive you to the capital and put you on a plane to the States. Start reading the want ads because you won't be a Bureau agent much longer." Matthews stood. "Next time you're told to do something, asshole, you'll do it." He knocked on a door, and Frank was led back to the cell.

During the night, Frank was tormented by his failures. Savalle is dead or a captive because of me, Frank thought. Then I got Rafe killed. Now I'm going to be fired. No one is looking for Savalle. And no one is spreading the alarm about Sarin nerve gas. All because I insisted on hurrying to come here myself instead of trying to work in the system and convince others to follow up. This has been a disaster.

The next morning, Frank was led from the cell back to the small room, but he wasn't handcuffed this time. He was surprised to see a cup of coffee and a plate of fruit and cheese on the table. His police escort smiled, nodded to him to sit, and motioned for him to drink and eat. Frank was baffled at the change in his treatment but sat and ate hungrily. After finishing the meal, he was sipping coffee when the door opened. Matthews walked in with a sullen look on his face.

Frank stood. "What is this, Matthews, my last meal? Or..."

Another man came in behind Matthews. The first thing Frank noticed was his lively eyes. He was maybe in his late 40s, medium height, stocky, with thinning reddish brown hair and a ruddy face adorned with a bushy mustache. Matthews stood aside, and the man extended a hand to Frank. "Frank, I'm Robert Collins," he said with a broad smile. "Please just call me Collins." As they shook, Collins said. "I'm taking over from Matthews. You won't be seeing him anymore." Collins paused a beat before continuing. "I hope you won't mind." Frank detected a wry smile. Collins nodded sideways toward the door. "Come on, Frank, let's get you out of here. We have some work to do."

CHAPTER 13

Frank and Collins sat in a cramped and secure room within a U.S. Consulate, far from the jail where Frank had been held. The windowless room lacked proper ventilation but was protected from foreign intelligence services attempting to eavesdrop. Collins "read in" Frank to the highly classified WMD alert program, dubbed "Flashpoint," and Frank signed a form acknowledging his criminal liability should he leak any secrets.

"As I explained," Collins began, "based on your information and other intelligence, the site you discovered has just been designated at Flashpoint Level One. This means a limited amount of national resources are automatically at our disposal. In addition, we've arranged for a satellite to target the location starting in the next few days." Frank felt a sense of relief; finally, something was being done.

"We checked NSA," Collins continued. "As you know, NSA's computers analyze billions of intercepted conversations picked up worldwide every day. The computers can search for and recognize the voices of high-priority targets."

"I'm familiar with that," Frank said, "and that NSA targets the leaders of countries, militaries, and terrorist groups for interceptions."

Collins nodded. "All of those, as well as key nuclear scientists and others involved with WMDs. NSA searches for the voices of key targets and conversations using key words, phrases, and locations." Collins paused a moment. "But intercepting the conversations is the easy part. The tricky part is dealing with the overwhelming amount of data. Recordings of all intercepted conversations are kept, and many are eventually translated. But there are just too many conversations and too few translators. Computer programs produce quick translations and transcripts but miss things and have a significant error rate."

"Moreover, no one bothers to look at the transcripts," Collins continued. "There are just too many. So the actual transcripts are fed into other computer programs that identify items humans should read."

"You're saying the data is useless because we can't absorb it."

Collins nodded. "Almost true, but not quite. When we have someone of great interest, we can have the NSA search for intercepted conversations and provide us with translations. So, after your information was designated as a Flashpoint One, we had the NSA check for anything intercepted from the secret compound area that could be of interest. We got a hit, Frank. But it would not have meant anything without your information. About two months ago, NSA intercepted a phone call by a high-level Iranian target in Tehran to someone in the area of your secret camp."

Collins withdrew a document from a folder and slid it across the table to Frank. "Take a look at this, Frank. It's a transcript of that conversation. The Iranian target in Tehran is Izad Ghorbani. I'll tell you more about him later. The man he's talking to is called Yazdan. He hasn't been fully identified." Frank read the transcript.

BEGIN REPORT

Izad GHORBANI is referred to as IG.

YAZDAN, full name unknown, is referred to as Yaz.

Unintelligible or Inaudible conversation is referred to as U.I.

[Ringing sounds. Phone answered.]

Yaz: Yes?

I.G.: Yazdan, you are taking too long to [U.I.]. When will it be ready?

Yaz: I am sorry. But it is not easy to get things done here. Something simple can take days here. There are different languages. Trucks, food...

I.G.:No! Stop making excuses [U.I.]. You should have [U.I.].

Yaz: But, I...

I.G.: Enough. The [U.I.] be ready for shipment by [U.I.]. You must [U.I.]. Do you understand?

Yaz: Yes, sir.

[Call ended.]

END REPORT

When he finished reading, Frank looked at Collins. "Frank," Collins said, "that conversation didn't mean anything before you discovered the site in the mountains. NSA pinpointed Yazdan as being in that general mountain area when the call occurred. But it didn't mean anything to us then. The intercept confirms an important Iranian connection to the compound."

"And the conversation backs up what the truck driver told me and Savalle," said Frank. "About different languages and shipments."

"Exactly. But there's more. NSA found a more recent intercept from the mountain area. Again, Izad Ghorbani in Tehran and Yazdan at the secret camp were identified through voice recognition. The call occurred two days after you found the camp. Here's that conversation," Collins said, handing another transcript to Frank.

BEGIN REPORT

Izad GHORBANI is referred to as IG.

YAZDAN, full name unknown, is referred to as Yaz.

[Ringing sounds. Phone answered.]

Yaz: [Unintelligible] two of them.

I.G.: What? Who are they? What were they doing there?

Yaz: [U.I.] made it inside and got away, and then [U.I.]. We are searching [U.I.] American and we [U.I.] other one. He is French.

I.G.: You must [U.I.] they were there, and who knows [U.I.]. Keep [U.I.].

Yaz: Yes, sir. [UI].

[End of call.]

END REPORT

"Frank, if they found out you're American and Savalle is French, then they must have..."

"They must have captured Savalle," Frank said excitedly. His face brightened. "He's alive. That means if we hurry, we can..." Collins held up a hand. "What?" Frank said.

"With Flashpoint, the priority is finding WMDs, not your friend."

"But... ."

"We will move quickly, but only because of WMDs and not him. I want to make sure you understand the priorities here. Savalle is irrelevant to us."

Frank's face hardened. "You know, Collins, that's pretty damn cold."

"Sorry, but that's the way it is."

"Well, here's one thing to consider. If we hurry and find Savalle alive, he can tell us more about the operation. The things he's learned since being captured."

Collins pursed his lips and nodded slowly. "Good point," he said thoughtfully. "I'll mention it to my people. Okay?"

"Okay. Fair enough. Now, what about Izad Ghorbani, the one in Iran who was calling the compound? You were going to tell me more about him."

"Ghorbani is an operations commander with Iran's assassination and sabotage group, Unit 400. We know he's been in contact with people in Iran's nuclear weapons and chemical warfare programs. So," Collins said, "that makes his communications with the compound especially significant. In fact, there's talk about upgrading this to Flashpoint level two, which may happen within a few hours."

"That means that in the morning," Collins continued, "we're going to be flooded with WMD experts, Special Ops, and others arriving. So let's see how much we can get done tonight because tomorrow we won't even have time to think." Frank knew the feeling. He remembered other times when he was barraged with overwhelming demands competing for his time and attention, coming so fast it felt like trying to drink from a fire hydrant. Everything was urgent, no time to think, and finally staggering to bed in the early morning hours, physically and mentally drained, his mind numb. He cringed, thinking about tomorrow, but was excited things were moving fast.

Frank and Collins worked late into the night. Afterward, Collins took Frank to a nearby cottage where they would spend the night. Frank dropped his backpack in a bedroom and rejoined Collins in the small living room. Seated on a couch, Collins nodded to an easy chair, and Frank plopped down. A bottle of Scotch whisky sat on the coffee table, and Collins poured two generous drinks. "Cheers," said Collins as they clinked glasses. Sipping the Scotch, Frank felt the whisky relaxing and infusing him with warmth. It had been a long, tiring day and night. It felt good to unwind after more than a week of constant and brutal tension.

After refilling his glass, Frank took a deep breath. "Collins, I need to tell you about something." Collins cocked an eyebrow. "A local crime boss named Kruger and his muscleman beat up Jean Paul Savalle's woman, Nicole. I found them and broke some bones." Frank began explaining about the attack on Nicole and Frank's fight with Kruger.

"Wait," said Collins, holding up a palm and shaking his head. "Hold on. I don't need to hear anymore. You broke some bones. I understand that. Okay? But did you *kill* anyone?" Frank shook his head. "Then we don't give a damn about that crap, Frank. This is not the Bureau, okay? Now, let's get back to our drinks. There's going to be a lot going on tomorrow. So let's relax while we can."

As daylight broke, Special Ops teams, WMD experts, and others swarmed in. Frank woke to a bustling clamor in the building. Voices, shouted questions, thumps of equipment hitting the floor, engines idling outside, radio operators transmitting, radios squawking, doors banging. Rousted from bed, Frank was immediately swamped with incessant demands. "Go over this satellite image with us," said one Special Ops leader. Then, as Frank began tracing his route to the mountain camp, two WMD experts interrupted and wanted him to describe what he had seen in detail. While the special ops leader was still waiting, Frank's discussion with the experts was interrupted by a conference call from Langley, which was then interrupted by a conference call from FBI headquarters.

"No, I didn't see anything like that," Frank said into one phone while holding another to his other ear. "I'll explain it, but hold on a moment; NGA is on the other line," he said, then he spoke into the other phone. "What was it you needed to know right away?" He was besieged with incessant demands. By mid-afternoon, his head was spinning, and the noise in the room was a constant buzz. Someone was holding a phone out to him while another held up another document they needed him to review.

"Wait," Frank finally said. "Wait!" He shook his head and waved them off. "Not now. I've got to clear my head." He walked out of the building, leaving the clamoring din behind.

Outside, the silence was a welcome change, and Frank savored the peace. He walked a short distance, stopped, and looked up. The sun felt good on his face. His chest was tight with tension. He took deep breaths to clear his head and tried to hold his scattered thoughts at bay. One thought, however, kept returning to him—Kathy. He longed to hear her voice but had been ordered not to contact her because it might compromise his location. He looked at his watch, wondering what she was doing. It was 5 PM in Africa and 11 AM in Washington.

WASHINGTON, D.C. 11 AM

At that moment, Kathy was at work in Washington and thinking about Frank. Although she had been reassured he was alright, she still worried. Outside her condo building, Iranian assassins lurked, waiting for Frank to return so they could carry out their orders to kill them both. However, time was becoming a problem, and they were becoming impatient. The longer they waited, the more likely their presence in the U.S. would be discovered. If Frank didn't return soon, they would have to pull out or kill Kathy Foster before leaving. Once psyched up for a kill, holding the blood lust at bay was difficult. The mornings and evenings when she left for work or returned home would be the best times.

TEHRAN, 7:30 PM

In Tehran, eight and a half hours ahead of Washington time, it was 7:30 PM, and Marwan was thinking about Foster and the hit team in D.C. He knew his killers were eager. He looked at the decoded message again.

The leader of the death squad pointed out the increasing likelihood of discovery if they stayed in D.C. much longer waiting for Marsh to return. He asked Marwan for instructions.

Marwan considered the options: order the team to leave now, wait just a little longer for Marsh, or have them kill Kathy Foster and leave. Marwan stood at the window in his office, staring into the distance. After long moments he returned to his desk and wrote a message to be encrypted and sent to D.C.

WASHINGTON, D.C. 11:30 AM

Sitting at her desk in the Old Executive Building next door to the White House, Kathy rubbed her forehead while staring at a draft NSC document on her computer screen. She was working on a policy proposal for expanding NATO cooperation with non-NATO nations, but she couldn't concentrate. She had not heard from Frank for two weeks and had no idea when she would see him again. "He's fine," the FBI assured her. "Frank's in Africa, but we can't tell you what he's doing. We're not sure when he'll be back." She felt frustrated and depressed. Maybe it would be good to go out tonight for a change instead of staying in and worrying. Kathy rose and walked down the hall to find out if her friend Susan would like to go out to dinner. They could go to a nice Italian restaurant within walking distance of her condo. While Kathy talked with Susan, Nazar read Marwan's decoded message and summoned his team.

AFRICA 5:30 PM

Frank sighed. It was time to go back inside and rejoin the chaos. Maybe if—"Frank," someone called from the doorway. He turned and saw

Collins motioning him to come back. "Hurry, Frank," Collins said urgently. "Something's come up."

Collins led him to a room where an analyst sat in front of a laptop on a desk. "Take a look at this," Collins said. The analyst got up, and Frank took his place. "NSA just sent us an intercept they had overlooked. This is the transcript. Remember Yazdan? He was at the mountain camp talking with Izad Ghorbani back in Tehran." Frank nodded. "Well, NSA picked up a call between Yazdan and someone unidentified. This was five days ago." Frank looked at the transcript on the computer screen.

YAZDAN, identity and full name unknown, is referred to as Yaz.

Unknown Subject is referred to as USub. Probable location: Tehran, Iran

Translated from Persian.

Yaz: We have nearly finished abandoning [unintelligible].

USub: Is [unintelligible] still alive?

Yaz: [Unintelligible]

USub: What about the shipment?

Yaz: [Unintelligible] a ship two days ago. It is already [unintelligible].

USub: All of it?

Yaz: [Unintelligible]

Frank looked up at Collins. "They've abandoned the site?"
"That's what it looks like. We may be too late."

"What about asking if someone was still alive? That could be Savalle. We need to get up there as soon as possible," Frank said anxiously.

"Frank, it could be, but we're more concerned in what is—"

"Collins, I understand you don't give a damn about anyone's life," Frank snapped. "Only in finding WMDs, but we need to get up there fast, if not for Savalle, then to find what's there. All we've been doing is talking. People here are rushing around, but none are heading to the mountain yet." Frank looked directly at Collins. "So when are we going?"

Collins winced. "There's a little problem with that."

"Problem? What kind of problem?"

"SOCOM rejected the operational plan for a raid on the mountain, which was submitted by the Special Ops team leader. Instead, they want him to revise the plan to include a more thorough risk assessment and specify additional measures for force protection and risk mitigation. He's working on it as quickly as he can. But before the Special Ops team can go in, SOCOM and the Pentagon want Marines with the Marine Special Task Force stationed in Spain to be flown to an airfield in Cameroon. They will act as a quick reaction force, a QRF, in case the Special Ops team gets in trouble."

"But—"

"I know. It will take hours just to fly the Marines from Spain to Cameroon."

"Are they on the way?"

Collins shook his head and frowned. "No. Not yet. The U.S. regional commander for Africa hasn't given his approval yet, but they hope to get it any moment. Unfortunately, the State Department has gotten wind that something is up in Africa. The Deputy Secretary of State is demanding to know what's going on. So now there's a tug of war going on between the Secretaries of Defense and State. And now the SecDef wants to see the ops plan himself. My agency and the Flashpoint Executive Committee are trying to get the White House Chief of Staff and the President's National Security Advisor to intervene and approve the raid. But now, those two want full briefings before they will do any-thing. Everyone is demanding briefings and PowerPoint slide presen-tations. So," Collins said with a deflated look, "that's where everything stands right now."

Frank shook his head slowly. "Incredible. Just incredible. We're fighting ourselves—and we're losing. Most people outside the gov-ernment have no idea. Damn." Frank looked away, then back at Collins. "Collins, I've seen things like this too many times, and so have you. If I understand correctly, then DoD and SOCOM are demanding risk mitigation, but CIA and the Flashpoint Executive Committee are pushing the mission. State resists everything, and DoD never likes to be told what to do. And the White House Chief of Staff and the President's National Security Advisor probably have their own little turf battles going on between themselves. Is that about right?"

Collins shrugged.

"What the hell happened with Flashpoint being the highest priority for all agencies?"

"Flashpoint *is* a priority, Frank, but we're only at level two now. Turf battles, bureaucracy, and egos still get in the way at this level. So we're trying to get it upgraded to level three."

"How many *months* will that take?" Frank said sarcastically.

Collins ignored the comment. "I do have some good news. In a few hours, NSA will start monitoring the area to hear any conversations on the ground, not just phone calls. They'll be able to pick up anyone talking, maybe not all of it, but some. And later tonight, the area will have drone coverage."

That was small comfort for Frank. He felt frustrated and helpless. His friend Savalle was somewhere on the mountain. Perhaps Jean Paul is dead, but if he *is* alive, Frank thought, then time is running out to save him.

IN THE ATLANTIC OCEAN OFF THE WEST COAST OF AFRICA

A Virginia Class nuclear submarine was transiting off the coast of West Africa. The USS South Dakota, SSN 790, cruised silently below the surface at 22 knots per hour. Commander Randy Sharp sat in the operations center and stared at a computer screen. Evans, the Operations Officer, noticed the look on Sharpe's face. "Something wrong, sir?"

Sharpe looked up. "They want us to launch the drone—to assist a land mission," he said sourly.

"A land mission? Our only drone?"

"Prepare to launch the drone in one hour at 200 feet below the surface, through the tube—but wait on my command."

"Eye, eye, sir. Prepare to launch in one hour at 200 feet below the surface."

Commander Sharpe turned back to the computer screen and began typing a message. Evans understood Sharpe's irritation. It was the sub's only drone, and it was also non-recoverable. After completing a one-time mission, the drone would be flown back over the ocean and crashed into the deep. After that, the submarine would not be equipped with another drone until it returned to its home port at the end of the patrol. That was another 45 days away.

Commander Sharpe sent a message advising that the sub would be ready to launch the drone as ordered but respectfully requested reconsideration. Meanwhile, a battle about using the submarine's only drone raged within the Pentagon between the Navy Chief of Operations, CNO, and the Office of Secretary of Defense. Using and then destroying the drone would be expensive and limit the submarine tactically. Surely, alternative land-based drones must be available. In the end, the arguments were rejected, and the orders stood.

At 6 PM local time, off the coast of West Africa, USS South Dakota launched its drone from 200 feet below the ocean's surface. Contained in a small canister launched from the sub's signal ejector, the drone flew out of the canister after breaking the surface. However, the drone developed engine trouble shortly after gaining altitude and crashed into the sea before reaching land.

One hundred miles away, Collins frowned at his computer screen. He waited a moment and then looked at Frank. "Bad news. The drone from the sub crashed. We'll have to wait until we can get one from Niamey."

"Niamey? In Niger?" said Frank.

"The U.S. Air Force and the French share a base at Niamey supporting French Foreign Legion operations in Mali. The French fly fighter bombers out of the base, and we have two MQ-9 Reaper drones there. We tried to get one of the Reapers to recon the mountain compound, but one Reaper is tied up with a French operation, and the other is out of service for maintenance. So that's why we went to the drone from the sub." Collins shrugged. "Now, we'll just have to wait until we can get one from Niamy."

Frank could only shake his head. With current technology, people think you push a button, and things instantly happen. But it doesn't work that way in real life. Frank was feeling powerless to personally make things happen. He was accustomed to leading investigations, coordinating agencies, and getting things done. But here in Africa, the CIA was in charge, DOD and DOS were involved, and there were too many moving parts to make things happen quickly. Now, all he could do was wait. But others weren't waiting, Frank thought. According to NSA, the Iranians were abandoning the compound and moving WMD materials out. But where?

Late that night, Frank collapsed in bed after a long day of bedlam with CIA, Special Ops, analysts, and WMD experts working frantically. His mind was numb, and he quickly drifted off to sleep. Suddenly, someone shook his shoulder. "Frank. Wake up. You awake? Frank, you awake?" He blinked his eyes open, trying to focus. Collins was shaking his shoulder. "Come on, Frank. Get up. We've got something. Come on."

Rubbing his face and glancing at his watch, Frank saw it was two in the morning. He pulled on trousers, threw on a shirt, and put on his boots. Collins led him to a room where an analyst and a special ops member huddled around a laptop. "Look at the screen," Collins said. "We finally got a drone, and this live video is coming from it. It just reached the mountain site. I knew you would want to see."

In a greenish light on the screen, Frank saw a compound of small buildings surrounded by barbed wire in the middle of a thick jungle. Two men with rifles guarded the entrance, and two others patrolled the back side of the compound, where another small track led out and into the jungle. "That's it," Frank exclaimed, pointing to the screen. "That's the compound where I was. And that's the building," Frank pointed at the screen, "that's the one with the Sarin and barrels inside."

After an hour of watching, nothing had changed, and Frank went back to bed, but Collins woke him again an hour later. Collins said the raid on the mountain site was finally on, and the FBI insisted that Frank should go too. Collins led him to a room filled with a dozen heavily armed special ops men, all bearded, dressed in bush clothing, and wearing baseball caps. Collins introduced him to the team leaders, Rick and Eric.

"You'll be going in with our backdoor recon team," Rick said curtly. It was clear neither Rick nor Eric was happy with Frank going along. "Just do what you're told and stay out of the way," Rick said. "Jason will take you in with his three men to cover the back side of the compound. But don't get in the way—understand?" Frank nodded. He was given gear to don for the raid.

With daybreak still more than an hour away, Frank climbed aboard an M-60 Blackhawk helicopter with Jason and three others. After a 40-minute ride, they rappelled down to the jungle and crept quietly on a narrow, rutted path. Frank stayed close to the team leader, Jason, who whispered, "Be quiet and stay out of the way. If shooting starts, just hug the ground."

At daybreak, the point man, Tony, stopped and motioned that he had heard or seen something ahead. The men edged into the jungle and stood listening. After long moments, Jason motioned for Tony to go on. Tony carefully stepped out of the jungle onto the dirt path and began easing forward. A burst of gunfire erupted ahead, and the team started firing back furiously.

Frank dove to the ground. Bullets cracked and zipped above his head. Jason was kneeling and firing a few feet away, changing magazines and firing rapidly at gun flashes. Up ahead, Tony cried out, "I'm hit, I'm hit." He lay crumpled in the middle of the path. Jason shouted above the din of gunfire, "Don't move. We'll get you." But with torrents of incoming fire, no one could move.

Bullets were shredding leaves inches above Frank's head and bursting pieces of bark off trees. He was frozen with fear, wanting to get up and run away from the mayhem. The firing escalated into a deafening roar. Suddenly, Frank jumped up and ran toward Tony. It was a dozen yards to Tony's crumpled figure, but it felt like a hundred to Frank. The gunfire rose to a furious crescendo and focused on him as he ran.

Something knocked his left foot out from under him, and Frank stumbled to one knee, unable to move for a moment, which made him an easy target. He rose and stumbled toward Tony. Even though his left foot wasn't working right, he limped forward, grabbed Tony's vest, and dragged him out of the road and into the jungle. Frank fell backward and lay panting hard, staring at leaves snapping off just above his face. He felt an exhilarating rush at being alive but cringed at his recklessness.

Several explosions erupted ahead, followed by scattered gunfire and then sudden silence. Then, just as abruptly as it had begun, the firefight was over. The compound was secured. It was quickly but thoroughly searched and examined by WMD experts. Except for a few guards, the compound had already been abandoned, and the guards were all killed by the raiding party. The warehouse where Frank had seen

Sarin and explosives was empty, and nothing of value had been left for the raiding party to find. A large smoldering burn pit was still hot.

While searching for anything of value, Frank was startled when a helicopter landed on the far side of the compound and quickly took off less than a minute later. He realized it must have been a medevac for Tony, the wounded special ops man.

Moments later, Rick, the special ops raid leader, approached Frank. "I think we found your friend, Savalle," Rick said grimly. Frank felt his heart drop. "We blew away two guys near the burn pit. They were a hardcore element left behind to take care of anything important left inside the compound. That's why they were at the burn pit, and that's where we found him." Frank cringed, waiting for more. "We're pretty sure it's Savalle, the Frenchman," Rick continued and paused. "He was in bad shape and kept mumbling in French."

"He's alive!" Frank exclaimed, wide-eyed, almost unable to believe it. "He was alive? Alive! Is he *still* alive?"

Rick explained that Savalle was found on the ground beside the two men at the burn pit. "They were going to finish him off before they left," Rick said, "but we interrupted." Savalle had been wounded when he was captured and badly tortured but would probably live. He had already been lifted out by the helicopter and was being flown to a hospital. Frank sank to his knees, settled back on his heels, and bowed his head. Tears rolled down his grimy cheeks.

Several hours later, the raid party was lifted out by helicopters and returned to base. The wounded Special Ops member, Tony, had been flown out with Savalle to be treated for gunshot wounds to his legs. He might lose a leg.

Frank discovered he had not been hit when his left foot was knocked out from under him. Instead, a bullet had blasted off the heel of his boot, and the shock of the impact had numbed his foot. Now, the feeling was back, and Frank replaced his boots with track shoes at the base. Everyone was exhausted after the raid. The special ops group was already preparing to leave, and helicopters were warming up to take them away.

Feeling exhausted, Frank sat on the edge of his cot and was taking off his shirt when Collins stuck his head in the doorway. "Take a short rest, Frank, and then we'll get together in an hour to debrief about what was found at the compound. D.C. is already yelling for information." Frank was too tired to respond and simply nodded. "By the way, Frank, I heard what you did. Pulling the special ops guy to safety." Collins gave Frank an admiring smile and a thumbs up.

A few minutes later, Collins returned and led Frank into a room where the special ops team was gathered and ready to walk out to waiting helicopters. They became quiet as Frank entered the room, and he felt everyone watching him. The commander, Rick, stepped forward and said, "Mister Marsh." He came to attention and saluted as the others stood watching.

Jason stepped forward and said, "We have something for you." He handed Frank the dirty, worn boot Frank had been wearing when the heel had been shot off. On the side of the leather boot, something had been written in a black permanent marker. "The Royal Order of the Boot, presented to Mister Marsh for bravery in action." Jason shook Frank's hand, "Well done, sir." A minute later, they were all gone. Frank stood staring at the boot in his hands. A weary smile spread across his face.

CHAPTER 14

Downtown D.C. bustled with early evening traffic as taxis dropped off passengers in front of brightly lit hotels and restaurants. The sidewalks teemed with tourists and restaurant-goers. Inside a cozy Italian restaurant, Kathy and Susan perched at the crowded bar, sipping martinis while waiting for their table. The room was bathed in the warm glow of low lighting and small table lamps with ruby lampshades, infusing it in pools of warm golden lights. White-jacketed waiters glided among tables. The air was thick with the aromas of comfort food, and the hum of conversations filled the room, accompanied by the clinking of glasses and the glow of smiling faces.

As Kathy finished her first martini, the tension in her chest and shoulders began to ease. She heaved a deep sigh, relieved to relax after worrying about Frank. "Have you heard anything more about Frank?" Susan asked.

Kathy shook her head. "No, but they would have told me right away if something had happened to him. So," Kathy said, lifting her second drink, "no news is good news." She forced a brave smile.

In a restaurant across the street, Basir sat at a table at a front bay window. He watched the Italian restaurant, waiting for Kathy and the other woman to emerge. When she came out, he was to alert the others waiting down the street near her apartment building.

He leaned closer to the window and glanced down the street to see if the wino was still on the route toward Foster's apartment. A young black wino with dreadlocks had been sitting on the sidewalk propped against a wall, drinking from a liquor bottle wrapped in a brown paper bag. A black Steelers cap with a flat brim was cocked partially sideways on his head. It was pulled low and hid his eyes. The wino flashed a gold tooth when he tilted the bottle up to take a swig. Basir couldn't tell if the wino was still there. He was probably gone by now. If not, he would probably be passed out when Foster left the restaurant to walk back.

Later that night, Kathy and Susan walked out of the restaurant. Susan caught a cab, and Kathy began walking alone to her apartment building, a few blocks away, past closed restaurants and shops. Basir followed, walking quickly to catch up to her in a darkened area ahead. The others were waiting in an SUV parked ahead on a side street. Traffic had thinned to an occasional passing taxi, and the streets were nearly deserted. Basir quickened his pace. Reaching under his coat, he pulled out a pistol. Basir suddenly heard something right behind him. He stopped and turned just as Stick's pistol slammed across his face. The blow hurled Basir to the sidewalk, and the gun flew out of his hand. "You ain't gonna be robbing nobody for a while, Muthfucka," Stick declared. He pointed his silenced pistol at Basir's moaning figure and fired. Basir emitted a piercing scream. Stick turned and ran. An SUV from a side street sped toward Basir.

As she neared her apartment building, Kathy heard a noise somewhere behind her, a thud followed by a piercing yell. Glancing over her shoulder, Kathy saw darkened figures a half-block behind her scurrying on the sidewalk next to an SUV. Unable to make out what was happening, she quickened her pace to the apartment building. More crime, she thought. *D.C. is getting so bad.*

"Yo, Uncle Tyrone, you gonna have to pay me more," said Stick over a cell phone. "I'm having to bust more caps in this shit than in the dope business."

Tyrone Williams winced. "What the heck's happened?"

"Well, somebody was following her ass after she was out eating last night—but I took care of it."

"Took care of it?" A cringing pause. "Anyone *dead*?"

"Naw, just messed up a little."

"A little?" Williams winced.

"Yo."

"What about Foster? Is she all right? Where is she now?"

"Oh, yeah, the woman's okay," Stick explained. "I saw a dude look like he gonna rob her, and I took care of him before he got close."

"Took care of him? What do you mean? Wait... don't tell me. You said he's still alive, right? He's alive?"

"Yo. But he ain't gonna be walking so good."

Williams bit his lip and shook his head. "Damn. Is there going to be heat on you now?"

"Naw, I don't think so. They rushed off in a van. I don't think the woman even knew."

There was a pause. "Look here, Stick. There are cameras all over this city. Whatever you did is probably on camera. You hear what I'm saying?"

Another pause. "You mean I need to lay low? Maybe leave?"

"Look, the firearms laws here are real strict. Even if you did right, you could do time. Hear what I'm saying?"

"I feel you. Be out of here in a minute. What about some traveling money?" After the call, Stick thought about what he should do. Head home to the delta and keep dodging Big Al's boys? Or head to Chicago and have it out with Big Al? His stomach knotted just thinking about his choices. Damn, man, Stick thought, why it gotta be like this? The following day, Stick was on the road heading away from D.C., still undecided about what to do.

TEHRAN, IRAN

As a meeting of Iranian Quds Force leaders ended, Major General Qassem Soleimani, the Quds Force Commander, looked at Marwan.

"Stay, Marwan. I want a word." When they were alone, Soleimani frowned and looked at Marwan. "I have heard concerns about you."

"About me?"

"Yes, you. Some think you are obsessed with killing the American, the FBI agent. Wait," Soleimani said, holding up a palm when he saw Marwan was about to speak. "Killing the American is not a problem. But," Soleimani said, glancing at Marwan's amputated leg, since replaced with a prosthesis, "*if* you are doing it for personal reasons, then some question the wisdom of using our resources for that." He paused a moment. "I share that concern."

Marwan waited a moment before responding. "I lost my leg because of the American—Marsh. But I would not do it for that reason alone. I do not want to be a symbol that we can be attacked without consequences. Killing Marsh would send a message to the Americans and to our own people that those who harm us cannot escape harm. The Jews in Israel follow the same policy, and with good reason. That's why I want to find and kill Marsh. But if you want me to stop, Excellency, I will stop." Marwan knew his rationale about sending a message was thin, and the general knew it. It was a personal vendetta.

Soleimani stared silently at Marwan. After a while, he said, "I understand you sent men to Washington to go after this man, Marsh. You have my consent to proceed but with three conditions."

"Yes, Excellency," Marwan said with a nod.

"First, it must not be done on American soil. Second, it must not interfere with other missions. Third, you may kill Marsh, but we must not be linked to it. Killing an FBI agent will have repercussions. The Americans would use it to inflame their public and other countries against us. I did not say anything when you tried to kill this man, Marsh, and the woman in Greece because you did that to try to protect your high-level source, 'Magician,' from being compromised. It is different now. You may kill him, but only if you can make it look like a robbery, an accident, a suicide, or otherwise untraceable to us. We cannot be linked to it."

Marwan nodded. "Yes, Excellency. I understand."

Marwan left the meeting feeling relieved but also worried. Relieved he could continue to go after Marsh, although he would have to pull his men out of Washington. But someone had complained. One of his rivals, Marwan thought. *Someone trying to undercut my standing with General Soleimani.* He needed to figure out who it was.

WASHINGTON, D.C.

Reza had a problem. Marwan's urgent new instructions directed him to return to Iraq immediately. That would be simple, but Basir had been wounded in the attempt to kill Foster last night and wouldn't be able to travel. They had gotten him to a safe house in Maryland, just outside D.C. A bullet had smashed a bone in his thigh; he was in great pain and needed surgery. Reza couldn't take Basir to a hospital because they would report a gunshot victim to the police. They couldn't take Basir with them when they left and couldn't leave him behind. Reza was already wondering where they could bury the body.

CHAPTER 15

AFRICA

A few hours after the special ops team departed, Frank and Collins huddled over burnt fragments of papers found at the mountain compound. The writings were in various languages—English, Persian, Arabic, and French. Collins had the writings hurriedly translated through an encrypted link. Now, they were examining each one on a laptop screen.

BURNT FRAGMENTS OF PAPER: LEGIBLE LETTERS AND WORDS:

ITEM 1

...por...... freighter ... via Morocc......... fis.. v..sal...coast ......lorr... war...

ITEM 2

...spec... rge... sum... release....remem...

ITEM 3

.........zar ...

"Using computer programs," said Collins, "our analysts searched for the most probable words and meanings. Unfortunately, items two and three lacked sufficient clues to be reconstructed. But item one was partially reconstructed as: 'port...freighter... via Morocco...fishing vessel... coast... lorry (truck)... war...'."

"Which may mean," Frank said, "that something went by freighter via Morocco. Something that would be offloaded onto a fishing vessel off a coast somewhere. And then it would be transported in a truck." He looked at Collins. "That's going to the Sarin and explosives I saw in the warehouse," he exclaimed, his voice rising. "We need to move quickly. Maybe satellites and vessel tracking."

Frank remembered a briefing he had received on tracking ships. More than 180,000 ships are tracked in real-time and historically by the AIS, Automatic Identification System. AIS transponder signals from ships are captured by ground and ship transceivers and satellites. However, vessels can turn off their transponders and "go dark" in the AIS to avoid being tracked. That was usually done by drug or arms smuggling ships or trying to evade sanctions on countries such as North Korea, Iran, and Russia.

Frank's voice was tinged with urgency as he spoke to Collins. "Something's going to happen in Europe. We need to..."

"Hell, something's *always* going to happen in Europe," Collins said dismissively. "You're jumping to conclusions."

"Maybe I am, but I can feel it. It's linked to the mountain site here. I don't know when or where, but it's going to be in Europe. And probably soon, now they know we are on to them."

"Calm down, Frank. Those pieces of paper we found at the compound might refer to places in Europe, but it doesn't mean anything yet as far as we are concerned."

"But what about..."

"I didn't want to have to tell you this, but here it is. No evidence of WMDs was found at the mountain site. *None.* And it lost the designation as a FLASHPOINT matter. No more resources. No more priority."

"But what about the barrels and canisters I saw? Sarin nerve gas, explosives, heavy water? What about..."

Collins was waving a hand and shaking his head. "No, Frank." He sighed deeply before continuing. "Your report of seeing the barrels and canisters and their markings is no longer considered credible. After nothing was found, it was assessed that the concussion you suffered when escaping had confused your memory of what you thought you had seen at the site. And your suspicions aren't enough. So something vague that might happen in Europe is not a priority." Collins paused and looked at Frank sympathetically. "I'm sorry, Frank."

Frank grimaced and shook his head slowly, eyes downcast. He thought about all that had happened and blamed himself. Jean Paul had been captured and tortured, Rafe was dead, and Nicole had been beaten. Now, a special ops team member would likely lose a leg—all because he rushed to Africa in search of Marwan. I'm a fool, he thought. He slumped and rubbed his face with both hands. A fool.

After a moment, Collins said, "I'm leaving tomorrow. "But before I go, I want you to know you did a damn fine job. Evidence of WMDs at the mountain compound was inclusive. But something was going on there that needed checking and shutting down. Thanks to you, that was done."

Frank nodded and sighed heavily. He felt like a loser being congratulated for at least trying. The price was too high for the little that had been accomplished. He thought again of Rafe, Nicole, and Jean Paul.

Thinking about Jean Paul reminded Frank of something he had been dreading. He had one last thing to do before leaving Africa. His duty to turn in Jean Paul on the arrest warrant for killing a man. Even though it was self-defense while Jean Paul was trying to keep a human trafficker from beating Nicole, the man he killed was local crime figure protected by the police. There wouldn't be a chance of a fair trial. But Frank still had to turn him in. There was no way around it.

"Could you do me a favor?" Frank said to Collins. "An off-the-record favor, if there is such a thing?"

"It depends," Collins said. "But if I can, I'll try."

"I'm sure you have contacts and sources throughout the region, especially in security and police forces." After Frank explained what he had in mind, Collins made a couple of calls. And then gave Frank a name and a phone number.

Two days later, a burly police captain escorted Frank and Nicole into a hospital and summoned a doctor who spoke English well. "His condition was poor when he was brought in," the doctor said. "A gunshot wound, broken ribs, a broken jaw, trauma, swelling and bruising all over his body." A low moan escaped Nicole's lips. "But he has been improving rapidly," the doctor quickly added.

When they entered Jean Paul's room, Nicole rushed to him and grabbed his hand. She kissed his forehead and began caressing his hair. She smiled at him through tears, whispering her love. Jean Paul was heavily bandaged. He looked haggard, and his face was still bruised and swollen on one side. His eyes showed surprise when he saw Frank move to the other side of the bed. Jean Paul spoke in a low, weak voice. "I thought you were dead." He took another breath before continuing. "The camp? What about..."

"All done," Frank said, gripping Jean Paul's other hand. "Shut down. Time for you to rest and get well, my friend. The doctor says you'll be able to leave in another week. I'll step out so you and Nicole can have some time."

Frank knew it was time to do his duty to turn in Jean Paul. He motioned to the police captain, and they stepped outside the room. After an earnest conversation in the hallway, Frank rejoined Nicole and Jean Paul.

Two days later, the police captain completed a report on Jean Paul Savalle. According to the report, Savalle arrived at the hospital in critical condition and died three days later. A death certificate accompanied the report.

The next day, the arrest warrant for Jean Paul was dismissed.

Frank smiled about finally doing something good in Africa. Jean Paul was no longer a hunted man. He and Nicole would live happily and without worries, above the Legion Bar.

Frank couldn't foresee that events unfolding in Europe would soon thrust him into a critical role.

PART TWO

CHAPTER 16

The first inkling of a major terror attack is often some small, insignificant event. Nothing that by itself raises alarms.

Assistant FBI director Bill Nelson was finishing a call when Larry Welch, deputy chief of the National Counter Terrorism Center, NCTC, arrived at Nelson's office. He knew Nelson liked to get down to business, so as he sat down, Welch was prepared to get right to the point. But as Nelson hung up the phone, he spoke first. "What the hell is it, Welch? The only time I see you is when you have bad news." Nelson had been a tough street cop before his FBI career. He not only looked like actor Fred Thompson, but he also had the same gruff demeanor.

Welch winced. "It's about the level of chatter related to terrorists. There's been a spike between Iran and Belgium." Slight and balding, Welch removed his dark-rimmed glasses and rubbed the bridge of his nose before replacing them and continuing. "CIA doesn't assess that it's significant, but it's the first time we've ever had a spike between Iran and Belgium. I don't know what it means, but it must mean something. I thought you would want to know because you have the Legats in Europe."

"Hell, Welch, we get that stuff all the time. It doesn't mean much without more. You know that."

After Welch left, Nelson recalled that a month ago, he had been worried about intelligence related to Europe in the President's Daily Brief. One Top Secret/SCI passage had bothered Nelson. "Britain's MI-6 reported that a source in Europe had been contacted last month by Middle Eastern terrorists who wanted to acquire a Stinger anti-aircraft missile. However, the terrorists recently indicated that their plans are now on hold because they could interfere with 'something bigger.' CIA assesses the probability of a significant attack soon is small." The CIA had dismissed the report, but Nelson remembered his gut feeling that something was going to happen. But what? And where and when?

With that and Welch's concern about the increased chatter, Nelson decided to move up a trip already scheduled to visit Legats in Europe. He also considered contacting Gabrielle Lemaire, the New York Police Department Liaison in Brussels. But it meant going to the Bureau's biggest rival, the NYPD Intelligence and Counter-terrorism units, the best in the country. Turf battles between the Bureau and NYPD were a constant source of tension.

Some of the worst clashes between the FBI and NYPD came overseas, which the Bureau considered its exclusive turf. FBI Legats had long been stationed in many foreign capitals. But after the September 11th attacks in 2001, NYPD started stationing its own intelligence liaison officers in some foreign capitals. NYPD liaisons gathered intelligence on terror tactics and threats to New York City. However, they dealt directly with foreign agencies instead of going through the FBI, which generated clashes with the Bureau.

A trim, petite blonde, Gabrielle was a native of France who had become a naturalized U.S. citizen. After becoming an NYPD officer, she served with the NYPD Counter Terrorism and Intelligence Bureau when she was selected for the NYPD International Liaison program. She was stationed in Paris but also maintained an apartment in Brussels for liaison work with NATO. She was bright, creative, and resourceful.

Nelson had back-channeled Gabrielle once on another matter. Now might be the time to ask her for help again. Nelson flew to Brussels three days later and checked into the Royal Windsor Hotel Grand Palace. From the room, he called Gabrielle and arranged to meet the following afternoon.

BRUSSELS, BELGIUM

After calling Lemaire, Nelson thought again about the intelligence on terrorists holding off on an anti-aircraft missile because of "something bigger" and Welch's concern about increased chatter between Iran and Belgium. He grimaced and hoped he was worrying for nothing.

Gabrielle Lemaire had her own reasons to worry. Something may happen soon, she feared, but she didn't know what. Gabrielle was anxious for more information and impatient to hear from her source, Masud.

A 22-year-old whose parents had emigrated from Algeria to Belgium, Masud had been staying in New York on a student visa when he was recruited as a source by officers with the NYPD Intelligence and Counter Terrorism Bureau. Thin, with thick, curly black hair and big brown eyes, Masud had recently rejoined his family in Brussels. His NYPD handler in New York told him to contact Gabrielle if anything came up. Masud passed bits of information to Gabrielle, but the most important was about an Iranian immigrant named Ahmed.

After Bill Nelson called about meeting, Gabrielle returned to reviewing her notes about Ahmed. The first report concerning Ahmed was from a month earlier. "Source Masud reported conversations with a friend named KIZER, who resides in Brussels. Kizer is a male in his late teens or early 20s who is an immigrant from Iran. The source says Kizer is sympathetic to Hezbollah and Iran. Kizer told source that his uncle AHMED (no other identifying info), an Iranian immigrant who resides in Brussels, occasionally travels to Paris on private business. Kizer thinks Ahmed secretly works for Iran or for Lebanon's HEZBOLLAH."

Gabrielle had run checks on the partial name "Ahmed," but there were too many with that name, and she couldn't identify him without further information. So, she dismissed Masud's information. Without more, it was worthless speculation. But a week ago, Masud called her with more. Masud talked quickly, rushing his words.

"There's a boat," Masud said in a low voice. "It's coming soon."

"A boat? What boat? Who?"

"Ahmed's boat. Kizer told me his uncle Ahmed is waiting on a boat coming soon. It will have important cargo. I tried to find out more, but Kizer wouldn't say anything else. And he... I have to go," said Masud breathlessly. The phone went dead.

After the call, Gabrielle renewed inquiries on the name Ahmed, but nothing matched. Finally, taking a chance, she passed the name Ahmed to Marcel Bernard, her closest French intelligence contact, but without revealing all the information she had received. Bernard, a rugged 38-year-old ex-paratrooper, was assigned to NATO headquarters in Brussels. They had been together in NATO meetings and occasionally met to exchange information. The two had become close, and their relationship hovered on becoming intimate. She pretended the name Ahmed had come from a tip to NYPD in New York City. But Marcel was unable to identify him. Gabrielle felt frustrated. And then events began moving quickly.

Two days ago, Masud called back about another important development. She re-read her notes.

"Source Masud reported conversations with KIZER concerning AHMED. Ahmed gave Kizer money and instructed him to rent a self-storage unit in Kizer's name. Kizer rented the unit. According to Kizer, a padlock then appeared on the unit, and Ahmed warned Kizer to stay away from it. Kizer did not reveal the location of the storage unit. Kizer said he was helping Ahmed with something 'secret and important.'"

Following the call, Gabrielle hurriedly met Masud in her car that night. She urged him to find the storage unit's location, but he hesitated. "These people are dangerous," Masud protested. "If I ask questions, they will be suspicious."

Gabrielle pushed anyway. "That's smart of you to think about that, Masud," she said. "But they would just think you are merely curious."

"But they..."

"Masud," she said, with a reassuring pat on his forearm, "it's natural to feel people might become suspicious, but that's just because *you* know *why* you ask questions. You see? But they don't know why you ask. They will just think you are curious or eager to help. *Okay?*" He had a pained look but gave her a slight nod.

"Find out where the storage unit is located. It's important," Gabrielle said emphatically. "We need this to get your student visa to the U.S. renewed. Okay?"

He nodded again and then took a deep breath and blew it out.

"Good," she said, nodding. "And if you are afraid to ask questions, then offer to help them. You must find the unit. Understand?"

He stared back silently for a few moments, looking like a scared child. Then, "Okay," he said quietly. Masud's narrow shoulders slumped; he climbed out of the car and hurried away into the night.

That was two nights ago, and she had been waiting to hear from Masud since. She briefly wondered why Assistant FBI Director Bill Nelson wanted to meet with her but pushed the thought away. I need to focus on Ahmed. Focus: important cargo coming in a boat, a storage unit, something 'secret.' Things are moving quickly. If only...

The cell phone she used for Masud rang.

"Yes?" she said anxiously.

"Kizer is going to the storage unit tonight," said Masud, speaking low and quickly. "Maybe you can follow him and find it. He said he was going to meet his uncle Ahmed tonight."

"Why? Did Kizer say why they were going?"

"No. When I said something about going out tonight, Kizer said he couldn't go because his uncle wanted to meet him at the storage unit. He mentioned the boat again. That's all he said, and I was afraid to ask questions. So I offered to help," Masud said in a rushed voice. "They, uh..." The call went dead.

Gabrielle faced a crisis. She wanted to follow Kizer to find the storage unit. But it would require a surveillance team, and she couldn't call for help. She wasn't supposed to be 'operational as an international liaison officer.' She was restricted to conducting liaisons with foreign intelligence agencies. Gabrielle had already violated that restriction by actively handling Masud as a source. If she tried to conduct surveillance of Kizer, she could jeopardize her career and more. If officials in Belgium found out, they would likely file a protest with the State Department. They might even cancel the NYPD Liaison program in Belgium. She recalled the most important instructions about her assignment: "Don't embarrass NYPD, and don't ever do anything that could jeopardize the program."

Displaying initiative and being resourceful had always been among Gabrielle's strengths. But she had sometimes pushed too far, to the point of being fired or praised, depending on how things turned out. If she tried to get help now, even from her French intelligence contact Marcel, she would have to admit she had run a source. But something needed to be done. Perhaps she could make an anonymous call to the counter-terrorism agency in Belgium. But she quickly realized it wouldn't work. They wouldn't take it seriously enough to put urgent surveillance on Kizer.

She left the apartment and went for a walk, trying to clear her head and figure out what to do. Fate intervened when she walked by a shop. She stopped and looked up at the sign and then stepped inside. Fifteen minutes later, Gabrielle walked out of The Spy Shop with a shopping bag containing a magnetic vehicle tracking device. An international chain, The Spy Shop stores carried various electronic surveillance devices available to the public. Gabrielle returned to her apartment and took the tracking device out of the bag. An hour later, she was ready to use it. She put it in her purse and then filled the purse with extra tubes of lipstick, sticks of eye shadow, and lip gloss.

Late that afternoon, Gabrielle drove to the immigrant area of Brussels. She found the street where Kizer usually parked his car, a dented 14-year-old faded red Corolla. The street was narrow, and cars were parked bumper to bumper on both sides. Small groups of young men sat on building steps or leaned against cars, smoking and talking.

Gabrielle parked several blocks away and walked back to the street, drawing stares and catcalls along the way. She was in jeans, sneakers, and a casual top but stood out with her blonde hair, although she wore a head scarf. It was risky, but she couldn't wait until late at night when no one would be on the streets; Kizer would have left for the storage unit by then.

Now, with men watching Gabrielle's every move, it would be difficult to attach the tracking device to Kizer's car without being caught. As she walked past a group on the street corner, Kizer's car loomed 30 yards ahead on her left, jammed between other parked cars. She heard taunts behind her. Ahead, at the far end of the block, three men stood talking and watching her approach. She wondered if Kizer was one of them. If so, it would be even more dangerous.

The car now was only a few feet ahead, and she would be abreast of the rear bumper in moments. She sucked in a breath. If she was going to try, she had to do it now. She would only get one try. Gabrielle cringed, and her body tensed. Hanging loosely from a strap over her shoulder, a large black purse was on her left hip, her hand resting against it. With a discreet tug of the bag, she pulled it off her shoulder and toward the rear of Kizer's car. The bag fell to the curb at the rear bumper, and a dozen items rolled out, scattering on the pavement.

"Oh!" she uttered as if startled, holding a hand up her mouth. Out of the corners of her eyes, she saw that the men at both ends of the block had stopped talking and were staring. She dropped down on one knee and began scooping up lipstick tubes, eyeliners, and gloss. She went down to both knees and bent under the bumper as if reaching for something that had rolled under the car. As she reached under the car, she slipped the tracking device out of the purse and slapped it onto the car's bottom. She pretended to grasp something in her hand from the pavement underneath the car, put it in the purse, and then continued picking up items scattered on the pavement. She prayed her body had blocked the view of the men behind her and that the parked cars blocked the view of the men ahead.

"What are you doing?" someone demanded harshly, the voice coming from behind and above.

On her knees, Gabrielle looked up over her right shoulder. Three men hovered over her. How long had they been there? A terrifying thought shot through her mind—did they see her attach the tracking device?

"Wha..."

One grabbed her arm and jerked her upright. She tried to yank her arm out of his grasp but couldn't.

"What are you doing?" he demanded, thrusting his angry face inches from hers.

"I, I was just..."

Another man yanked the purse out of her hand, opened it, and began rummaging inside.

"Hey, that's my bag. Give it..."

"What are you doing here?" a third man demanded. "You don't belong here." He saw something on the ground and suddenly knelt down on one knee at the rear of Kizer's car. He bent down and looked underneath the car and reached his arm underneath. Gabrielle's heart skipped a beat. She felt terrified and helpless.

"What is it?" one of the men asked. "What do you see?"

The man edged back out from under the car and excitedly held something up in his hand. "This!" he exclaimed, grinning. He held up her beige clutch. It contained money and credit cards. She had forgotten it was in her purse.

"Let me see," said the man gripping her arm. He let go and reached for the clutch. Gabrielle grabbed it and spun away to run, but a hand grabbed her shoulder. A fist hit the right side of her face and staggered her. She shook her head, struggling to remain conscious. A hand grabbed her arm, but she twisted loose and swung blindly with a backhand Karate chop. The back edge of her hand hit a man in the throat, and he crumbled to the ground. Other hands clutched for her; she twisted and tried to run, but someone grabbed the tail of her blouse. She jerked away, the blouse tore, and she took off running. She dashed between parked cars into the middle of the street and sprinted as fast as she could.

She heard shouts behind her. "Get her! Stop her!" It was followed by the sounds of men running. Reaching into her clutch, Gabrielle threw money to the pavement as she ran, hoping the money would slow her pursuers. She dashed around a corner and then another and another until finally she glanced over her shoulder and didn't see anyone pursuing.

She slowed to a walk, panting hard, trying to suck in air; her heart hammering. Taking a circuitous route, she reached her parked car. She locked the doors, started the engine, and roared away. After checking the rearview mirror and side mirrors, Gabrielle sighed with relief. The side of her head throbbed where she had been hit.

"Damn," she muttered as she drove." She shook her head. "Just *damn*." As an NYPD detective, she had been in tense situations but always had others with her. This was different. She was on her own. If she disappeared, no one would know who did it or why.

After reaching her apartment, Gabrielle poured a large scotch. She plopped down and noticed that her hand shook slightly as she drank. That was close, Gabrielle thought. And I could have been ... She stopped and forced herself not to think about it. Her head hurt, and she knew she would have bruises on her face and arms. The scotch spread warmth throughout her body. Gabrielle sucked in a breath and slowly blew it out. "Damn," she muttered with a grimace. "Just damn."

After finishing the scotch, she picked up her phone and logged on to the app for the tracking unit on Kizer's car. A detailed street map appeared on the screen and showed Kizer's car as a blinking red dot. It was still parked. To extend the tracker's battery life, she used the app to switch the tracker to motion-activate, which came on only when the car began moving. The vehicle's vibrations would cause the device to turn on and remain on for 20 minutes after the car stopped moving. She set the app to send an alarm to her cell phone when a tracker signal was detected.

After setting the tracker alarm, Gabrielle went into the bedroom to undress and shower. She glanced at the picture of her daughter on the nightstand beside the bed. Blond curls, big happy eyes, rosy cheeks, and a heart-melting smile. Gabrielle's eyes welled with tears, and she forced herself to look away. She felt a lump in her throat and compressed her lips to keep from crying. Focus on Kizer. Keep your mind on him. Mary was three when she was killed in a car accident. Gabrielle was on duty, and her husband had just picked Mary up from daycare. He sustained a broken arm and collarbone. The marriage ended a year later in a divorce. After that, Gabrielle began living on the edge. Her recklessness in the job bordered on a death wish but was attributed to extraordinary courage. She devoted herself to work and finally toned down her wildest impulses.

Every night before turning off the lamp and going to sleep, Gabrielle would reach out, touch Mary's face in the picture, and whisper, "I love you, my precious angel, my Mary. You're always with me." Gabrielle would do it again when she woke every morning. It was the only time she could think about Mary without going to pieces. She had to force herself not to think about her little girl. But despite her efforts to keep it at bay, grief sometimes came in waves. Just seeing a mother and her little girl could occasionally trigger it. Gabrielle would become overwhelmed, sob uncontrollably, and curl up in a ball. Now, she wiped away tears in the bedroom and tried to focus on work, a refuge from constant heartbreak.

Dusk descended, the room darkened, and Gabrielle switched on the lights. She showered and dressed. The right side of her face felt tender. Peering into a mirror, she saw her cheek was red and swollen. She applied a dab of makeup to cover the redness. While finishing up, she heard the tracker alarm beeping and hurried to her cell phone. Kizer's car was moving. A street map on the screen showed a blinking red dot moving slowly from a parked position into the street. The red dot moved along side streets and then turned onto a main thoroughfare, where it began traveling more quickly. She was excited.

The red dot turned onto Highway E40, heading west from Brussels, and the car's speed increased. An hour later, the dot reached Ostend on the coast of the North Sea and then began traveling north, parallel to the coast. Soon, the red dot slowed and turned to the left, off the highway, moving west. Then, the car slowed to a crawl in an area where marked streets disappeared from the map. Finally, the red dot edged forward for half a mile and stopped. After being stationary for 20 minutes, the tracking unit automatically shut off, and the red dot disappeared from the screen. This must be where the storage unit or warehouse is located, Gabrielle thought. She would be able to ping the tracking device with her cell phone to turn it back on.

She searched the internet and found a satellite picture of the location where the car had stopped. The photo had been taken during daylight a year before. As the image came into focus, she saw a two-story, metal rectangular building inside a fenced compound surrounded by thick forest. A narrow parking lot bordered the building on the front and sides. The nearest road, a two-lane highway, passed a mile away, and a heavy forest stood between the highway and the warehouse. From the highway, a narrow, single-lane drive wound through the woods to the compound. Forest crowded the sides of the lane. The ocean was less than a mile west of the warehouse.

Peering at the image, Gabrielle noticed something odd. Although the satellite image was made during the middle of the day and vehicles were on the highway, the parking area inside the compound was vacant and appeared to be overgrown with weeds. The compound appeared untended and unused.

Gabrielle wondered again about the boat, the storage unit, and what Ahmed and Kizer were going to do. Maybe I should tell Marcel, she thought. We could follow Kizer together. She called Marcel's number, but thought better of it and hung up when he answered. He'll have to report what I've been doing. Marcel called back, but she didn't answer. He called again a few minutes later, and she ignored the ringing.

Minutes later, Gabrielle was driving out of the city to find Kizer's car and the building where he had stopped. An hour later, as she drove in the dark along a desolate highway toward the vacant building, she had no idea what she might find or how this would turn out.

CHAPTER 17

It was nearing midnight, and traffic had thinned out. Gabrielle had been so focused on what might be at the warehouse that she only now realized that the highway was deserted. It had been more than ten minutes since she had seen another car.

She wore a black jacket over a dark blouse and jeans to avoid standing out at night. Thinking about what could go wrong, she felt the jacket pocket to confirm her cell phone was handy. Maybe she should call this off and go back. She slowed the car but, after a few moments, took a deep breath and resumed her speed. It was a test of drives for Gabrielle: her aggressive and bold approach against her prudent and more reasonable side.

Just past midnight, she found the entrance to the winding drive that led from the highway to the vacant warehouse. It was on her left. She nearly missed it because there wasn't any lighting at the turn-off. She drove past, turned around, and went back. A hundred yards or so before reaching the turn-off to the lane, which was now ahead on her right, she saw a narrow grassy track on the same side leading into the dense woods. She slowed and turned onto the track. As her car crawled slowly into the woods, branches, and bushes swept along the sides and roof, producing loud drumming and scraping sounds inside the vehicle. The racket reminded her of going through a deafening carwash. The track ended about 30 yards into the woods, far enough to hide the car. Gabrielle turned off the headlights and the motor.

Using her cell phone app, Gabrielle checked the tracker's activity log to find out if Kizer's car had moved while she was traveling. According to the log, his car had moved but had gone only a short distance and stopped. It had left the warehouse and moved along the winding drive back toward the highway. But before reaching the highway, the car turned off to its right, moving west. After turning off, Kizer's car traveled less than a mile and stopped at the ocean.

Gabrielle thought over everything again, trying to fathom what all the pieces meant. First, Kizer's uncle Ahmed, who traveled to Paris to meet people from the Middle East, told Kizer a boat was coming with something 'important.' Second, Ahmed had Kizer rent a warehouse or storage unit in Kizer's name. Third, Ahmed put a padlock on the warehouse and warned Kizer to stay away. Fourth, despite warning Kizer to stay away, Ahmed wanted Kizer to meet him at the warehouse tonight. And now, Kizer's car had just moved from a warehouse to the ocean.

It was only speculation that Ahmed might be working with Iran or Hezbollah. But Ahmed is involved in something "important and secret." *What?* Gabrielle wondered. What the hell is going on? A boat bringing in immigrants? Weapons, explosives? Frustrated, she bit her bottom lip. Whatever it is, I need to find out. She realized something else. She could have found a way to turn over Masud and his information to her French intelligence contact, Marcel. But then she would have been excluded from leading efforts to follow up. *She* wanted to be the one to track down the information. Maybe it was her ego, but she felt she could do it better than anyone else. Recklessness won over prudence. Although they had never met, Gabrielle and FBI Agent Frank Marsh were kindred spirits.

Gabrielle switched her phone ringer to mute, shoved it in her jacket pocket, and got out of the car. For emotional fortification, she recalled a command one of her NYPD colleagues used: "Stand back, youse SOBs, NYPD is here." Her lips firmed. She took a deep breath and let it out. "Let's do it," she said to herself.

Which should be checked out first: the warehouse or the location where Kizer's car stopped at the edge of the sea? Gabrielle decided Kizer's car and the seashore were more important right now. She moved off, picking her way through dark woods toward the winding drive that ran from the highway to the warehouse. Ten minutes later, Gabrielle stepped out of the woods and onto the narrow drive near where it joined the highway. She turned and started walking in the direction of the warehouse. It was difficult to see ahead in the dark, but her eyes had adjusted to the night. She would follow the drive until she found the path on her left leading to the ocean, the one Kizer's car took.

Afraid she might encounter Kizer's car coming out, Gabrielle walked slowly and quietly, alert for any sounds. After rounding a curve in the drive, she heard a low rumbling sound and froze, ready to dash into the woods if car lights appeared ahead. The sound grew louder, and Gabrielle suddenly realized it was coming from behind. She looked over her shoulder and saw headlight beams swinging in an arc around the bend behind her, sweeping fast and lighting everything in her direction. No time to run; in a moment, she would be caught in the glare of headlights. Gabrielle dove to the ground and landed on her stomach several feet to the right of the drive. She hugged the ground, pressed the side of her face in the dirt, and folded her arms over her head. She lay motionless, hoping her dark clothes would help and no one would look closely. Headlight beams lit trees and ground and washed over her, bathing her in brilliant, ghostly white light. She felt caught and helpless. Fear made her legs and body feel heavy. Gabrielle was terrified she would move in slow motion if she tried to escape. Fighting panic, she suppressed a desperate urge to jump up and run.

The vehicle was closing in from behind and then began slowing. It crawled toward her, the motor growling like a huge lumbering creature. It stopped beside her, and the dark shape of a truck, the size of a rental truck, loomed over her. The headlights flashed off, plunging everything into impenetrable black ink. The hulking truck sat still with the motor rumbling, sounding like a malicious snarl. Gabrielle cringed, expecting doors to swing open and men to jump out and grab her. Time had no meaning. Her life existed only in this moment and place. She shuddered, panting in quick, shallow breaths. Then, suddenly, she heard a metal screech. A gear shifted, the motor revved, and the truck began edging forward with its lights off. A few yards further, it started turning left onto a narrow path through the forest on the opposite side of the drive from Gabrielle, heading toward the ocean. Brake lights glowed bright red as the driver used the brakes to negotiate the sharp turn. Seconds later, the brake lights went out, and the truck disappeared in the dark.

The rumbling motor became fainter as the truck moved further away toward the sea. Gabrielle audibly sighed. She lifted her face from the dirt, raised to one knee, and then stood, breathing deeply and blowing it out. While wiping dirt from her face, Gabrielle suddenly felt chilled. She had become soaked in sweat while cringing on the ground. Shivering in the cool night air, Gabrielle realized how lucky she had been. She realized that the men in the truck must have been looking for the path on the left side of the drive, and that's why they ignored a motionless clump on the right.

Suddenly, she heard the truck's brakes screeching. The rumble of the motor changed and began idling. She strained to hear. A truck door squeaked open, and she heard muffled voices that carried far in the night air. Several seconds later, the truck door shut with a metallic thud. The motor revved, and the truck began moving again. The sounds of the truck engine became fainter as it moved farther away until the sounds disappeared completely. The sudden silence made Gabrielle feel isolated and all alone.

She wondered what the truck door opening meant. Maybe someone had to relieve himself. But that can't be it because the door was open for only a few seconds before being shut. Perhaps they put someone out as a lookout. A worrisome thought.

The silence was suddenly shattered by a distant gunshot. Gabrielle flinched and felt a surge of fear. The gunshot had come from the direction of the truck and sea. Then another sharp pop erupted. She flinched again and held her breath for a few moments. Motionless, she stood listening intently. Several minutes passed without any more sounds. Heavy silence shrouded the darkness around her, the night as black and silent as inside a burial vault.

Gabrielle felt an urge to leave but pushed the thought from her mind. She could try to creep down the path to the sea to find out what was going on, but it would be impossible if a lookout was on the track. Maybe I can position myself at the junction where the track to the ocean joins the winding drive to the plant, she thought. And perhaps see a license number on the truck when it leaves.

At the junction, she found that the path to the sea was a rutted dirt lane, crowded with towering heavy brush on both sides and only enough room for a single vehicle to pass. She edged against the brush on the left side of the path and stood still, waiting and listening. She was still shivering in the cool night air. She pulled the jacket collar up to ward off the chill and hugged her chest with her arms.

After several minutes of unbroken silence, she began moving along the path. Gabrielle knew that her strengths included a strong curiosity and boldness. But she also knew that a strength can become a weakness when taken to extremes. She thought this might be one of those situations but couldn't restrain herself. Gabrielle crept forward along the left edge of the path, taking one cautious step and then another. She stopped every minute or so and listened a few moments before continuing.

From ahead in the dark came the sudden squawk of a radio. Gabrielle froze in mid-step. The squawk was followed by a low murmur, another radio squawk, and then silence. A lookout using a portable radio. She had been able to make out one word. It sounded like "leech," which is Arabic for "why." Her heart raced, and she tensed, ready to hide or run. About 50 feet ahead, a small bright flame abruptly flared and moved upward as a man struck a match and lit a cigarette. His face was a hideous mask in the glow of the flame. She glimpsed another man standing beside him in the match's light, holding a two-way radio. The smoker blew out the match. Then, the tip of his cigarette glowed red in the dark, glowing bright each time he inhaled.

She cautiously began backing up, but a twig snapped. One of the men uttered an exclamation, and Gabrielle froze. The smoker responded in a questioning tone, and the red tip of his burning cigarette flew to the ground. The men spoke in Persian and Arabic in hushed, urgent voices. A radio squawked as one spoke into it. Gabrielle carefully backed into the brush, trying not to make any sound. She felt branches and leaves closing around her, forming a wall between her and the path. The radio squawked again, and the two men talked in low voices.

From the direction of the men, a flashlight beam shot out and danced around the path and surrounding brush. It lit the branches and leaves in front of Gabrielle and then moved further, searching. Then, the light abruptly moved back to her position and stayed there. She felt like she was in the glare of a spotlight. The man holding the flashlight began walking toward her, the light hovering on her position as he walked. Her heart was racing. Then the second man called out, and the flashlight beam swung away from her to the other side of the path. The men called back and forth to each other. Finally, the man with the flashlight walked past her, within a few feet, searching with the flashlight.

Gabrielle took advantage of the noise the men were making to back deeper into the brush. As she did, the brush thinned out toward the sea, and she saw a chance to move silently and quickly away. Moving toward the sea, Gabrielle smelled salt air, felt a sea breeze on her face, and heard heavy waves washing against the shore. Then, she heard something else above the sounds of waves—low rumbling engines ahead to her right front. She moved toward the sounds and up a rise to the crest of a low bluff overlooking the sea. Below and to her right was a small cove.

Deep-throated sounds of rumbling engines came from the cove below. Gabrielle lay down on her stomach on the crest, among small scrubs, and peered at the cove, trying to penetrate the black night. After several moments, she made out large black shapes at the cove's edge. Just then, a sliver of the moon emerged from behind dark, drifting clouds, and the scene below was painted in a pale ghostly light.

In fleeting light, Gabrielle saw a fishing trawler idling next to the shore, its diesel engines rumbling. A ramp extended from the trawler to the beach at the water's edge. The large truck Gabrielle had seen was backed up to the end of the ramp.

"Here's another one," someone called out in French, the voice carrying far in the night air. A flashlight switched on and lit the ramp. She saw two men roll a drum down the ramp and load it into the back of the truck. Gabrielle counted at least six men, some around the back of the truck and others on the boat, speaking in Persian, Arabic, and French. A loud thump and simultaneous yell of pain erupted at the truck. A figure limped from the back, cursing. A laugh. A sharp rebuke. A command shut down the exchange.

"Just a few more," someone said in French. Dark figures began moving up the ramp toward the boat. "When we get there," said another, "we'll form a chain and unload the barrels quickly. And..." A portable radio squawked, and anxious voices talked in Persian. The dark figures moving stopped in place. The man using the radio called out to the others in Persian and then repeated his orders in French. "The lookouts said someone might be lurking around on foot. Quick," he said urgently, "stop what you're doing and check the area. Now!"

Men fanned out with flashlight beams bouncing and swinging in wild arcs. Two men a dozen yards apart headed in Gabrielle's direction, walking up the slope of the bluff toward her position at the crest. Their flashlight beams were sweeping ahead, lighting the crest. Gabrielle ducked her head just before a beam of light swept across where she lay. The flashlight beams and voices of the men were closing in. She began desperately crawling backward down the slope in crablike movements with her hands and feet. Then she got up, bent over in a crouch, and ran through scrubs, breathing hard, frantic she might be caught. She suddenly fell into a depression in the ground and hurled forward, landing face-first, her breath knocked out. Unable to move, helpless.

The two men reached the top of the crest and moved down the slope in her direction, their flashlight beams crisscrossing just above where she lay in the depression. They would be upon her in moments. She was trying to breathe again but was still unable to move. Even if she could get up and run, they would see her. Gabrielle felt trapped. She finally caught her breath just as the men were approaching on both sides of the dip in the ground where she lay. She turned on her side and curled into a fetal position, her arms covering her head. A shout erupted from the far side of the slope, and the men stopped. Someone shouted again.

"Come back," came a distant yell, "come back, no one is around. Let's get finished."

The men stood a few yards away from Gabrielle. If either shined his flashlight in her direction, they would see her. She recoiled. One grumbled and said something to the other. The other responded, and as they talked, Gabrielle could tell they had turned and were walking away. She crawled to the edge of the depression and peeked over the rim. She saw two figures moving up the slope, their flashlight beams jigging and lighting the ground ahead. Finally, they disappeared over the crest of the hill. She breathed an audible sigh of relief.

Gabrielle stood and began moving away, carefully giving a wide berth to the path where she had encountered the lookouts. Scrubs changed to heavier brush and then to forest. She moved slowly and quietly in a wide semi-circle and emerged from the forest onto the winding drive from the vacant plant to the highway. She stepped out on the plant drive and moved right, following it back toward the highway and her car.

As she walked, Gabrielle thought about hiding in the forest to watch for the truck leaving but decided she had enough close calls for one night. So instead, she would get her car and park at a distance where she could watch the junction where the plant drive joined the highway. Then, Gabrielle would wait for the truck to leave and follow it. This is too big, she decided as she walked, and when I get back to my car, I'll call Marcel for help even if it reveals that I've been operational.

Just before the plant drive joined the highway, Gabrielle moved into the forest on the left side of the drive. Paralleling the highway, she walked just inside the forest's edge until she finally reached her car parked in the woods at the end of the narrow path. A short distance behind her, Farhad, who had followed her from the plant drive, watched her in the green glow of night vision goggles. Following the alarm raised by the lookouts on the path to the cove, he had been dispatched from the cove with the NGVs to watch the plant drive. While watching Gabrielle move toward her car, Farhad pressed the transmit button on a Bluetooth device in his left ear, whispered in Persian, and then acknowledged a response. As Gabrielle reached the car, a dark figure dashed toward her.

Gripping the car door handle, Gabrielle felt a rush of relief. She was safe. Suddenly, she heard rustling behind her. As she turned, Farhad's fist hit the side of her head. The blow flung her against the car, knocking her breath out. Uttering a cry, she crumpled to the ground, landing on her back, dazed and frantically struggling to breathe. Farhad's dark figure loomed over her, and she felt a vicious kick in the ribs. Sharp pains shot through her body. She was gasping for air. Farhad pounced on Gabrielle, straddled her waist, and swung a fist back to punch her again. Suddenly, a dark figure darted forward and kicked Farhad in the face, knocking him backward. He landed on his back with a thud. Lifting his head, Farhad grabbed for a gun at his waist. The dark figure dove on top and hammered him with punches; within seconds, Farhad lay unconscious, his face mashed and bloody.

The dark figure rose and hurried to Gabrielle. His face was covered with a balaclava except for his eyes and mouth. He knelt at her side, lowered his head inches from her face, and whispered in French.

Despite the stabbing pain in her ribs, Gabrielle weakly struggled, but he held her down and kept whispering. Then, finally, she heard his whispers. "Gabrielle, it's me," he whispered. "It's me, Marcel. Marcel." He pulled the balaclava off his head.

"Marcel...?" she said uncertainly, her voice feeble and her eyes searching his face in the dark. "Is that..." She stopped with a sharp moan. Severe pains stabbed her ribs when she breathed. Each breath felt like her chest was being pierced all the way through. She tried taking shallow breaths. Her head throbbed with excruciating pain.

"It is okay, Gabrielle. You're safe now." Marcel lifted her head and shoulders and held her gently. "You're safe," he repeated. The adrenaline that had fueled Gabrielle was now gone, and pent-up emotions were released in a flood. Tears rolled down her cheeks. Her body shook with sobs. A knife stabbed her ribs with every breath. Cradled in Marcel's arms, Gabrielle put an arm around his neck and buried her head in his shoulder. They held each other silently in the dark night, the only sound being her muffled sobs.

Standing in the cove near the boat, Ahmed tried again to reach Farhad on a two-way radio. Still no answer. But from Farhad's last radio call, Ahmed knew where the woman and her car were located—just inside the forest, about a hundred yards to the left of where the S-shaped plant drive joined the highway. Ahmed barked orders, and three men armed with Uzis hurried to a Peugeot and drove off without lights on the lane running from the cove to the plant drive.

"Gabrielle," Marcel spoke urgently, his voice barely above a whisper, "are there others? Other men, who may be after you?"

After a moment, she stopped sobbing and said in a low voice, "A boat..." She took a painful breath. "More men..." another breath, "unloading drums onto a truck and..." She flinched. A knife was stabbing her right lung with each breath.

"We need to get out of here now," Marcel said quickly. "We'll use your car to get to mine. It's close, and I'll call for help. Can you walk if I help you?" Gabrielle nodded weakly. He lifted her to her feet and then into the passenger seat of her car. It was too painful for Gabrielle to reach into her pocket for her car keys, so he had to do it.

As Marcel started the car, Gabrielle clutched her left arm across her chest, wincing as she tried to relieve the pain in her right side. "Are you okay?" he asked before shifting to back out.

"Yes,' she rasped and took a shallow breath. "Okay," she said breathlessly. She hurt so badly.

Marcel backed the small car toward the highway. As they cleared the forest, backing up, he saw the highway was deserted. A hundred yards to his left, a Peugeot without lights slowly emerged unseen at the highway. Three men in the Peugeot saw bright red brake lights as Marcel finished reversing.

Marcel turned on the headlights and began driving toward his car, parked half a mile ahead. The darkened Peugeot turned onto the highway and sped to catch up. The pursuers readied their weapons.

As he drove, Marcel spoke, his eyes on the road ahead. "I was worried about you. I knew you were probably doing something you shouldn't. I should have reported it, but I didn't want to get you in trouble." He was concentrating on the road and didn't notice the black shape in the rearview mirror. It was approaching fast and looming larger.

"After you called but didn't speak, I tracked your cell phone, and you here. I found your car but didn't know where you had gone, so I waited in the woods." He glanced at her. "Do you understand what I'm saying, Gabrielle? I care about you and ..."

Gunfire erupted, shattering the back window, and Marcel slumped over. The car swerved toward the opposite lane, and another burst of gunfire made Gabrielle snap into action. Ignoring her pain, she grabbed the steering wheel, which was slippery with blood. The car veered onto the shoulder and sped down an incline toward a tree line. Gabrielle saw trees racing toward her in a blur, and she braced for the impact. With a sickening metallic crash, the car collided with a tree head-on, crushing the front end and sending debris flying. The car crumpled from the front bumper to the front doors. The mangled vehicle lurched and settled. Clouds of steam began hissing from under a twisted hood. Broken car parts were creaking and ticking. Odors of steam and burnt oil filled the air. A dozen bullet holes had riddled the car. A deflated airbag partially covered Gabrielle's slumped and motionless body. The driver's door stood open from the impact, and Marcel's bloodied upper body hung out of his seat, arm dangling almost to the ground.

The darkened Peugeot parked at an angle on the shoulder. Its headlights flashed on and illuminated the smashed car. Smoke and steam from the wreckage eerily curled in ghostly shafts of headlight beams. Two men with Uzis emerged from the Peugeot and began walking down the incline toward Gabrielle's smoking car.

CHAPTER 18

As the men descended the incline toward Gabrielle's wrecked car, they felt a sudden disturbance in the air and ground. They froze, listening intently as a low hum grew louder, approaching from the direction in which they had been chasing Gabrielle's car. Headlights abruptly lit up the curve ahead. A large transport truck was rounding the curve, followed closely by another.

The driver of the Peugeot shouted, and the two men scrambled back to the car. The driver switched off the headlights, and the Peugeot made a tight turn, speeding away and turning off the highway at the drive leading to the vacant plant.

Meanwhile, Ahmed finished a cell phone call at the dark cove near the boat and then barked orders. Men scrambled to pull the ramp back onto the boat and close the doors on the back of the truck. Then, moving without lights, the dark shape of the trawler slowly backed away from shore, swung around toward the open sea, and disappeared into the black night.

The Peugeot emerged from the forest and stopped in front of the truck. The driver hurried to Ahmed. "What about the woman Farhad followed?" Ahmed said.

"We saw a car coming out of the woods and caught up with it," said the driver. "It must have been the woman because it came out of the forest where Farhad said it was. We began shooting, and the car went off the road and crashed. We must have hit her. And then—"

"Did you make sure she was dead and get her identification and phone?"

The driver shook his head. "We were going to do that, but some trucks came, and we had to leave. The truck drivers would surely stop at the wrecked car and call the police."

"What about Farhad? Did you find him?"

"We couldn't stop and look for him because of the trucks."

Ahmed instructed the driver to take one of the men and return to the plant drive to search for Farhad, who had gone missing after finding the woman. "But hurry. We only have a few minutes." The men left in the Peugeot.

Ahmed gathered the five remaining men. "Kizer and his friend Masud must have talked. Get them out," he said, pointing at Kizer's small car. Both had their hands tied behind their backs. The men pulled Kizer and Masud toward the water's edge and made them kneel.

"No, please," begged Kizer in a quivering voice. "Uncle, please. Please let me go, please, uncle." Masud whimpered and sobbed, his body shivering.

"Do it," Ahmed barked.

"No, please!" Kizer cried. One of the men grabbed Kizer by the hair and pulled his head back, exposing his throat. "Please, no..." He slit Kizer's throat with a large knife. Gushing blood, Kizer's body fell sideways to the ground, wiggled, and became still.

Another grabbed Masud by the hair and pulled his head back. "Mama," Masud cried, "I want my mama! Mama, help me..." The man slit Masud's throat, half severing his neck. Masud's body fell forward and became still in moments. "Drag them to the woods," Ahmed said. "And hurry."

A few minutes later, the truck rumbled away from the cove with its headlights off. Ahmed followed in a darkened car, and behind him, one of the men drove Kizer's car. After the vehicles disappeared into the night, the deserted cove fell silent except for the ocean's mournful murmurs. Weeping waves washed gently at the shore, near pools of dark blood. Despite a steady sea breeze, a sweet, sticky smell of blood and an odor of terror lingered in the air.

The men sent to look for Farhad found him unconscious. They loaded him in their car and caught up with the small convoy. Ahmed felt relieved. He could not risk leaving any of his men behind alive. Now, he worried about the woman who had been watching them. What had she seen? Who was she working for? Had she reported anything by phone or radio? Probably not, he thought, because they would have been caught if she had. Ahmed shook it off. Despite the problem with the woman, the plan for the ship's cargo seemed to be working. The pieces were coming together.

CHAPTER 19

The incessant ringing of a mobile phone on the nightstand woke FBI Assistant Director Bill Nelson from a deep sleep in his Brussels hotel room. He saw the call was from the FBI command center in Washington. Nelson was stifling a yawn when the first words jolted him awake.

"Something's happened," an FBI official said quickly. "A few hours ago, a bullet-ridden car was found in a remote area near the Belgium coast. Inside were a French intelligence agent and an NYPD international liaison officer. One is dead, and the other is in a coma and—"

"NYPD? Who? Do you have a name?"

"Someone named Lemaire, a G. A. Lemaire. I don't know the full name yet. But, I think Lemaire is a female and..."

"Who was killed?" Nelson said, dreading the answer. "Which one?"

"It was the French agent. Marcel Bernard. He was killed by gunfire, and Lemaire is in a coma. Not sure if she will survive. I've got Deputy Director Walters on this same line, and he wants to talk to you."

After a pause, "Bill, this is Sam Walters," said the FBI Deputy Director. "I know you're there on something else, but it's good you're in place to help on this."

"I'll do what I can, Sam. What do you have in mind?"

"The immediate thing is to establish Bureau jurisdiction. We'll treat it as a terror attack on an American citizen—the NYPD officer, Lemaire—which gives us jurisdiction under the statutes."

"Is that what it was, Sam? A terrorist attack?"

"We don't know yet. For all we know, it could have been something else. No one knows why Lemaire and the French agent were together.

The French and NYPD don't seem to know anything about it. They're in an uproar, searching for answers. France and Belgium are spun up, as you can imagine. The White House is already demanding answers, and the President's National Security Advisor is throwing his weight around again. But worse than that, we have to deal with Delgado with NYPD," Walters said tensely. "You remember him, Bill? The head of their counter-terrorism division?"

Bill Nelson grimaced. "I know him well. Delgado and I bashed heads several times over who had the lead on terror cases in New York. He's a prick."

"Exactly. You know how they are. It's hard enough to keep them out. But with one of their own down, they'll want to charge into Belgium and France like they're NYPD precincts. They can be good partners," Walters continued, "but we don't want them screwing this up. This is *our* jurisdiction, Bill. They can advise and consult, but they have to stay out of the way. I've called a meeting with my staff about the attack, but part of the agenda will be how to keep NYPD at arm's length on this."

Walters paused. "Now, Bill," Walters continued, "this what I need you to do. Clear the way with our French counterparts for the Bureau to take the lead or at least be equal partners with the French in investigating the attack. That won't be easy since their man was killed. You know what they can be like. The Flying Squad will take off for Brussels in a few hours. Just do what you can with the French and Belgium to keep NYPD from actively participating in the investigation. Like I said, NYPD can provide information and consult, but the investigation is ours alone."

"Keeping NYPD out is going to be hard," Nelson said, "especially because we'll need to find out from them what Lemaire had been working on. Who her contacts were and—"

"I know, I know," Walters said, exasperated. "Just do what you can, Bill. Gotta go; I've got NSC on the other line."

Bill Nelson picked up a pen and began making a list of what he needed to do and the officials he needed to contact. Getting the FBI off to a quick start with the French and Belgian security services would be the best way to keep NYPD relegated to a supporting role. He knew there would soon be an urgent flurry of overwhelming demands on his time and attention. The French Interior Minister, the French Intelligence service, and the security services in Belgium would all demand information and answers. As would NATO, the CIA, the State Department, and NYPD. All within the framework of power struggles and turf battles. Nelson took a deep breath and then began making calls.

Brussels, Belgium: NATO Headquarters

Bill Nelson sat at the head of a conference table in a secure room at NATO headquarters in Brussels, three hours after dawn and 100 miles from Gabrielle Lemaire's wrecked car. The vast NATO complex, home to delegations from member countries, was shaped like an inverted "U," with a majestic entrance at the inside base. A Secure Video Teleconference (SVTC) began. A large flat screen on the conference room wall displayed a dozen small squares, each filled by one or more participants from various agencies. The meeting was chaired from Washington, D.C., by the president's deputy national security advisor, Ann Covington. Nelson hoped the SVTC would achieve some actual coordination and resolve the inevitable turf battles that were part of high-profile incidents.

After the participants had introduced themselves, Ann Covington briefed them on the situation. "So in summary," she concluded, "Gabrielle Lemaire, the NYPD international liaison, and Marcel Bernard, the French intelligence agent, were attacked, and no suspects have been identified. At this stage, we don't know why the two were together or what they were doing. The investigation is just beginning, but because the victims are intelligence agents, we assume it was a terrorist attack. Consequently, we have ordered increased security at U.S. installations throughout Europe and the U.K." Each participant in the SVTC then briefed what their agency knew and what they were doing to follow up.

Sam Walters, the FBI Deputy Director, spoke up. "Ann, the FBI is sending our international response team, The Flying Squad, pending approval from Belgium and France, to work closely with our international counterparts. The team will depart in a few hours. Assistant Director Bill Nelson happened to be in Brussels and is already coordinating with the French and Belgium security services."

After other participants described their resources supporting the investigation, Ann Covington called on the final one, who had yet to speak.

"Now, let's hear from New York PD. I believe that's Joseph Delgado, the Deputy Commissioner. Commissioner Delgado, be assured that we will make every effort to identify and arrest the perpetrators. We will leave no stone unturned."

"That's right, Joe," added FBI Deputy Director Sam Walters, "the FBI team will be leaving soon and on the ground 10 to 12 hours from now. We'll set up a forward command center in Paris or Belgium. And we'll coordinate closely with NYPD; you can be assured of that, Commissioner Delgado. With your approval, your detectives will be part of our joint command center and fully involved every step of the way."

Bill Nelson knew this was 'Bureau-speak,' which meant the FBI didn't want NYPD meddling and wanted any NYPD detectives to be stationed at an FBI command center, where they would be carefully controlled and limited.

"Thank you," Delgado replied, "I appreciate all the federal government is doing to help *us* investigate the attack on *our* detective, Gabrielle Lemaire, and the French agent." Nelson took note of Delgado's carefully chosen words and emphasis, a sharp rejection of the FBI's assumption that it was in charge of the case.

"The FBI is going to take care of it," Sam Walters snapped. "As I said, your detectives will be at the joint command center, and our FBI team will be leaving..."

"Our team left for Europe two hours ago," Delgado said defiantly.

Sam Walters's mouth dropped open. "What? But..."

"A major case team of NYPD detectives, analysts, and crime scene specialists, all cleared for Top Secret SCI, are in the air right now. They'll land in Paris in nine hours from takeoff."

Ann Covington jumped in. "But...you...uh, while we want NYPD fully involved," she protested, "international interests dictate that the operation must be led by our national security agencies, the FBI, with the assistance of CIA and other agencies. You are welcome to..."

"For those who may not know it," declared Delgado, "NYPD has 34,000 officers and hundreds of thousands of retired officers. Our officers, active and retired, expect us—and *require us*—to take care of our own, as we always have, regardless of where our officers are attacked."

"This is Reynolds," said a bespeckled, gray-haired man, speaking from one of the small squares on the screen. His voice was cultured and nasal as if talking with a head cold. He enunciated words slowly and precisely. "Reynolds, with the State Department, Commissioner. You must realize that maintaining international relations is a delicate matter. That's why it is entrusted to professionals," he said condescendingly. "You may not fully appreciate that—"

"I'll tell you what I *fully appreciate*," Commissioner Delgado interjected, his gruff voice rising. "I fully appreciate what former New York City Mayor Michael Bloomberg once pointed out. The Mayor said, and I quote, 'I have my own army in the NYPD, which is the seventh biggest army in the world. I have my own State Department, much to Foggy Bottom's annoyance. We have the United Nations in New York, and so we have an entree into the diplomatic world that Washington does not have.'"

Delgado paused for a moment to let it sink in. "I don't know how much you know about the New York Police Department, Mister Reynolds. Focusing on international affairs, you may not be very familiar with our American institutions," he said sarcastically.

"Well," said FBI Deputy Director Sam Walters, "you make a good point, Commissioner Delgado, but of course, when it comes to—"

"And you know what Mayor Bloomberg said about the FBI, Sam Walters? He said the Bureau is only one-quarter the size of NYPD, and we have more Arabic speakers in just one precinct than you do in the entire Bureau."

"Well—"

"NYPD is going to investigate the attack on our officer, Lemaire," Delgado said flatly, "and we welcome help from everyone, *including* the Bureau." Long moments of silence followed.

"This is Reynolds again, with the State Department," interjected the gray-haired man on the screen. "We understand your position, Commissioner Delgado. But have you obtained all the necessary approvals from Belgium and France to conduct active investigations? It's a delicate subject with those countries. I just want to make sure that—"

"We're applying for all the approvals needed," Delgado said abruptly.

That means, Assistant FBI Director Bill Nelson thought, that NYPD doesn't have all the approvals it needs from those countries yet. So we need to move quickly to block them.

"May I make a suggestion," Bill Nelson offered. "It's important that we all work closely together. Everyone knows it's best to have a single person and agency in charge of an investigation. Otherwise, there will be duplication of effort, confusion, cross-purposes, and missed leads. And the French and our other international partners will be confused about sharing information."

"That's correct," said Sam Walters quickly. "The established protocol calls for the FBI to lead terror cases overseas." As Walters spoke, Delgado looked ready to erupt again.

"Exactly," Bill Nelson agreed, "The FBI normally leads overseas in the usual circumstances. However, Commissioner Delgado has a point. This attack was directed at an NYPD intelligence detective and the French. NYPD has a critical stake in the investigation, something our international protocols had not anticipated." As he talked, Nelson noticed Delgado was listening closely. "Consequently, this should be a joint investigation." Nelson proposed a three-man team to oversee the investigation, one each from the FBI, NYPD, and the French. In the end, Delgado grudgingly agreed. Given the opposition voiced during the meeting, Delgado realized the State Department and the White House would quietly urge foreign governments to bar an active investigation by NYPD.

After the SVTC ended, Bill Nelson was retrieving his cell phone from a secure pouch in the hallway when a member of the NATO staff approached him with several messages.

"Sir, FBI deputy director Sam Walters wants you on another SVTC beginning in 15 minutes. And here are several other messages," said the staff member, handing Nelson message forms. "Deputy NSC director Ann Covington wants you to call her immediately on our secure communications line. A secure phone is in the SCIF. The Interior Minister of France wants you to meet with him as soon as possible at the Interior Ministry in Paris. New York deputy police commissioner Delgado wants you to call him. The White House communications director needs to talk with you as soon as possible. The CIA station chief wants a meeting today in Paris, and you also have a call from MI-6."

Looking at the messages, Nelson shook his head slowly. He had been at the center of numerous crises and knew that urgent demands would soon overwhelm his time and attention. It felt like trying to drink from a fire hydrant. And much of his time would be spent putting out fires.

Minutes later, Nelson was sitting in the SCIF when the wall screen blinked to life and filled with the image of FBI Deputy Director Sam Walters at FBI headquarters. Walters didn't look happy.

"Bill, this is a damn mess," Sam Walters said irritably. "What the hell does Delgado think he's doing? We wouldn't have been in this crap if NYPD had kept their people in New York where they belong." NYPD international liaison detectives stationed in other countries had always been a sore point with Walters. A few years earlier, he had encouraged media contacts and think tanks to criticize the NYPD international liaison program. Despite the media campaign, NYPD didn't relent and actually expanded to additional countries.

"I agree with you," Nelson said, "but now we have to deal with the situation. We can't have NYPD running around Europe. That's why I suggested that we be the lead agency for the investigation but use a three-person team, with one each from the Bureau, NYPD, and the French. I thought that would co-opt NYPD trying to act on its own while at the same time making us the overall lead agency."

"It's a wonder Delgado half-agreed even to that," Walters grumbled. "They act like Europe is just another damn NYPD precinct. At least there's a silver lining in this; we should be able to gin up some critical media on the New York PD international liaison program. Paint NYPD as bumbling fools who don't know what they're doing and interfering with the Bureau and foreign intelligence services."

"You may be right, but if you generate negative media on it, Delgado will know the Bureau's behind it. It might cause them to dig in their heels when we want everyone to play nice right now to solve this thing."

No one said anything, and Nelson could imagine Walters clenching his jaws. "You may be right," Walters finally conceded. "I'll hold off for now, but I'm going to unleash as soon as this is over. And maybe the French are ready to boot them out now, too. You remember that years ago, we tried to get the French, the Brits, and others not to cooperate with the NYPD detectives but didn't have much luck. Now would be a good time to revisit that with foreign governments. I want you to get started on it while you're there."

"I agree. But again, the priority is to find out what happened and who's behind it, so I think we need to hold off until this is over."

Nelson heard Walters mutter a harrumph. "All right, but if the investigation begins to drag out, I want you to go ahead and convince foreign governments to kick NYPD out or shut off cooperation."

"Yes, sir. There's one more thing," Nelson said. "For our agent on the joint investigation team, I want Frank Marsh."

"Marsh? Isn't he in Africa right now? With the special ops force, JSOC sent?"

"The operation is over, and the JSOC people have left, but Marsh is still in Africa getting some rest before returning. If I can have him, we can reroute him here. I want him as our lead agent on this team."

"Bill, you know Marsh sometimes causes problems."

"Marsh is a high-wire act who sometimes works without a net," Nelson replied, "but his work broke open the plot on the casino bombing, and he also identified the traitor with the NSC."

"Well, it's your funeral. Let's wrap this up. I've got an in-person meeting with the NSC. They are spun up, and the White House wants the latest information. Plus, the White House wants to know how to handle the attack publicly—low profile or high profile? They would rather downplay it off the record to the media as a possible romantic dispute rather than as a terror attack. Which the Brit Townsend helpfully suggested was the case during our SVTC. By the way, the State Department is also spun up and wants to boot NYPD out of foreign countries. I've told them we definitely agree. So they might carry water for us on this."

Nelson changed the subject before Walters could launch into another rant about NYPD.

The following day, a U.S. Air Force C-17 cargo jet took off from Malabo International Airport at Punta Europa, Bioko Island, Equatorial Guinea. Despite being capable of carrying a payload of 170,000 pounds and hundreds of combat troops, the C-17 only carried 180 pounds, a single passenger—FBI agent Frank Marsh, six-foot, lean, and athletic, who was trying to ignore the aches he still felt from his recent ordeal. Earlier that morning, Frank had been instructed to hurry to Malabo airport to board a special flight. The C-17 pilots had received urgent orders to get him to France as quickly as possible. The aircraft had flown to Malabo from Camp Lemonnier in Djibouti, the only permanent U.S. military base in Africa, home to the Combined Joint Task Force-Horn of Africa (CJTF-HOA) of the U.S. Africa Command.

Frank was still exhausted, and following takeoff, he curled up in a sleeping bag and quickly fell asleep on the metal deck. After departing from Malabo, the C-17 climbed to 28,000 feet and began cruising at 515 miles per hour. Nine hours later, after a refueling stop, the plane landed at Charles De Gaulle Airport in Paris. The FBI Legat in Paris met the plane and took Frank to the U.S. Embassy to meet with FBI assistant director Bill Nelson, who had arrived that afternoon from Brussels to confer with the French Interior Minister. "Mr. Nelson will brief you himself," was all the Legat would tell Frank.

CHAPTER 20

Kathy was excited. After discovering Frank was going to Europe, she arranged an NSC trip to Belgium and Paris to meet with foreign counterparts about matters on the National Security Council's agenda. While changing for her overnight flight to Brussels, Kathy caught sight of herself in the mirror. She couldn't help but notice the faint scars where Marwan had seared her cheek and her breast with liquid nitrogen. Despite Frank's assurances that they weren't noticeable, Kathy saw them every time she looked in a mirror. Frank pretended he couldn't see them, but she knew better.

Worse, the scars always reminded her of shrieking in pain while being tortured. The image in the mirror became blurry as tears welled up and rolled down her cheeks. Kathy wiped her eyes and washed her face, but puffy and red-rimmed eyes stared back at her in the mirror. She stood for long moments staring at her scars again—but this time thoughtfully. She scrunched her mouth and bit one side of her lips. Then, looking at her eyes in the mirror, her chin rose, and her mouth firmed.

This is the day I change, she decided. The scars always reminded me of my fear and pain. But from now on, they will remind me of my strength and courage. Holding out under torture until I was delirious. Enduring months of painful treatments. The fire is back. I'm "me" again, she thought, only stronger than before. Kathy felt like she was seeing herself again for the first time in many months. She smiled excitedly. I can't wait for Frank to see the old "new" me.

The following day, after an overnight trans-Atlantic flight, Kathy landed in Brussels and checked into the Royal Windsor Hotel Grand

Palace. She sent word to let Frank know where she was staying. He replied that he would be able to join her in a few days for at least one night together.

CHAPTER 21

TEHRAN, IRAN

An aide handed Marwan a decoded message from COMET, the source in Washington. It read: "Katherine Foster is going to Brussels or Paris for meetings. Frank Marsh may join her there." The two people responsible for the loss of my leg, Marwan thought, would both be in one place. He thought about Zorak.

TEHRAN

Relaxing at home in Tehran, Zorak smiled at the sounds of his two sons, aged eight and ten, laughing while playing electronic games in their room. In his mid-forties, he looked like a gentle family man with a kind face and prematurely graying hair. His father was Persian, and his mother was from England; in his early years, he had been educated in England and Switzerland. He was fluent in English, German, Italian, and French. With his command of languages, refined appearance, and self-assured manner, Zorak easily passed for a European businessman, a good cover for his real profession. Zorak was a Quds Force assassin. To be more precise, he was an assassin who had been forced into retirement.

It had been two years since he had killed a target. Before retirement, he occasionally taught new assassins how to kill and, more importantly, how to avoid being caught. Anyone can kill, he thought, but to kill in foreign countries *and* get away with it required thorough planning, ingenuity, and the ability to be unfazed by the unexpected.

He tried to train this into the latest generation of assassins. But things had changed, he thought with a frown. The profession was not what it once was. Because of ubiquitous surveillance cameras in cities and the ability of intelligence services to track travelers, the preferred methods for assassinations have changed. A bullet in the head had been replaced by spraying lethal poison in the target's face or putting radioactive material in his drink or food. Or on the target's home doorknob, as the Russians had done in England and several European countries. Those methods allowed time for the assassin to avoid detection and to leave the country before the target died and before it was discovered that the death was an assassination.

Although no longer preferred, a bullet in the head was still occasionally used. Zorak felt professional satisfaction in doing his killings well, more than 20. Lately, however, he had begun second-guessing the need for some. He even regretted a few and was glad he was retired. Quds Force sometimes asked for his advice on complex assassinations, but he no longer participated in the actual killings. That's probably what Marwan wants to see me about now, he thought—my advice on planning a difficult one.

Bursts of laughter and shouts from the back interrupted his thoughts. "Be quiet, boys," Zorak yelled but smiled at the fun they were having. He took off his glasses and pinched the bridge of his nose with two fingers. He set his glasses down and lit a cigarette. As he was finishing the cigarette, Marwan arrived carrying an attaché case.

They sat in the living room, and Zorak served a glass of chilled sharbat, a traditional Iranian beverage. Then he went into the kitchen and returned with a chilled bottle of vodka and two glasses. Alcohol was forbidden, but the wealthy and powerful drank behind closed doors. He poured generous helpings and handed one to Marwan. They lifted their glasses and nodded at each other over the rims. They drank and talked about old times. Zorak lit a cigarette when the glasses were empty while Marwan opened his attaché case on the coffee table. Zorak cringed when he learned what Marwan wanted.

"You want me to kill the American FBI man, Marsh, and the woman named Foster?" Zorak said. "But why me? Why not use the men you have?" Marwan explained that an assassination team in Washington, D.C., had recently been thwarted in killing Foster. He was adamant about bringing Zorak back for this one hit. "I want the best," Marwan declared firmly.

Zorak knew Marwan showed him respect by coming to his home to personally seek his help. He had heard rumors that Marwan had become obsessed with killing the Americans. He also knew that Marwan was ruthless.

"It's good that your wife and your sons enjoy this home and a good life," Marwan said pointedly. "They depend on you. And *I* depend on you." Zorak's stomach churned at the comment. One rival of Marwan had been mysteriously killed when someone on a motorcycle shot him while the man's car was stopped at an intersection. The death was attributed to Mossad, the Israeli intelligence service that had assassinated nuclear scientists and other officials in Iran. But Zorak suspected Marwan was behind the killing. A second rival had simply disappeared without a trace. Zorak realized he was trapped. The well-being of his wife and sons lingered in his mind and hovered over the meeting. He forced himself to appear ready to help.

"Here is the file on Frank Marsh and Katherine Foster," Marwan said, handing a folder to Zorak. "It includes descriptions, photographs, and personal histories. Neither has any personal security protection as far as we know."

Zorak began leafing through the pages while Marwan continued. "We believe Marsh and Foster will be in Europe soon. Either Brussels or Paris. We will be informed of their location and the hotel where they are staying. Our cyber unit believes it will be able to track the location of Foster's personal cell phone in real time, and you will have that information, too. It should be all you need to plan and carry out the killings. You will be supplied with passports and papers in several identities and whatever disguises and backgrounds you decide to use."

Zorak nodded. "How long will they be in Europe? How much time do I have to do it?"

"I think they will arrive this week and stay for a week or more, but—"

Zorak interrupted. "We don't have much time," he said, frowning. "Once we know where they will be, I've got to plan the kill and my exit from the country."

Marwan nodded and said, "We don't have much time. You have to leave tomorrow for Paris. We'll send updates on their location. There is one more thing. This must be done, and you must be out of the country before the 27th of April."

Zorak looked at Marwan questioningly. "April 27?"

"That's the Jews' Holocaust Memorial Day in Israel, called Yom HaShoah, but it's commemorated by Jews across Europe. We have something planned for that day in Europe. It will be difficult for you to get out of the country if you're still there. So you need to complete your mission and leave before the 27th." Zorak pursed his lips and nodded. That was just days away.

That afternoon, Zorak was setting things out for an overnight bag when he heard a knock and opened the door. An older man stood, staring silently at him. Zorak frowned. "As my wife's father, you are welcome in our home, but as my former colleague, you are not." He paused. "So, which one visits me today?"

Haddid bit his lip. "I come as both. And also as the deputy commander of a Unit 400 section. When I explain, I think you welcome the visit."

"I'll be the judge of that," Zorak snapped. "Come in," he said, with a sideways nod toward the living room. After they settled in easy chairs, Zorak waved a palm. "Go ahead."

"It's about Marwan." Haddid paused. "He's becoming a problem and … Wait, please, let me finish," Haddid said, holding up a hand. "I heard Marwan wants to send you to Europe to kill an American FBI agent and a woman with the American National Security Council staff.

Since losing his leg because of these two Americans, Marwan has been obsessed with killing them. But killing them now would cause problems for the country. The Americans and other nations would react and increase sanctions, or worse. We would be further isolated. For that reason, Marwan has been ordered to do it *only* if the killing can be made to look like an accident or robbery. It must not be linked to us. To make it impossible for Marwan to even try, he's been restricted from using the number of men necessary to do it properly. But now I hear he wants to send you *alone* to kill them." Haddid paused. "This is reckless. You shouldn't do it," he said, shaking his head. "It wouldn't—"

"I always do what I'm told," Zorak retorted.

"I know, but—"

"You've always been critical of Marwan. And jealous."

"This is not about that," Haddid protested. "It's about what is good for our country. Don't you see?"

"What would you have me do?" Zorak said sarcastically. "Refuse to do it? I do what I'm told. You wasted your time coming here." Zorak rose, signaling the visit was over.

Haddid stood. "There's one more thing. Something big is planned in Europe. Marwan convinced some of our leaders to allow it, but it may have serious consequences for our country. So maybe now you will change your mind about doing what Marwan wants."

Zorak stared at him and then nodded toward the door. "You never stop." He followed Haddid to the door. At the doorway, Haddid stopped and turned.

"You and I have had a problem since Budapest," Haddid said. "You changed after that. After Budapest, Marwan was going to put you in prison or worse. That's right—*your hero* Marwan. You didn't know that, did you?" He was met with silence.

"For my daughter's sake, I persuaded him to let you retire instead. Now that Marwan is going to use you again, you need to know this. If you refuse to do the killing, there will be repercussions. But if you go to Europe and fail, it will be even worse for you. It will be bad for our country if you succeed in carrying out the killings. There are only bad choices." Haddid said, shaking his head. "You should refuse to—"

"Go," Zorak said curtly. They stared silently at each other for a moment; then Haddid turned and walked away.

After he left, Zorak paced the room. He stopped at a window and stared into the distance. He thought about Budapest. Long repressed images bared themselves. A man crawling on his stomach after being shot, reaching out and clutching Zorak's ankle. Zorak shot him again. But the lifeless hand still gripped him.

Now, Zorak recalled the rest. Standing frozen in the apartment hallway, the bloody hand on his ankle. Then, Haddid's urgent voice. "What are you doing? We're waiting for you in the car." Haddid and Ehsan, the driver, stood on the other side of the body, staring at him. "Hurry. Come on."

Suddenly, there was a tiny cry behind the two men. A woman carrying a baby appeared, eyes terrified. Ehsan turned and swung a silenced pistol toward her. He fired. With two small pops, her chest erupted crimson, and her body dropped. She fell on her back, bent legs sprawled awkwardly. Dead hands dropped away from the baby lying on her breast in a spreading cradle of dark red. The baby crying from the jarring fall. Ehsan pointed the gun at the baby.

Without thinking, Zorak swung his gun toward Ehsan. Haddid lunged at Zorak, hitting his arm as he fired. A muffled pop, and Ehsan spun around with blood flowing from his shoulder. Haddid wrestled Zorak's gun away. Then he scooped Ehsan's gun up from the floor and pushed both men toward the door and outside to the idling car. Zorak heard the baby crying behind them as they rushed out. He sat numbly in the speeding vehicle, staring vacantly ahead. Holding his shoulder, Ehsan rocked and moaned; his face contorted with pain and rage.

Zorak's memory was blank until days later when he stood in front of Marwan's desk and heard that he had been retired. His years of dedicated service had been wiped out by a few seconds of weakness, a spark of humanity. Zorak felt shame. He would forever be remembered for those fleeting moments of weakness rather than his lifetime of accomplishments.

But now he could redeem himself and become the stuff of legend again. He was grateful to Marwan for giving him a second chance. He would prove himself. Frank Marsh and Katherine Foster would die at his hands.

That night, Zorak was summoned to a last-minute meeting with Marwan.

"Everything is set," said Marwan. "They're going to Brussels. You will leave tomorrow for Brussels, and Ehsan will join you there."

"Ehsan?" said Zorak, dumbfounded, his eyebrows raised. Maybe he didn't hear correctly. "Ehsan?"

Marwan nodded. "You two need to work together again."

Zorak's brow furrowed. "But," he protested weakly, "I..." Marwan's look stopped him.

"He'll contact you in Brussels," Marwan said flatly and nodded toward the door.

Zorak went home and finished packing an overnight bag for the trip. "What's wrong?" his wife said. "You look worried." He just shook his head. She knew not to pursue it.

The next day, Zorak flew to Paris by way of Istanbul and Geneva. After landing at Charles De Gaulle Airport in Paris, he boarded the TGV high-speed train from the airport to Brussels, which would take just over an hour. Acting on information COMET sent to Marwan, Zorak planned to stay near the Royal Windsor Hotel in Brussels.

ISRAEL

"Where was he?" asked Colonel Tamir Hayman. As head of Mossad's Europe operations division, Hayman was accustomed to urgent alerts and trying to make sense of fragments of intelligence. Sitting in a control room in front of a wall with four large video screens, he was looking at the magnified image of a passenger's face, a recent arrival at Charles de Gaulle Airport in Paris. The picture was from a French security camera in the terminal. Hayman saw a clean-shaven, bespectacled man with graying hair who appeared to be in his mid to late 40s. He wore gray slacks, a light blue dress shirt, and a navy sports coat. A businessman carrying an overnight bag.

"He was at Charles de Gaulle yesterday, arriving on an incoming flight," replied an intelligence analyst sitting next to Hayman. "Our facial recognition program identified him with a 78% probability of being Zorak, the Iranian Quds Force assassin we have been trying to track for several years. Two years ago, he dropped out of sight. This is the first potential sighting we've had since then."

Although normally unflappable, Hayman was agitated. "Where is he now?" he demanded.

"We don't know yet, sir. We're still checking other government and private security cameras in Paris, but the camera images are data-intensive, and it takes our computers time to process them with the FR program. Do you want us to make this the highest priority?"

Hayman pursed his lips, trying to remember if Zorak was still on the list of targets. Then he recalled that the case for killing Zorak had been presented to the Prime Minister, and the PM had approved adding him to the list of kill targets. But that had been three years ago, and the procedure required the PM to periodically reaffirm his approval. "Make it an urgent priority," he said, rising and heading for the door. "And keep me informed," he said over his shoulder.

Minutes later, Hayman was in his office preparing a request for the PM to renew the approval to kill Zorak. Just as he finished, Danny Gold, his second in command, came in. "I just got word about Zorak in Paris," Gold said. "What do you need me to do?"

"I'm going to see the PM for fresh approval. Have Nedov get a team ready to leave immediately for Paris. Have the shop rush passports, documents, and cover stories for them. I want Nedov on the ground in Paris as soon as possible."

"What about our embassy and personnel in Paris?"

"Put them on heightened alert, but don't share the information about Zorak. Find out if we have any government officials or conferences in France. They could be targets."

"What about the French? Should we try to get their help finding Zorak?"

Hayman shook his head. "No. Remember, we had that blowup with the French over our last kill on French soil. They're not over it yet. If we ask for French help finding Zorak, they will bar us from doing anything ourselves. And we don't want them to somehow discover that we are tracking Zorak by hacking into French security cameras. Through the Sentry Light operation."

Hayman rose. "I'm going to the PM's office. Get Nedov's team moving into place. We still don't know Zorak's target. And he must have a team with him. Find out if...."

Hayman's desk phone buzzed, and he pushed a speaker button. "Yes?"

"Sir," said an analyst in the control room, "we've spotted Zorak again. At the train station in Paris. We don't know which train he was catching, but we're still searching. Wait," the analyst said excitedly, "I think we just got him again, sir." After a pause, the analyst continued. "It's a high-speed train. He took the train for Brussels, sir. Last night."

After the call, Hayman instructed Gold to send Nedov's team to Brussels. Hayman left to see the PM. When he returned to the office, Sentry Light videos were being processed to locate Zorak's arrival at the Brussels train station and track his movements from there. Nedov and his team were in the air on a flight to Brussels.

ISRAEL

"Sir, we have a problem," said a Mossad analyst to Hayman. Hayman sat beside an analyst in the windowless control room, watching one of the giant screens on a wall. It displayed passengers stepping off train cars and onto the railway platform. "This is Brussels' central train station," said the analyst, glancing at Hayman and then back at the screen. "And that's the high-speed train from Paris. It's the train we think Zorak took."

"So what's the problem?"

"The facial recognition program, FR, didn't pick up Zorak among the arriving passengers in Brussels. We've watched the video several times and can't find Zorak coming off the train or at the train station."

Hayman hunched forward, staring at passengers coming off the train and walking along the station platform. Overhead cameras showed them streaming into the station. "Show me inside the station." The video switched, and he searched the faces of passengers crowding into the station, mingling with others purchasing tickets, waiting for trains, and coming off other trains. Hayman sighed. He sat back and looked at the analyst. "This was the direct high-speed train? The one with no stops along the route, correct?"

"That's correct, sir."

After a moment, Hayman said, "Zorak must have put on a disguise during the trip. So here's what I want you and your team to do. Take his image as he boarded in Paris and manipulate it by adding a mustache. Then a beard, change his hair color, make his hair longer and shorter, show him without glasses, puff out his cheeks. Anything he might use to change his appearance."

"Check the clothes he wore when boarding in Paris. Did anyone get off in Brussels wearing similar clothes? He probably changed, but check anyway. Pay close attention to the shoes he wore when boarding in Paris. He may not have changed footwear. If you saw him with luggage, check for anyone carrying the same thing in Brussels." Hayman paused. "One more thing. Zorak is a smoker. If we have a video of Zorak smoking in Paris, then pay special attention to anyone smoking at the station in Brussels and compare it to him in Paris. How they light a cigarette, hold it, and smoke. If we can identify passengers who may be Zorak in disguise, then start searching hotel videos for those who look similar." Hayman stood. "Get it done as quickly as possible," Hayman said firmly. "I'll be in my office. Keep me posted as soon as you know something. An hour later, the analyst told Hayman they couldn't find Zorak. He had slipped by them.

BRUSSELS, BELGIUM

Kathy visited officials at NATO headquarters in Brussels to solicit their views on future Russian moves against countries aligned with the U.S. They were concerned about indications that Russia might attack Ukraine. That afternoon, Kathy received a message that Frank had arrived and was waiting for her at the hotel. He had received approval to meet her for one night in Brussels. She cut her last meeting short and hurried back to the hotel.

Frank was showering when she arrived. "Kathy, is that you?" he called from the shower.

"Yes, but stay where you are. I'm joining you in the shower," Kathy said, kicking off her shoes and undressing in a rush. In the shower, they embraced, their lips locked together, her breasts pressed against his chest. His hands clasped her bottom and pulled her tight against his hips. As the water fell in cascades on their bodies, Frank kissed her neck and shoulders and then moved to her breasts.

Afterward, they lay in bed on their stomachs, faces resting on crossed arms, looking at each other, their bodies caressed by the soft breezes of a slow-turning ceiling fan. Looking into each other's eyes, they talked in low murmurs.

"Frank, you drive me wild. I felt chills shooting all through my body."

Frank smiled. "I know, baby. I heard you yelling and screaming. Or at least I think I heard you. I wasn't sure because I was suddenly yelling so loud myself. You drive me out of control, you know that? Totally out of control." After a few moments, he continued. "But I still want to know one thing."

Kathy opened her half-closed eyes a little wider. "What?"

"I still want to know how you became *you*. How did you get to be so stunningly beautiful and enchanting, brilliant and ingenious, fascinating and captivating, sexy and exciting? I want to know. How did you become *you*?"

"Oh, Frank." She lifted her head and kissed him on the cheek. "I think you're biased."

"I've said it before, Kathy. I wish you could see yourself with my eyes. Then you would see how special and how wonderful you are."

They continued talking in low voices and soon fell into a contented slumber. Later, Frank woke up feeling Kathy tracing her fingers lightly on his back. She was lying on her side, her arm bent and her face resting on a palm.

"I was trying not to wake you," she said quietly.

"Hey, my beautiful woman," Frank murmured, still drowsy. "What are you doing?"

"Just tracing the scars on your back, Frank." She circled her fingers on a golf-ball-sized scar on the back of his left shoulder. "This scar is where you were wounded by shrapnel in Iraq." She paused. "I don't like to think of you being hurt. Or that you were nearly killed." She bent down and lightly kissed his knotted scar.

Frank sighed, savoring the feeling of intimacy between them. He knew this was one of the precious moments he would remember for the rest of his life. He felt her fingers move to the back of his right shoulder. "And this is where you were stabbed in a bar fight, right?"

"Right," Frank said, "and you know something?"

"What," she said, smiling.

"You're beautiful." He rolled over. "I'm going to give you pleasure galore again," he said, lifting his head to kiss her. After a long, lingering kiss, she moved her head away slightly and squinted. Her fingers touched the outside of his left eyebrow. "Frank, is this another scar? I can barely see it and never noticed it before."

Frank touched the faint scar. "I guess it is. But guys are supposed to have scars, right?"

Kathy crunched her mouth. "Maybe so, but not like you, Frank. What was this scar from?"

"Another bar fight," he said with a rueful smile.

"I should have known. You never told me about that one."

"Not much to tell. A fight. A scar. No big thing."

"Well, I want to hear *all* about it." Kathy reached down and felt him growing in her hand. "Please."

Frank sucked in a deep breath. "Whoo. Okay, but you've got me too distracted. You'll have to let go and promise to resume after I tell you about it."

"It was when I was in the Marines on port liberty in Lisbon, Portugal. Our Navy transport ship had docked at Lisbon for several days. A buddy and I were in one of the bars in the red-light district around the port. We were sitting at a table with three working girls when..."

"'Working girls?'" Kathy cocked an eye. "Frank! You mean prostitutes? You were with *prostitutes*?"

"Yeah, but... see, it wasn't like that," Frank said with a head shake. "We were just drinking with them. They were just friends. One, I think her name was Rosa, was the madam, and she took a liking to me, so she and two of her girls settled at our table just talking and passing the time. Occasionally, one of the girls would leave to turn a trick and then come back."

Kathy peered at Frank. "And what did this *'madam'* look like," Kathy said.

"Maybe in her mid-30s. But I was in my late 20s, so she was an older woman. At least to me."

"You didn't answer my question, Frank. What did she look like?"

Frank bit the corner of his mouth. "Maybe a little like Sophia Loren, I guess." Then, seeing Kathy's eyes widen, Frank quickly added, "Just a little, though. Really, not much like her. Really."

"Frank, you're full of it. But I love you anyway. Go ahead. Tell me the rest."

"A half-dozen French Navy sailors were drinking at a table near us, and they kept making remarks to the women in French. I couldn't understand what the women said back, but they clearly didn't want anything to do with the French sailors. Then, they began calling each other names. Rosa left to go to the bar a little later but had to pass by the French. When she came back, one of the French sailors grabbed her arm. Rosa jerked her arm away and snatched the navy cap off his head. She tucked the cap under her dress, rubbed it against her crouch, and then flung it back at him, yelling. He shouted, jumped up, and went for her. The others jumped up, too. I leaped up and grabbed him. He swung at me, and I slugged him. And then the fight was on." Frank paused. "A hell of a fight," he said with a wry smile.

"Sooo, Frank, you got that scar when you got in a fight *over prostitutes*."

Frank shook his head. "Kathy, it wasn't like that. See, we were..."

"Yes..."

"We were...see, we were just..."

"Yes?"

"We were just protecting their honor."

Kathy shook her head and smiled. "Frank, you won't do."

Knowing that the best defense was a good offense, Frank moved his head down to Kathy's breasts, and his mouth was soon distracting her.

"Oh, don't, Frank. Don't. Don't stop!"

Several floors below, Zorak walked through the hotel lobby, his face obscured from overhead surveillance cameras by a wide-brimmed hat and sunglasses. Zorak strolled around the hotel area, spotting surveillance cameras covering sidewalks and streets—and identifying the blind spots. He walked the area to gauge the amount of pedestrian traffic. Then, back in his hotel room a few blocks away, he sat and considered the options. If Marsh and Foster walked to a nearby restaurant, he could kill them both on the sidewalk. But too many witnesses would be present, alarms would be sounded, and it would be difficult to get away.

Zorak decided that the only way to kill them both and to have enough time to get away would be to kill them in their hotel room. He would wear a disguise, knock on their door, step inside, and shoot them both. Or he would enter their room while they were away, using a device that would open any hotel door. Then, he would wait and kill them when they returned. Their bodies wouldn't be discovered until he was on his way out of the country.

Now that he had a plan, he could relax. He would pick up a silenced gun tomorrow. Zorak poured a glass of vodka and leaned back in the easy chair in the room. He wanted a cigarette, but smoking was prohibited in the hotel. As he drank, he began thinking again about assassinations he regretted. One was in the narrow corridor in an apartment building where the target lived, a man in his thirties. After establishing the target's routine, Zorak waited in the hall for the man to come home from work. As the man approached, Zorak was surprised to see a woman with him. But it was too late to stop. Zorak raised the gun and shot the man twice in the chest. He remembered the stunned look on the man's face. "Why are you killing me?" the man uttered, then collapsed. Zorak pointed the gun at the woman. She had backed against the wall, her big dark eyes terrified. "Please don't," she whispered. "Please," she begged. The bullet hit her under an eye, and she slid down the wall, leaving a broad bloody smear on the wall from the gaping hole in the back of her head. She sat against the wall; her unseeing eyes seemed to ask, "Why?"

One killing turned out to be a mistaken identity. Someone who resembled the man he was supposed to kill. Another killing Zorak regretted was of a man who crawled on his stomach after being shot and reached out and clutched Zorak's ankle with his hand. Zorak shot him again. That hand clutching his ankle occasionally came back in nightmares. It wouldn't let go. Zorak shuddered and filled his glass again. He didn't regret the murders; he regretted not doing them cleanly. Marsh and Foster would be a clean killing. Tomorrow would be their last day alive.

CHAPTER 22

The next day, Zorak emerged from a tiny luggage shop in Brussels carrying a small computer bag slung over a shoulder; just another businessman carrying essentials of his trade. He finally felt whole again. Zorak made a surveillance detection run, SDR, after leaving the luggage shop to ensure he wasn't under surveillance. Halfway through the SDR, he stopped at a restaurant for lunch and watched for signs of anyone out of place or paying him undue attention. He raised his wrist during lunch and looked at his watch as if checking the time. As he did, he looked to see if anyone else did the same, a natural reaction of anyone watching him, one of the minor tricks of the trade. No one reacted. Good. Soon, he would leave without finishing lunch and continue the SDR. He planned to head for his hotel once he felt confident he was clean. He would relax there and kill the Americans tonight.

While Zorak was having lunch, an analyst called Hayman. "We found him," the analyst said excitedly. "Though live videos in Brussels. He was on the street and just went into a restaurant. We're watching it live through the business and government cameras we hacked."

Nedov and his men were on standby in Brussels and, within minutes, were heading toward the restaurant. The analyst was on the phone with Nedov, giving him directions and relaying what they were seeing on the live video feeds. Nedov and his men could monitor and talk to each other and the analyst through inconspicuous earpieces. "Keep focused on the door of the restaurant," Nedov said. "We're on our way, but it will take 15 minutes." They were driving a rental car through busy streets. They had already stopped to retrieve silenced handguns from a Mossad support contact stationed in Brussels.

Then, through a secure connection, the videos from hacked cameras were transmitted live to Nedov's phone.

"There he is," the analyst said excitedly. "See him? The one coming out now. Wearing glasses and a hat."

Nedov looked at the small figures on the screen on his phone. "The one who just stopped and lit a cigarette? Carrying a computer bag?"

"Yes, that's him! Look, he's walking up the street now."

Nedov looked up from his phone and spotted Zorak walking from the restaurant. "That's him," he told the driver. "Stop here." The driver let Nedov and Uri out, and the two men began trailing Zorak on foot. Nedov kept a discreet distance behind him while Uri followed on the other side of the street. The driver drove past and parked two blocks in front of Zorak, his eyes glued to the rearview mirror and side mirror. Ever wary, Zorak stopped twice and window-shopped. Each time, he glanced over his shoulder and examined reflections in store windows to scrutinize the appearance and movements of anyone behind and across the street.

"Stay further back, Uri," Nedov said. "I thought we could get him here, but it's too busy. We can keep him in sight on the video feeds.... Wait... he just went into a hotel. See it?"

Nedov, Uri, and the driver met in a coffee shop in sight of the entrance to the hotel. The driver stayed in the shop watching the hotel while Nedov and Uri scouted the surrounding area on foot, looking at side streets, alleyways, and outside cameras. The analyst in Israel checked cameras around the hotel for blind spots—places where the team could make a hit without being videoed—and relayed several locations to the team.

Back in his room, Zorak placed the computer case on a desk and poured a glass of vodka to celebrate. He sat and stared at the case as he sipped, enjoying the anticipation of opening it. Putting the empty glass down, he opened the computer case and removed a signal device that would detect surveillance cameras. After placing it on the desk, he reached back into the case and removed a black pistol with a silencer. Gripping the gun with both hands, he pointed it at a window and sighted down the barrel. He felt a familiar buzz of excitement and savored the anticipation of using it. Zorak imagined hearing the muffled sound of a silenced gunshot, feeling the recoil, and seeing bloody mists as Frank Marsh's and Kathy Foster's heads explode and their lifeless bodies drop. Without realizing it, he was smiling. He lay the pistol down and refilled his glass. It would be dark soon and time to head to the Royal Windsor. He would knock on the Americans' door and execute his mission.

* * *

In a Brussels hotel room, Zorak snapped bullets into a pistol magazine. Nearby, Frank and Kathy relaxed in their room. Nedov and his team were watching Zorak's hotel. In the Molenbeek district of Brussels, Reza and his men were cleaning weapons and reviewing final plans for the Paris attack. In Paris, twelve-year-old Melanie Levy was practicing reading from Anne Frank's Diary for Holocaust Memorial Day. In Tehran, Marwan was anticipating the success of the terror attack and assassinations.

* * *

That evening, there was a bustle of discreet activity. "Zorak just came out of the hotel," Uri said over his earpiece, "and is walking heading north." As he walked, Zorak pressed his elbow against his left side for a moment. Just long enough to be assured that his gun was firmly secure under his sport coat. The Royal Windsor Hotel was just a few blocks away.

"I see him," Nedov replied over his earpiece. "He's heading in our direction. We'll walk toward him. Move up quickly behind him, Uri. He'll be at that side street soon. Get ready."

The following day, Frank left Brussels early and headed to Paris. Kathy went to NATO headquarters in Brussels for more meetings. Nedov and his team were in the air, flying back to Israel. Zorak was never heard from again. The Israelis never learned why Zorak was in Brussels. Frank and Kathy were unaware of their close call.

CHAPTER 23

At the Paris headquarters of the SDAT, the Anti-terrorism Task Force of The National Police, three men sitting at a table warily regarded each other. Their first meeting had gotten off to a rocky start. Rizzo De Luca, 44, a burly man with buzz-cut hair, got up from the table scowling. "You two fuckers" he said, looking down at Frank Marsh and Alain Boulanger, a French intelligence agent, "can do whatever you want. I don't care. But I'm getting a translator and start pounding the streets. I didn't come over here to be part of some three-man show team. I'm hitting the streets."

Frank suppressed a surge of anger. De Luca is not only smart but clever, Frank reminded himself; otherwise, he would not have been selected to be the lead NYPD detective assigned to the team.

"No, you're not," said Frank.

"The hell I'm not..."

"Your commissioner agreed that the three of us would work as a team. You'll be kicked out of France if you can't do it." Frank looked at Alain Boulanger. "Isn't that right, Alain?"

"Yes, it is true. My agency, the R.G., will have you ejected from France." Alain spoke with a French accent, but his English was good. "Me, I would prefer to have you here."

"That's bullshit," De Luca snorted. "You can't do crap."

"You are right, me, I cannot, but the director of the R.G. can. The director told me personally to let him know whatever I needed. If I make a phone call, you will be sent back to America." Boulanger shot De Luca a questioning look. "So?"

"So you see, De Luca," said Frank with a shrug, "we have to do what our agencies want, not what *we* want. They want us to work as a team. Like Alain here, I want you on the team. But you won't be able to do any good if you're sent back to the U.S., right?"

Frank was the voice of reason. However, he was concerned that De Luca would be headstrong and might act impulsively on his own—something Frank himself had sometimes done, but he trusted his own instincts and judgment. After learning that De Luca would be assigned to the team, Frank called the FBI office in New York for any information about him. He learned that De Luca was a loner, not well-liked, but a tenacious and highly-regarded detective. He was effective, brash, and bull-headed.

Frank had also checked out Alain Boulanger, the French intelligence agent, but the FBI Legat in Paris had limited information. He learned that Boulanger was 34 and married with children. He was thought to have single-handedly cracked some significant cases. With a medium build, neat black hair, a trim mustache, and black-rimmed glasses, Alain Boulanger looked more like a mild-mannered accountant than a crack agent.

"I know all about *you*, Marsh," De Luca snorted. "You think you're a real hot shot. Well, I've worked with lots of bureau agents, and many thought they were hotshots, too. You wanna know how many turned out to be worth a damn? None. They didn't know fuck about how to break a case, and most couldn't raise a pimple on the ass of a real detective." De Luca paused before continuing. "And I found out that you don't like to work with others, Marsh. You always want to go it alone. Yet, here you are—telling me to work as part of a team. *Bullshit*," De Luca sneered.

Frank didn't like what he heard, but it increased his respect for De Luca. At least he had checked me out—like I did him, thought Frank.

"And you," De Luca said to Boulanger, "*Bowl-longer*." De Luca drew out 'Bowl Longer,' and anger flashed in Boulanger's eyes. "I checked you out, too. Yeah, that's right, damn right. You think you some kinda hot shit too. Well, I know how you Frenchies work. It's *who* you know. And they tell me you're a loner, too. So, as far as I'm concerned," De Luca said, looking at the two men, "you can both fuck off."

A long, tense moment hung in silence. "Monsieurs," said Boulanger, "I, too, checked on both of you. And I learned the same things. So..." Boulanger shrugged and held out open palms, looking from Frank to De Luca. "And my name is *Boulanger*," he said to De Luca, slowly pronouncing his name, "*not* 'Bowl Longer.'"

"Well, I can't pronounce that French crap, so to me, you're 'Bowl-longer.'" The two men glared at each other.

Frank rose to his feet, and Boulanger followed. Damn, thought Frank with a sudden realization, the three of us are just alike: aggressive investigators who each want to lead and prefer to work alone. This will never work.

The three men stood silently, staring at each other. Then, after a moment, they each started to say something at the same time and stopped. Frank held up a hand. "Okay. How about this? We each have a say right now. And then, if we can't all agree to try to work together, we ask to be replaced." De Luca and Boulanger looked skeptical.

"We don't know what the attack on Lemaire and Bernard was about or if more attacks are coming," Frank continued. "And we need to find out fast before another attack does occur. So, here's what I can do. I think I can dig up more leads and get us more information than other FBI agents. And I'll share all of it with you. What I get, you get too." He looked from De Luca to Boulanger. "If you have worked with the bureau before, you know that seldom happens. Most of the time, the FBI holds back information. I won't. I don't have an agenda or care who gets the credit. You can always accomplish more if you don't care who gets the credit. I just want to get this done. And I want to work with investigators who feel the same way."

They were still eying him warily, but Frank saw a spark of recognition in their eyes. Boulanger cocked his head slightly to one side. "Me," said

Boulanger, touching his chest with the tips of his fingers, "I am the same as you, Frank. I am good at what I do, and I, too, will share everything. However, only the French government has authority here. I should be conducting this investigation on my own, but the Interior Minister agreed that we try this. I am not happy about doing this, but I will try. And I remind you that both of you are here with our permission. If either of you interferes or causes problems, you will not be allowed to stay in France. Do you understand this?" He looked at the men, from one to the other. Frank nodded, but De Luca just stared back.

Frank looked at De Luca. "Well?"

De Luca chewed the inside of his lip and finally said, "All right, you fuckers, I'm going to stay and give it a try. But just to show you how it's fucking done. And I'm reminding you, our detective was attacked—and we always take care of our own. So just don't get in my fucking way, understand?"

They fell silent for a moment. "Well," said Frank, "it looks like we're going to try to work together. Let me suggest that we each check with our agencies for more information and try to identify leads. Then, we get back together in two hours and discuss what we know."

"Who the fuck put you in charge, Marsh?" De Luca snapped.

"Well, okay, De Luca, what's your idea then?" said Frank, his voice rising.

Boulanger waved a hand toward Frank. "Me, I think Frank, he is right."

Boulanger and Frank looked at De Luca. He waited a few moments before responding.

"Alright, fuckers. Two hours." De Luca turned to leave.

"Ah, monsieur '*Loco*,' said Boulanger with a smirk, "if you cannot pronounce my name, maybe you should just call me 'Alain.' Yes?"

"Fuck you, *Bowl Longer*." De Luca turned and stormed out.

Watching De Luca disappear through the doorway, Frank just shook his head. What a circus this is going to be, he thought.

He held back on suggesting that Sarin nerve gas could be involved. Although Frank thought Sarin might have been moved to Europe from the mountain compound in Africa, his claim of having seen Sarin was no longer considered credible. Plus, nothing indicated that the attack on Gabrielle Lemaire and Marcel Bernard was connected with a Sarin plot. Still, his mind was spinning. Did terrorists really bring Sarin to Europe, he wondered. If so, what is their target, and how long do we have to try to prevent an attack? He felt anxious.

SDAT HEADQUARTERS, PARIS, FRANCE: 1000 HOURS

The three men sat at a small conference table with laptops in front of each and a large video screen on the wall at the end of the table. Frank and Alain Boulanger sat next to each other on one side of the table, and De Luca and an intelligence analyst sat on the opposite side.

"Monsieurs," said Alain Boulanger, "if you have no objection, I will go first. For each of you, here is a portable media, a thumb drive," he said, placing a thumb drive in front of each. "It has the latest reports and the list of items collected by our crime scene specialists at the place of the attack. It also has reports from the National Police in Belgium, medical persons, and security officials. And it includes the statements of the two truck drivers who arrived first at the scene of the attack. All have been translated into English for you."

Hours later, each man and the analyst had gone over everything they had. A search of Gabrielle's apartment for leads had been unproductive. RG agents found burner phones that used encrypted programs, as well as an encrypted laptop. All data on the laptop self-destructed when an impatient new agent tried to access it instead of submitting it to experts. There were no matches to the shell casings found at the scene of the attack. The investigation seemed at a dead end.

Then, Frank Marsh spoke up. "We have a lot to go over. But the most pressing thing is to review the reports of the NYPD detective, Gabrielle Lemaire, and the French RG agent, Marcel Bernard, to find out what they were working on that night. Why they were together. But I still haven't received their reports from NYPD or the R.G." He paused and looked at Alain Boulanger. "Alain?"

"I am sorry," he said with a painful grimace, "but my superiors will not let me release Marcel Bernard's reports. At this time," he added.

"But you've surely read them," Frank insisted. "You can at least tell us what his reports say about what they were working on together. Right?"

"All I can say, Frank, is that they were not working on anything jointly," Boulanger said.

"But," Frank pressed, "did Marcel's reports indicate what *Gabrielle* was working on?"

Boulanger shifted uncomfortably and bit his bottom lip.

"Well?" Frank said.

Boulanger sighed audibly. "All right. I will tell you this. I am not supposed to. But I will tell you. Marcel, he was supposed to report all conversations with Gabrielle Lemaire." Boulanger looked down and shook his head slightly before looking at Frank and continuing. "Marcel, he was supposed to try to recruit Lemaire as a source for the R.G. But that's traditional," he quickly added. "Everyone does that."

"So?" Frank said.

"Marcel, he was not able to recruit Lemaire as an R.G. source. His reports on her and the things she was interested in began decreasing. Even though we know he saw her often because they were both rep-resentatives to NATO, he wrote fewer and fewer reports about her. We found a few text messages between them, but then nothing. We think they switched to using Signal for encrypted texting and calling." Boulanger sighed again. "The R.G., they wonder if Marcel and Lemaire became too close to each other. We don't know," he said with a shrug.

They fell silent. Frank remembered hearing the U.K. had suggested that a romantic rival may have carried out the attack, although he didn't believe it. But it was possible that Gabrielle Lemaire and Marcel Bernard had become close and had even been in a relationship.

"What about you?" Frank said to De Luca. "I have not seen any New York Police reports by Lemaire or reports about what she was working on."

De Luca scrunched his lips. Then, finally, he said, "If the Frenchies won't give up their reports, then by God, we won't either."

"That's bullshit, De Luca," Frank protested. "You didn't give us NYPD reports about Lemaire even before you knew whether the French would share their reports. So don't give me that crap. Where are Lemaire's reports?"

De Luca glanced away, then hunched forward and crossed his arms on the table. Looking down at the table, he growled, "The P.D. doesn't want me to share reports either."

All fell silent again, thoughts boomeranging.

"Screw that," Frank finally said. "Tell us anyway." De Luca looked up, and Frank held his eyes. "Tell it. Now, damnit. Go ahead," said Frank with a nod. "Go ahead."

De Luca shot Frank a fierce look and then took a deep breath. "All right, you fuckers. She was supposed to keep tabs on everyone she worked with, including the Frenchie, Bernard. And her reports on their conversations began tapering off over time. Like they did with the French RG. But there was nothing in the reports about what she was working on, besides the usual NATO stuff. So there was nothing there." He paused. "Okay?' he demanded.

Frank nodded. "Okay." Boulanger nodded too, "Okay."

"Well," Frank said, "there are some things we are following up on. But meanwhile, I propose we do what De Luca suggested." They looked at him questioningly. "Let's hit the streets."

CHAPTER 24

Frank stood on the shoulder of the highway with Alain Boulanger and Peter Mertens, an agent with Belgium's security service, examining the scene where Gabrielle Lemaire's car had crashed. Rutted tracks remained where a wrecker had pulled Lemaire's car up from the bottom of the slope. Mertens pointed downhill. "The car crashed into that tree," said Mertens. "We searched the area and just found bits of car parts. Marcel Bernard, the French agent, was driving Lemaire's car, and she was in the passenger seat," Mertens said. "Bernard's car was found parked further up the road, and they were attacked while traveling in the direction of his car."

He turned and motioned down the road. "Scattered along the road, we found nine-millimeter shell casings." Mertens showed Frank and Boulanger photographs of shell casings strung along the road, with a yellow evidence marker next to each one.

"Do you have any idea why the attackers chose this spot to attack them?" Frank asked. Mertens shook his head.

Taking photographs marking shell casings, Frank and Boulanger walked along the road, visualizing where they were found. The casings had been strung out about 100 yards. Finally, Frank reached a spot where the shell casing furthest from Lemaire's car was found. "This must be where the attack began," Frank said. "Why here?" Looking around, he saw only forests lining both sides of the road. He resumed walking without knowing what he was looking for, perhaps an overlooked shell casing. After another hundred yards, he stopped and was turning to go back when he saw something on the right shoulder of the road. "Look," he said to Boulanger.

Frank knelt on one knee. "Right here." He leaned over and pointed, "Look, you can barely make it out. Tire tracks in the dirt here at the edge of the road."

Boulanger shrugged. "After the attack, the emergency vehicles, they made tire tracks," he said dismissively.

"Yes, but those tire tracks are far back where Lemaire's car went off the road. And these tracks are different. They show a vehicle coming onto the road, not parking on the shoulder like emergency vehicles would. Take a look." Boulanger crouched down and saw faint tire tracks. They entered the road from the forest some 20 yards away, down a gentle slope.

The two men stood up and peered at the forest. Now that they knew what they were looking for, they saw it—a break in the woods and a narrow vehicle path underneath tree limbs. They moved down the slope and into the woods, walking along the path, which ended in a small grassy circle about 30 yards into the forest. The undergrowth was trampled and flattened, indicating a car had been there. "It looks like the vehicle that entered the road had been parked here," Frank said, examining the ground.

"Here," Boulanger said excitedly. He was squatting and pointing down at something half-buried in the ground. It was a cell phone that had been run over and pressed into the ground by a vehicle. Frank was excited. Lemaire's cell phone was never found, and this could be it. The phone was rushed to a lab for examination.

Several hours later, Frank and Boulanger sat at a table in the lab conference room while a forensic expert, Dupry, used a laptop to display images from the cell phone on a large screen on the wall. "Lemaire downloaded an app on her cell phone on the day of the attack," Dupry explained. "It's an app used to track a vehicle when a tracking device is attached."

"Will you be able to find out if Lemaire tracked a vehicle that day?" Frank asked. "And if so, where?"

"We can try, but we may need the help of the company that sells the tracking device and its app."

Mertens spoke up. "Give me the name of the company, and I'll get on that right away,"

Dupry continued with the briefing about the contents of Lemaire's phone. There was more to do, and he promised to rush a report to Frank and Boulanger that night.

* * *

It was after midnight, and Frank was tired. It had been a long day examining the scene of the attack, followed by a conference at the lab and then doing follow-up work at the office he and Boulanger shared with DeLuca. He sat at a battered old desk and rubbed the back of his neck. For the fifth time, Frank re-read reports of the attack that killed the French intelligence officer and critically injured Lemaire, the NYPD detective.

He tried to piece together what had happened and why. What brought Gabrielle Lemaire, Marcel Bernard, and their attackers together on the road that night? At first, he wondered if the attackers had been following the two and had planned to kill them, but the answer was found on Lemaire's cell phone. Frank focused again on a vital part of the report. Initially written in French and translated into English, a forensic examination of Lemaire's cell phone revealed why she was in the area where she and Bernard were attacked.

"The most recent activity on the mobile phone was the installation and use of a program to track the location of a mobile vehicle tracking device. The device was apparently attached to an unidentified vehicle earlier on the date of the attack. The first activation of the device occurred at approximately 1620 hours in the vicinity of the 1700 block of Rue Maleen in Brussels. At that time, the vehicle appeared stationary, and the tracking device stopped transmitting a signal 10 minutes later. This is consistent with a motion-activated vehicle tracking device and with the initial attachment of the device to a vehicle."

Frank knew exactly what that meant. Someone had reached under a vehicle and attached a magnetic tracking device. He had done the same thing in some of his cases. Discreetly walk by a car and quickly reach underneath to attach the device. Location data on Lemaire's cell phone revealed that she had traveled to Rue Maleen around the time the device had been attached to the vehicle.

Frank rubbed his chin. How could they identify the vehicle Lemaire had been tracking? He had already asked Boulanger to check the area on Rue Maleen for video surveillance recordings during the time and date when the device had been attached to the vehicle, but the area consisted of run-down apartment buildings, and no outside surveillance cameras were found. Frank returned to the forensic report and read further.

"The tracking program on Lemaire's cell phone revealed the following information concerning the vehicle to which the tracking device had been attached, from now on referred to as the Subject Vehicle—SV):

"At 21:30 hours, SV begins moving from the 1700 block of Rue Mallen. It traveled through the city to the edge of Brussels, where it then traveled on Route 19, heading north. At approximately 23:00 hours, the SV reached the general vicinity of where the attack occurred. The SV turned off the highway, traveled a short distance west toward the coast, and stopped.

Ten minutes later, the motion-activated device stopped transmitting. It never reactivated. This indicates that the vehicle never moved again, that the batteries on the device were depleted, or the device was discovered, removed, and inactivated."

Just then, Frank's phone rang, and he answered a call from De Luca, the NYPD detective. "I just left the area where the vehicle being tracked may have gone," De Luca said. "We went down a drive to an abandoned warehouse. Nothing there."

"Not even—"

"Hold on, damnit." DeLuca barked. "Then we found a lane running from the drive to the coast. It was rutted and looked recently used. We followed it to the seashore. That coulda been where the vehicle being tracked went, but no vehicles were around."

"But—"

"You wanna hear this or what?" De Luca demanded with a growl.

"Sorry. I'm listening."

"The lane ended at a small cove on the seashore. We found tire tracks and footprints at the cove. Maybe three or four vehicles. One set looked like truck tires."

"Did you look for—"

"Damnit, Marsh, you Bureau fuckers are all alike. You think you're the only sonofabitches that know how to investigate." De Luca paused. "Well?"

"Alright. Go ahead."

"I checked the ground. There were cigarette butts and one empty cigarette pack. Most of the butts were European cigarettes, but two were Egyptian. The empty cigarette pack had a French tax stamp on it. I told the French and Belgium investigators to check the butts for DNA. And then run the DNA against DNA databases for any matches. They'll send lab reports on any DNA to the Bureau, so you fuckers can check it too. I also had them take pictures and make molds of the tire tracks and footprints. And also, measure the distance between the pairs of tire tracks, just in case it will help identify or eliminate particular brands or models of vehicles. However, that's a long shot."

Frank was nodding as De Luca spoke, pleased with his thoroughness, doing everything Frank would have done.

"And I told the local guys to return to the cove tomorrow with a dog. To see if a dog can pick up anything sniffing around, but I doubt it. I smelled something in the air at the cove. Very faint odor, like a dead body, but I was the only one who smelled it. We looked around but didn't find anything. If something's there, a dog may find it. Alright, that's all. I'm on my way back to Paris."

"Good work, De Luca. That's—"

"Fuck off, Marsh." The phone went dead.

Several vehicles at the cove meant they probably met a boat, thought Frank. To unload from the boat to a truck? If so, what? And who? The critical lead was the unidentified vehicle Lemaire was tracking. Obviously, it had been driven from the area after the attack. Finding it was crucial, but how?

He focused on the reports again. Through the vehicle tracking program Lemaire had used, an analyst had retraced the tracked vehicle's route from the 1700 block of Mallen through Brussels and then on route 19. But checking businesses for outside surveillance cameras that might have recorded it as it passed proved to be a dead end. Some camera views didn't show the street or road, some images were blurred, and even when images were clear, there were too many vehicles to determine which one Lemaire was tracking.

Frank lifted his head at the sound of the door opening. Boulanger walked in with a leather satchel slung over his shoulder and sat down at his desk. Their eyes met, and Boulanger raised an eyebrow. "Still working on it, Frank? It is almost midnight. Do you ever stop?"

Frank sighed, leaning back in his chair. "Funny you say that," he said with a tired smile. "But here *you* are, back at work too."

Boulanger grinned, shrugging his shoulders. "I think you and I, we are alike, Frank. Police, yes?" As Frank listened to Boulanger, he couldn't help but agree. Cops everywhere were driven by the same desire to catch criminals, regardless of the differences in laws and methods. "Have you found anything new?" Boulanger asked.

Frank filled him in on De Luca's findings, and Boulanger pursued his lips and nodded approvingly. "De Luca, he is a crazy American cop, but he is good,"

"The most crucial thing now is to find out what was brought in by boat and where it went," Frank said. "To do that, we need to keep trying to identify the vehicle Lemaire was following." Frank explained that the reports he had been reviewing said nothing was found on surveillance camera recordings along the route the Lemaire's vehicle took. There were too many vehicles, or the videos were too blurry to be helpful. "But I want to look at the footage myself. The videos might be our only lead."

Boulanger grinned and reached into his satchel, pulling out a thumb drive. "Me, that is what I want to do, too. These are the camera recordings along the route taken by Lemaire's vehicle. They have been coordinated with the vehicle tracking program she used. Each video clip is from the approximate time frame when the vehicle would have passed by the camera. We can go through them together. Like you, Frank, I want to look for myself."

For over an hour, they hunched forward and scrutinized the footage on a flat screen. Finally, Frank's eyes grew heavy, and he slumped back in his seat, shaking his head. "There are too many cars. There's no way of telling which one Lemaire was tracking. It's like trying to find a needle in a haystack."

Hunching forward again, Frank propped his elbows on the table, rested his face in his palms, and stared dejectedly at the screen. Boulanger propped one arm on the table and rested a side of his face in his palm. He stared down at the table, his weary eyelids beginning to droop.

But then Frank sat upright, and his face brightened. "Let's look at it another way," he said, a glimmer of hope in his voice. "Identifying the vehicle from these video clips is like looking for a needle in a haystack. But we're looking in a dozen or so 'haystacks' or videos. So, to find the right vehicle, we just need to find the one that appears in *every* video. And if two or three cars appear in every video, then at least we've narrowed it down to those two or three." With raised eyebrows, Frank looked expectantly at Boulanger. "What do you think?"

Boulanger sat upright and nodded, and they went back to the footage. It was a slow and grueling process, pausing every few seconds to jot down the details of the cars on the screen. Frank shook his head. "This is taking forever. We need to find a quicker way to narrow it down."

He rubbed his chin. Both men stared glumly at the screen. Frank perked up. "Here's another idea. Let's find a video with the fewest vehicles in it. Those where the traffic had thinned out. The one Lemaire was tracking had to be one of those, right?"

"Right," said Boulanger, nodding.

"We'll write down the car descriptions. Then look at all the other videos, those with lots of cars, to find which car or cars were in every video."

Frank and Boulanger quickly narrowed it down to three vehicles. A small white van, a blue compact car, and an older red subcompact. All three were in the next several videos they examined. But then only the blue car and the red car were in the next two videos. Finally, they were down to the last video clip. It was of a four-lane street. There was no sign of the blue car or the red subcompact among the many vehicles. Frank's excitement evaporated. They had come so close but still didn't know which car Lemaire was following. He and Boulanger sat there, shoulders slumped, feeling defeated.

Frank stared at the screen for a long while as if he could make either car appear. Then he noticed it. "Here. Look here," he said excitedly, pointing to a car on the four-lane street. "Right here. You can just barely make it out. See it? There's a car on the other side of the car closest to the camera. The two cars are traveling side-by-side in the same direction, and the closest car almost completely blocks the other from sight." They couldn't see enough to identify it or the color.

They enlarged the image on the screen, but that didn't help. Frank stared at it until his eyes were burning. Finally, he sat back and rubbed his eyes. The car just couldn't be seen. He told himself it was time to stop trying but knew he wouldn't. After taking deep breaths, Frank hunched forward and stared at the screen again. Suddenly, he saw something. On the far side of the street, a large store window. He looked closely and saw reflections in the window. "Look," said Frank eagerly. "There in the window. The car hidden from view is reflected in the store window."

"Can you see what it is?"

Frank moved his head close to the screen. "It's an older model subcompact car. And the color looks to be ... wait, I can't tell. Let me look from another angle. It's...it's red." Frank looked at Boulanger. "It's red. The red subcompact is the only vehicle seen in every video clip. So it's got to be the car Lemaire was tracking."

As the night wore on, analysts examined the subcompact on the various videos. They were able to identify the make, likely model, and partial license plate number. Information fed into a vehicle database produced vehicle registrations of three possible matches. Just after daybreak, two were eliminated after the cars were located and their owners were interviewed. Frank sat at the desk where he had been working all night. He had a sinking spell before daybreak but had perked up a little at sunup. He was sipping another cup of coffee when Boulanger came back in. "What about the third car?" Frank said as Boulanger plopped down at his desk. "Anything yet?"

Boulanger sighed and gave Frank a tired smile. "The owner of the third car reported that he recently sold it to an immigrant. Neither the car nor the immigrant can be found. We've broadcast a wanted alert for both." Time was running out to find them.

Frank got De Luca on the phone and wasted no time getting to the point. "We've identified the car Lemaire was following when she was attacked. But we need to hurry. We're trying to find it as quickly as we can."

"Why the rush?" De Luca said.

"Think about it," Frank said. "It looks like Lemaire was attacked because she discovered a boat unloading something in the cove. She and the French agent, Bernard, would have only been there if terrorists had been involved. And the terrorists have to assume that Lemaire raised the alarm before they attacked her."

"Are you saying they're planning a terror attack? And that the boat delivered explosives?"

"It's just a guess, but it's logical based on what we know. We need to find that car, and fast before it's too late."

De Luca was silent for a moment. "Makes sense," he said with a grunt. "We probably don't have much time because the fuckers might have moved up their plans. I'll get the guys I'm working with here to get on it, and then I'll come on in. Give me a description of the car."

After the call, Frank felt a desperate tightness in his chest. Something terrible was coming. He couldn't shake the feeling that they were racing against the clock to stop a catastrophic event.

CHAPTER 25

PARIS, FRANCE

Melanie Levy, a twelve-year-old girl with long dark brown hair and inquisitive brown eyes, was excited. She had been asked to read a brief passage from Anne Frank's Diary at the annual Holocaust Memorial service at a Jewish center in Paris. Her resemblance to Anne Frank made her the perfect candidate for the job. But Melanie was nervous.

"Don't worry, Melanie, you will do fine," said her mother.

"But Mama, there'll be lots of grownups and kids there," Melanie protested.

As she learned more about Anne Frank and the horrors of the Holocaust, cracks appeared in her sense of security. She felt terrified at the thought that grownups were supposed to protect children, yet they had killed Anne and millions of others with poison gas. Sometimes, Melanie silently cried, but she was determined to do the reading well and become Anne's voice at the memorial service.

BRUSSELS, BELGIUM

Grownups were also excited and nervous about the Holocaust memorial service. In an apartment in the Molenbeek area of Brussels, several men gathered around a table to plan an attack on the Jewish center in Paris, 165 miles away. The men had put their cell phones in a ten-inch by ten-inch Faraday bag, used by intelligence services to prevent remote surveillance.

"Our men conducted surveillance of the Jewish center last year," Ahmed reminded the men at the table. "Here are the locations where guards were positioned then," he said, pointing to the diagram of a building and surrounding streets. "Here and here," he said, tapping the diagram. "One in front and one in the back. There may be a guard inside. All of you know your assignments. After you kill the guards, rush inside. Kill any guards inside. Kill the rabbi in front of the others. We make everyone lie on the floor, face down, with their hands on their heads. Kill anyone who hesitates to get down, including children who don't obey. I'll place one canister of nerve gas to release through the ventilation system and canisters at the front and back doors. The canisters release the nerve agent when I send the signal by cell phone. I'll do that the instant we leave the building. Remember to rush away." Marwan's instructions to Ahmed had been clear.

The men were excited about the impact of releasing nerve warfare chemicals during the service, as it would send a more terrifying signal than killing everyone with explosives. Moreover, it would demonstrate that Israel and other countries couldn't protect Jews. Only a solution to the Palestinian issue could do that.

In Paris, Melanie was excited about her new white dress and hair bow, which her mama had bought her to wear for the memorial service. She tried on the dress and practiced the reading from Anne Frank's Diary. Despite her nervousness, she was determined to make Anne proud of her.

CHAPTER 26

Frank, Boulanger, and DeLuca worked nonstop using phones and laptops, trying to locate the red car and the immigrant purchaser. All three were in contact with their agencies, scouring databases and intelligence reports that might contain clues. None had produced results—until now.

"I have a lead," announced Alain Boulanger excitedly, ending a call and turning to Frank and De Luca. "The seller had gotten one call from the man who purchased the car. We tried identifying the buyer's phone, but it was a burner phone. Then," Boulanger continued, "we checked the car buyer's burner phone record and found one call from it to a phone number in Paris. We don't know who uses the Paris number. But that same Paris number was also called by a Lebanese immigrant on our terror suspect list. The Lebanese recently fled the country. So, we have a common phone number called by the red car owner and the Lebanese terror suspect. It's crucial, yes?"

Frank spoke up. "Have you been able to—"

"Wait," said Boulanger brightly, "I have more. We used location information on the phone in Paris to put it at an apartment complex where another known terror suspect lives. It's a man named Saad. Maybe the owner of the red car we are looking for will contact Saad or go there."

"Let's go," De Luca said, rising. The men rushed out and hurriedly drove to the apartment building linked to Saad.

"There it is," Boulanger said as he drove, "just ahead on our right. That one." Frank saw a dull gray apartment building six stories high.

"It is there where Saad is supposed to live," Boulanger began slowing to park.

"No, don't stop," De Luca said urgently from the back seat.

"Wha..."

"Don't stop. Keep going. Keep going."

Boulanger resumed speed, and they drove past the building. De Luca looked over his shoulder, staring to the rear.

Frank twisted toward the back seat. "What is it, De Luca? You see something?"

"Yeah. Just a minute." He turned back toward the front. "Okay, Bowl Longer, you can slow down now. Just circle the block."

"Is someone following us?" Boulanger said, looking in the rearview mirror at De Luca.

"It's a car parked back there, just before the building. Something's not right about it."

Frank twisted again and looked at De Luca. "What do you mean? Not right. What didn't look right?"

"It was parked, and there were two guys in it. The driver and a guy in the back seat. Both looked like they were in their 30s. The driver had a beard, and the other guy looked like he might have a mustache."

"What was odd about that?" asked Frank. "They were probably just waiting on someone at the apartment."

"It just didn't fucking look right," De Luca said flatly as if that was explanation enough for anyone.

Frank understood. He had sometimes seen things out of place himself that wouldn't have been noticed by anyone else. But for Frank, those sights stood out like flashing red warning beacons. Something just not quite normal. A parked car in a parking lot with someone in it wasn't unusual, but maybe it was just a little too far from a building entrance. Most people would park as close as possible to their destination instead of intentionally parking further away. Or maybe the person in a parked car didn't appear to be waiting on anyone to come out of a building but instead was looking in a different direction. Or maybe men in two vehicles parked side by side in a far corner of a parking lot. Watch your surroundings and look for the presence of the abnormal or the absence of the normal. Frank was unusually able to recognize suspicious activity because he was sensitive to human nature and what people would typically do or say. Others, and perhaps De Luca was one, developed that ability from experience.

The front of the apartment building was on a one-way street. Boulanger circled and parked one block from the building and on the opposite side of the street. De Luca pointed out the car he had seen, a dark blue four-door Renault, parked at the curb in front of the building.

"Look in there, Frank," Boulanger waved toward the glove compartment. Frank retrieved a set of binoculars, and the three men took turns using them to watch the Renault. While using the binoculars, De Luca narrated what he was seeing. "Both in their 30s, driver, dark hair, beard, smoking a cigarette. One in the back seat may have a mustache. Both look Middle Eastern."

"Middle Easterners, it's no surprise," Boulanger said. "In this area here, many Middle Easterners, they live."

Frank took his turn with the binoculars. "The one in the back seat," said Frank while watching, "he's looking all around. Looks like he's trying to spot any surveillance."

"Yeah," De Luca said, "the fuckers aren't just waiting for a friend to come out. Might just be burglars waiting for their man to come out with the loot."

"You want me to call for uniform officers?" asked Boulanger.

"Naw," De Luca said dismissively, "we ain't here for that kind of shit."

"Then we go inside and find Saad, the terror suspect who lives there," Boulanger said.

"Wait," Frank said. "Let's see what they do first. Then, if they don't do anything soon, we'll go in, and... Look," Frank said quickly. "In front of the building."

A heavy-set man wearing a black windbreaker had left the entrance and stopped. He stood looking up and down the street.

"See him?"

"A lookout." Boulanger declared.

"Yeah, I see the fucker," De Luca said while looking through the binoculars. "The two fuckers in the car are watching him too. Oh yeah, something's going on."

The man in the black windbreaker scanned the nearby buildings and sidewalks. Then, apparently satisfied, he looked toward the blue Renault and nodded. The driver pulled out from the curb and stopped directly in front of the building entrance. A middle-aged man wearing a brown sports coat emerged from the building and settled in the front passenger seat. The man in the black windbreaker climbed in the back, and the car sped away.

"Write this down," De Luca said hurriedly, "Belgium license 9-BLG-616."

Frank jotted the number while Boulanger pulled out and began following the car discreetly. Heavy traffic helped hide their surveillance.

Boulanger called for registration information on the license and moments later shared the report. "The license was originally issued to a man in the Molenbeek suburb of Brussels. They are running a check on him now."

"Molenbeek?" said Frank. "Didn't the terrorists who attacked the Charlie Hebro magazine staff in Paris come from there?"

"Yes. It's what you call the 'hotbed,' a center for Muslim extremists in Brussels."

"We're watching suspects from there in New York," De Luca said. "Any fuckers from the Molenbeeek area need watching."

The Renault stopped at an apartment building. Boulanger pulled over and parked. A woman came out of the building and walked to the car. She bent down at the front passenger window and reached inside. Frank was watching through binoculars.

"What's she doing?" said De Luca. "Can you see?"

"I can't tell," Frank said. "Here, Alain, see if you can tell." He passed the binoculars to Boulanger. While Boulanger looked, Frank took photos with his phone camera.

"No, I cannot see her good either. The car, it is blocking the view."

She withdrew her arm and went back into the building. "Did she hand something in or get something from them?" asked Frank.

"Me, I could not tell," said Boulanger, shaking his head.

"Me neither."

The Renault pulled out into traffic, and Boulanger followed. Boulanger, Frank, and De Luca focused on the Renault in front and overlooked a black Peugeot that began following them from the last stop. Ahmed's cell phone rang inside the Renault, and he took it out of his brown sports coat.

"Yes."

"Someone is following you. Three men. We are behind them."

Minutes later, the Renault took a series of turns and was now traveling on narrow, winding streets in a migrant area of Paris. Men lounging in small groups shot hostile stares at Frank, Boulanger, and De Luca. "What do you think?" Boulanger asked. "Should we keep following or go back to find Saad?"

De Luca leaned forward from the back seat, resting his arms on the seat tops, staring at the Renault. "Let's stay on the fuckers a little while longer. Something's not right about them. They're up to something."

Frank and Boulanger exchanged a puzzled glance. Boulanger shrugged. "Yes, okay," he said. "We follow."

As they turned a few more corners, Frank noticed they were surrounded by deserted sidewalks and empty buildings covered in graffiti, typical urban decay.

The Renault stopped at a deserted four-way intersection and then continued through.

As Boulanger slowed to stop at the intersection, a car behind suddenly shot up beside him, swerved in front, and stopped abruptly, blocking Boulanger's car. Boulanger jammed the brakes just in time to avoid crashing into it. A second car screeched to a stop behind Boulanger's car, blocking it between the two vehicles.

The car's doors blocking the front flung open, and two men jumped out, raising pistols to fire. Doors swung open in the car behind, and men jumped out. Everything was occurring in an action-filled, slow-motion blur.

"Back up! Back up!" Frank shouted.

Boulanger threw the car in reverse and crashed into the car behind them, knocking it back several feet. The men who had climbed out of the car jumped out of the way.

"Go forward," Frank yelled. "The sidewalk, go go, go!"

Boulanger slammed the car into drive and floored the accelerator. Then, the car bounded onto the right sidewalk with a bone-jarring bounce. "Go, go, go!" Frank yelled.

The car bounded forward, tearing off the front passenger door of the car in front, with the gunman diving out of the way. Boulanger's car careened from the sidewalk, bounced onto the pavement, and sped off. Gunshots rang out behind them, punching holes in the trunk and back window.

"Gun!" De Luca yelled while bent over, "Give me a goddamn gun."

"The glove box," Boulanger shouted. Frank pulled out a pistol from the glove box and handed it over the seat to De Luca. As he did, he saw two cars chasing them. "They're chasing us. Two cars."

"Stop the car," De Luca yelled. Boulanger slammed on the brakes. As the car screeched to a halt, De Luca leaped out and charged toward the oncoming cars. "Come on fuckers," De Luca roared, striding forward and firing. The cars abruptly stopped. Men piled out and began firing.

Frank jumped out, braced his gun arm on the open rear door, and began firing well-aimed shots. Boulanger took cover on the other side of the car, firing rapidly. De Luca kept charging ahead and firing. In the blaze of gunfire, one of the attackers fell to the ground, and two others dragged him into the car. De Luca fired his last bullet but kept charging and yelling. "Come on, you fuckers! I'll blow ya ass off, mutherfuckers!"

The two cars quickly retreated, tires squealing, and disappeared from sight. Then, panting and fuming, De Luca stomped back to the car.

Boulanger quickly called for backup while the trio searched for the attackers and the Renault they had been following.

"The mutherfuckers," growled De Luca from the back seat.

Frank glanced over his shoulder. "De Luca, anyone ever told you you're crazy?" he quipped.

"Yes, Loco," Boulanger chimed in, glancing at De Luca in the rear-view mirror. "Me, I think you have the right name."

"Fuck you two. And next time, *Bowl Longer*," growled De Luca, "give me enough ammo." Boulanger and Frank exchanged amused glances.

After changing cars, Ahmed took out a one-time use cell phone and called a special number. "Yes," answered a man's voice in Arabic. "The wedding date needs to be moved up," Ahmed said. "Uninvited guests may show up soon." This was greeted with silence. "Did you hear me?" Ahmed said. "The wedding must be held early and at another place."

Ahmed heard the man grunt. "The date has been set. Follow the plans for the wedding."

At the National Security Agency, NSA, outside Washington, D.C., millions of phone calls were intercepted and translated, and an analyst filed a routine report of the date and time of the call.

"Intercept of a coded cell phone call insisting that the date of an event, a wedding,' be moved up because 'uninvited guests' may show up soon. Speakers could not be identified with confidence through voice identification. The call originated in Paris and was received in Syria. No prior intercepts of calling or receiving phone, indicating both may be one-time-use phones."

PARIS, FRANCE SDAT HEADQUARTERS

A frantic search for the cars involved in the attack on Boulanger, Frank, and De Luca was unsuccessful. That night, in the SCIF room at SDAT headquarters in Paris, a woman's face from the CIA headquarters in Langley, Virginia, appeared on the large flat screen on the wall. Small, trim, and wearing glasses, the woman spoke into the small black rounded bulb at the end of a pencil-thin microphone standing up from a small device on a table.

"If an attack is planned in Europe during the next five days," declared the analyst, "we assess more than 350 likely targets." Frank shook his head. It was like a weather forecaster saying rain is likely in Europe over the next five days, but we don't know where.

Kathy had just arrived from Brussels to join him for a few nights. Frank was excited and relieved. After going nonstop with little sleep, he could finally spend a short night with her, although he planned to be back in the joint office before daybreak.

CHAPTER 27

That night, Frank joined Kathy at their Paris hotel. They held each other tightly, their mouths locked in passionate kisses. After they made love, Kathy rolled onto her stomach. His body pressed against hers, Frank propped up on an elbow, his head resting on a hand, and began caressing her, his hand gently gliding over her back and round, bare bottom. He savored their intimacy and the sensual feel of her body. "That feels so good," she said sleepily. After a moment, she murmured, "Frank, what was the first thing you noticed about me?"

"The first thing?"

"You know, before you ever said a word to me, what was the first thing you noticed about me? Do you remember?"

"Do I remember? Of course. Your butt."

"My butt!" she said, slightly raising her head. "But I thought you liked my eyes and my breasts."

"Baby, I *love* your eyes, and your beautiful breasts drive me wild, but the first thing I ever noticed about you was your butt. When you first arrived in Iraq, I was going to a meeting with the CIA station chief, and you and I hadn't met yet. As we were going down the hallway in the embassy, you were walking in front of me, and I first saw you from behind. You were wearing dark brown slacks, and I remember your trim figure and your butt."

"But Frank, I don't have a big butt. There's nothing to notice."

"Oh yes, there is. Watching your firm little butt swaying as you walked, I thought, 'What a sassy butt.'"

"What? A *sassy* butt!"

Frank's hand glided over her round, bare bottom as they talked. "Yes, a sassy butt. That jumped in my mind as I watched you."

Kathy turned her head to the side and looked up at Frank. "What is a *sassy butt*, Frank?"

"I don't know, but that jumped into my mind. Maybe it means 'confident and sexy.' Yeah, definitely *sexy*."

She smiled. "And all this time, I thought you loved my breasts."

"Oh, I *do*," said Frank. "Roll over onto your back, and I'll show you how much I love them." Kathy rolled onto her back and pulled Frank's head down to her breasts. Moments later, her breathing quickened. "Oh my!" she uttered. "Now, the other one, Frank. The other one needs you, too," she said breathlessly. "Yes! A little harder."

Later, they showered and went out for dinner at a nearby restaurant. In the flickering candlelight on the table, Frank lifted his wine glass of Pouilly-Fuissé and clinked it against hers, their eyes locked in a silent embrace. "To us," Frank said. "As a poem says, 'I wish I had met you sooner so that I could love you longer.'" His face softened. "So that I could love *you* longer, Kathy. *You*."

Kathy sighed and smiled. "I love you, Frank," They were sipping wine when dessert arrived. "Now, Frank," Kathy said after they had finished dessert, "we were talking about the first thing you noticed about me." She cocked an eye. "My *sassy butt*—wasn't that it?"

Frank smiled. "Yes," he said, nodding. "Your *beautiful* butt."

"Well, then, what was the *second* thing you noticed about me, Frank?"

"That's easy," said Frank. "I'll never forget. It was *your eyes*. We had walked down the hallway at the embassy, and you were in front of me. That's when I saw your cute, sassy butt. Then, when we were seated in the conference room, I looked across the table and saw you from the front for the first time. Our eyes met. And silently communicated. I knew instantly that you and I *see* things others don't. We can *feel* things others don't. It's like we communicate in a secret language. I could tell you felt it, too." Frank reached across the table and clasped one of her hands in his. "You felt it at that same moment, just like I did. Didn't you?"

She sighed deeply. "Yes," she said, nodding. "I did."

"You know, I not only love you," Frank said, "I *adore* you. Beautiful, brilliant, and enchanting *you*. The love of my life."

Kathy couldn't speak. Her eyes moistened. She felt a catch in her throat.

The restaurant hummed with low conversations, glasses and silverware clinking, waiters in starched white tops gliding among tables, red candles flickering, and warm golden lights glowing and glinting off paneled rosewood walls. Frank and Kathy felt as if they were in a warm cocoon, distant from the world, lost in their own intimate, warm glow.

CHAPTER 28

The next morning, Frank rejoined Boulanger and DeLuca at their joint office. Working from their phones and laptops, they were busy pursuing leads when Frank received a call from Kathy.

"I've got something to show you," Kathy told Frank. "But we need a SCIF because it's classified. Meet me at the embassy. I'm there now." An hour later, they sat together in a secure room at the embassy, with Kathy using a laptop. She turned on a display on a large screen on the wall. The logo of the U.S. National Reconnaissance Office, NRO, appeared, along with a Top Secret warning.

"After you were assigned to investigate the attack on Lemaire, I began checking on anything that might help you," Kathy said. "Some results came in today." She paused a moment. "I've uncovered a lead that might tie into the attack on Gabrielle Lemaire and the French agent, Marcel Bernard, on the Belgian coast," Kathy said. Her words hung in the air, laden with intrigue. Frank leaned forward; his curiosity stirred. "The attack? What did you find?"

"Parking lots," Kathy said.

Frank's brow furrowed, and he squinted. "Parking lots?" he said, puzzled. "I don't follow. Parking lots?"

"Stock analysts and market researchers use commercial satellites to look at parking lots to analyze how well certain businesses are doing or how particular business locations are doing. For example, some analysts use satellite images to count vehicles in Walmart lots. And in the health field, medical officials check hospital parking to look for potential outbreaks."

Frank nodded, still wondering where she was headed. "Okay, but how does this relate to the attack?"

Kathy's eyes gleamed. "As you know, classified satellites monitor sensitive sites and can even capture details as fine as license plates. Specialists analyze the images to detect anything significant, anything out of the norm. For instance, at missile launch sites in North Korea."

"So, you're saying our satellites could reveal something about the attack?"

Kathy nodded. "Exactly. I've been looking into the Iranian Quds Force compound in Tehran. The building where the Quds Force commander and Marwan have their offices. Here," she said, keying a laptop, "look at these satellite images." The large screen on the wall displayed a satellite view of several buildings in a compound and parked vehicles. "It's the Quds Force compound."

She zoomed in on one large building. "The Quds Force commander and Marwan have their offices in this building. Imagery interpreters examine the parking lot for unusual activities, such as parking areas full of vehicles that would normally be empty. Especially outside normal work hours or days."

"Watch this." The screen displayed several dozen vehicles parked near Marwan's building and zoomed in on a large SUV. "This is Marwan's vehicle. If his vehicle is there at an unusual time, it may indicate that a significant Quds Force activity is occurring or has occurred somewhere."

"On a hunch," Kathy continued, "I had our people backtrack to the night that Gabrielle Lemaire and Marcel Bernard were attacked on the Belgium coast. It turns out there was a surge of activity on the night of Lemaire's attack, soon after the attack."

Kathy glanced at Frank and then keyed the monitor. "Look at this. It was right after the attack on Lemaire and the French agent." An image displayed dozens of vehicles at night. "All these vehicles normally wouldn't be there. This was in the middle of the night, in the early morning hours before daylight."

Frank turned to Kathy. "They looked at the Quds Force compound? Looked for Marwan's SUV?"

"Right," she said, nodding.

"And Marwan's—"

"Marwan's vehicle wasn't there, but—"

"Marwan wasn't there?" he said. "But if Quds Force was doing something in Europe, Marwan and Unit 400 would be involved. Why wasn't he at headquarters when everything erupted that night? That doesn't make sense, Kathy. If Quds Force was involved in the attack on Lemaire, Marwan would have been at headquarters."

"But Marwan *was* there," she said confidently. "Marwan occasionally changes vehicles for personal security reasons and to thwart surveillance. Knowing this, our analysts also follow the two people who are always with Marwan when he's on the move. His driver and his personal bodyguard. And their vehicles were at Quds Force headquarters the night of the attack."

"Which means that Marwan was there?"

"Exactly. Marwan was there right after the attack."

Kathy leaned in, and her voice was charged with excitement. "Think about it, Frank. It's the kind of activity that occurs when a crisis erupts. If Lemaire and Bernard stumbled onto something tied to the Quds Force, it would send them into crisis mode. That could explain the surge of activity that night."

"Kathy, you might be onto something crucial here," Frank said, his eyes narrowing as he absorbed her findings. As he rubbed his chin, his mind whirled with possibilities. "Remember the compound I found in Africa, where I saw explosives and Sarin? An interception linked Marwan to it. Paper fragments at the site indicated a shipment was going to Europe by ship. Perhaps a cargo that could have been offloaded at night on a coast. Maybe even the Belgium coast."

Kathy's eyes widened. "And no one followed up?"

Frank's expression darkened. "D.C. dismissed it after a raid yielded no evidence. They thought my head injury had muddled my observations. But now ..." Frank rubbed his face and the back of his neck. "I've got to do something," he said.

WASHINGTON, D.C.

"What's this?" FBI assistant director Bill Price said as his deputy handed him a memo.

"It's an urgent request we just received from Frank Marsh. He's on the joint team in France investigating the attack on the NYPD international liaison, Gabrielle Lemaire. He wants the NRO to allow him to share top secret satellite imagery of a parking lot that may show a link to the attack."

"A link? What kind of link?"

"It's in Marsh's memo. A satellite showed a surge of activity at Quds Force headquarters in Tehran right after the attack. Marsh mentions Africa and Sarin and says Marwan might be involved. He wants to share the intelligence with the French and NYPD. He explained—"

"Marwan!" Price barked. He spit out words angrily: "Marwan. Sarin. A parking lot!" He frowned and shook his head in disgust. "Marsh is fixated on Marwan. It warps his judgment. Just like the concussion affected his thinking in Africa." Price handed Marsh's memo back to his assistant. "No. Request denied. Answer: 'Request denied.'"

"Don't you want to read it first?"

"No, I know enough about Marsh and his fantasies. We're not about to embarrass the Bureau by asking NRO to authorize foreign disclosure of top secret imagery just because of Marsh. Denied!"

PARIS, FRANCE

Frank's laptop beeped with an incoming message. As he read the reply from FBI headquarters, Frank frowned and shook his head slowly.

"What's the matter, Frank?" said Boulanger, the French intelligence agent. Frank glanced at him across their desks. "You look downcast, Frank. Is it bad news?"

DeLuca, the NYPD detective, grunted and sneered. "It's probably your FBI fuckers jerking you around. You fuckers not only do it to everybody else, you do it to yourselves too." DeLuca started to say more but stopped when Frank shot him a fierce look.

Frank stood, stared distantly, and then headed toward the door. "I'll be back in a little while," he said over his shoulder in a low voice.

When he reached the street, Frank began walking aimlessly. He needed time to think. And to ask himself questions. What could I do? What should I do? How important or useless is information that may link the Quds Force and Sarin to the attack on Lemaire and Bernard? Did they discover Sarin or explosives coming in on a boat? Think of the danger Sarin would pose. And the explosives. Is Marwan planning a mass terror attack? Am I jumping to conclusions, just because of Marwan?

After walking several blocks, Frank stopped at a busy intersection. He turned and began walking back. And continued trying to decide what to do, if anything. Unauthorized disclosure of top secret information would end my career. And may even mean prison. Career. Prison. The intelligence may not even help identify and find those who attacked Lemaire and Bernard. And just knowing that there could be a Sarin attack somewhere in Europe wouldn't prevent it. Maybe the French would overreact. Maybe this. Maybe that. What to do? It's easy to do something when you know the right thing to do. But what if you don't know the right thing to do?

When Frank walked into the office, Boulanger and DeLuca stopped talking and watched him silently. Frank sat down, opened his laptop, and began working with his head down. Boulanger and DeLuca glanced at each other with raised eyebrows. A questioning shrug. They continued working silently.

A few minutes later, they were startled when Frank said somberly, "We need to talk." They moved to a table. All three hunched forward, elbows propped on the table with arms crossed. Boulanger and DeLuca looked questioningly at Frank, who looked from one to the other and sighed deeply.

"I'm not authorized to tell you this." His announcement hung heavy. Before continuing, he looked at each one again and saw they understood the gravity he felt of his dilemma. "Lemaire and Bernard may have stumbled onto a shipment of Sarin nerve agent being offloaded on the coast." Boulanger and DeLuca glanced at each other and leaned closer toward Frank, their eyes wider. He explained about discovering Sarin in the mountain compound in Africa, possible Iranian connections, and burned fragments referring to a cargo being shipped to Europe. Then, he revealed the surge of activity at Quds Force right after the attack on Lemaire and Bernard occurred. "Connecting the Quds Force and Sarin to the attack is plausible but may be wrong," Frank said. "And remember, my discovery of Sarin in Africa was dismissed in the U.S. But," he said, and then waited a beat before continuing, "what *if* a Sarin attack is coming?" He looked from Boulanger to DeLuca. The three men fell silent, lost in thought. How do we stop an attack that may or may not be coming at an unknown site somewhere in Europe, at an unknown time, by unknown terrorists?

"Beating the bushes," Frank said, breaking the silence. They looked at him questioningly. "Look, when you don't know more, you beat the bushes. Ask contacts about any reports of Quds Force activity in Europe, about any reports of possible attacks, no matter how improbable, and ask them to direct covert sources to probe for information." Boulanger and DeLuca nodded. "But please do it discreetly, without disclosing what I told you. I've risked my career by telling you this," he said gravely.

The men were soon busy making calls, jotting notes, calling out to each other, but with little progress. The FBI and CIA were asked by French security officials if they had any indications of a planned Sarin attack in Europe. Some found Frank's report of Sarin in Africa and of a Quds Force connection but discovered that his observations had been dismissed as unreliable. "Negative" was the reply to the French.

Hours later, Frank, Boulanger, and Deluca sat feeling defeated. A promising lead had come to a dead end. The sudden loss of momentum hung like a heavy pall, and the men avoided eye contact. Just then, Boulanger was summoned to the Ministry of the Interior.

Paris: The Ministry of Interior

Boulanger was feeling uneasy outside the office of the Interior Minister in Paris. He had been summoned abruptly, and he was anxious that his career was in jeopardy over the shootout. His immediate boss, Emile Arnaud, had already severely scolded him for not following procedures and working on the streets with the Americans.

"Why didn't you send our surveillance teams to watch the terrorists?" Arnaud demanded. "We could have identified their contacts, found out what they were doing, and captured all of them. But instead," Arnaud said between clenched teeth, jabbing a finger toward him, "you and your American friends went by yourselves and ruined everything. Got in a Wild West shootout like American cowboys and—"

"But, sir," Boulanger protested, "we didn't know terrorists would be there for certain. The Americans just wanted to see if—"

"The Americans!" Arnaud's face flushed redder. "We have procedures," Arnaud shouted angrily. "Procedures!"

Boulanger grimaced at the memory. He was glad Arnaud's wrath had been interrupted by a call from the office of Deputy Interior Minister Christophe Laurent summoning Boulanger. But now, Boulanger was worried. Being summoned by Laurent could not be good.

An aide escorted Boulanger into Laurent's office and waved him into a seat in front of the minister's desk. The aide sat beside the minister's desk and opened a notebook to take notes. A plump and balding man, Laurent stared at Boulanger through black-rimmed glasses.

"Sir," Boulanger began, "if this is about—" Laurent held up a hand. "Boulanger, you are here because you don't understand your true role in working with the Americans. You think the three of you are leading an investigation of the killing of our intelligence agent and the shooting of the New York policewoman, but that is not accurate."

Boulanger arched an eyebrow. "Sir?"

"That's correct. The Americans insisted on leading the investigation, and we agreed the three of you would work together. But you and the two Americans are just a mirage. A mirage to fool the Americans into thinking they are leading the investigation. The real work is being done by the security forces of this ministry. Your role is to keep the Americans from interfering. Do you understand?"

Boulanger felt deflated. "Yes, sir," he said numbly. "But what if—"

"No," Laurent said briskly, shaking his head. "No buts. No ifs. You will make a show of working with the Americans. You will keep them in the office. And you will report everything they do. Understood?"

On the way back to his office, Boulanger thought about his orders and frowned. He felt like a pawn in a senseless game.

He cleared security on the ground floor and was on his way to the elevator when someone called out, "Alain." He turned and saw Antoine, a fellow French intelligence agent, approaching. "I've been waiting for you," Antoine said. "We need to talk." Boulanger followed him to an empty office.

"Remember the cigarette butts found at the sea cove near the attack on Bernard and the New York policewoman?" Boulanger nodded, and Antoine continued. "The DNA from the cigarette butts at the cove matched the DNA of a terrorist known only as Ahmed. We first came across him a few months ago when his DNA was found on cigarette butts in the apartment of a terrorist we raided here in Paris. When questioned, the terrorist said the man smoking those cigarettes was known as Ahmed. He told us Ahmed travels between Paris and Brussels. We have not been able to fully identify him. But you need to know his DNA was at the cove."

"But why—"

"We are under orders not to share anything with you and the Americans. But it is not right, and you need to know. This Ahmed may have also been connected with Saad, the man at the apartments you and the Americans went to watch, which led to your gun battle on the street. Here is the address of a newspaper shop run by a man who may know Ahmed. His name is Omar. We questioned him, but he wouldn't say anything."

After joining Frank and De Luca in the office, Boulanger sat quietly at his desk, deep in thought. Someone should follow up on Antoine's information about Ahmed, he thought. Still, the Interior Minister ordered him not to do anything with the Americans. Just keep them in the office. If he did anything, it could end his career. He wished Antoine had not told him anything. "What's the matter?" Frank said. Boulanger looked up, startled. "You look like you have the weight of the world on your shoulders."

Boulanger grimaced and shook his head. "Sometimes, doing the right thing, it is not easy."

Frank nodded. "I often remind myself of something that helps me make the right decisions." Boulanger raised an eyebrow. "It's this," Frank continued. "You can always find an excuse to get out of doing the right thing."

Boulanger bit his lower lip and then spoke. "But what if you don't know what is the right thing to do?"

"That's a good question, Alain. Sometimes, there are only difficult choices. When your mind doesn't give you the answer, your heart will tell you. But you'll figure it out."

The men fell silent and resumed work at their desks. A few minutes later, Boulanger said, "I have something to tell you. Something important." He shared Antoine's information with De Luca and Frank. "So, what should we do?" he asked.

"That's easy," said Frank. "First, just to refresh what we know now. The people at the seaside cove near Brussels brought in something secret by boat. They're the people Gabrielle Lemaire was tracking, and they attacked her and Marcel Bernard. DNA from cigarettes found at the cove belongs to a terror suspect called Ahmed. According to your colleague Antoine, this man Omar is key to finding Ahmed." Frank paused. "We need to find Ahmed," he declared.

"Enough talking," De Luca growled while rising from his desk. "Let's go."

The three men rushed to the cigarette stand and cornered Omar in a back room. Boulanger questioned Omar in French. Omar responded in French with a sneer, and Boulanger flushed with anger.

"What did he say?" De Luca demanded.

"Omar, he said to me, 'I do not know anyone called Ahmed," Boulanger said. "He says for us to stop bothering him and to go screw ourselves."

De Luca's powerful gut punch bounced Omar off the wall and onto the floor, the air knocked out of his body. Frank and Boulanger grabbed De Luca's arms, but he easily threw them off. "Pull the fucker up and ask him again," De Luca demanded.

"You can't do that," Frank protested. "We can't—"

"You fuckers are trying to find terrorists," De Luca snapped. "But I'm after the fuckers who attacked an NYPD officer. And I'm going to find them," he declared, glaring at Frank and Boulanger.

Looking at Omar writhing on the floor and gasping for breath, Boulanger shrugged and held his palms out. "At least let us wait until he can breathe. Yes?"

Soon, a pale and whimpering Omar was pressed hard against the wall, with De Luca's hand gripping his throat and DeLuca's vicious face inches from his frightened eyes. Omar's lips quivered as he stared at De Luca. "Go ahead," De Luca snarled. "Ask the fucker again."

* * *

While Frank, De Luca, and Boulanger were pressing Omar, Ahmed, and others were hard at work in another part of the city. Inside the confined space of a small garage, two men packed explosives into the trunk of a gray car. Three large suitcases filled with white kilogram bricks of explosives lay on the floor next to the trunk. Amari was carefully arranging the bricks in the trunk, and Farid was attaching wiring to each one. They talked in low voices as they worked. "Hurry," said Farid. "We're already late."

"It couldn't be helped," said Amari, pausing to wipe the sweat off his brow with his forearm. "A car accident stopped us for a long time in traffic."

"No, you made us late," Farid retorted. "We wouldn't have been caught in traffic if you hadn't stopped to put petrol in the car." He was bent over working on wiring the bricks. He straightened up. "Stop a moment, and hand me the timer in the satchel."

The men worked quickly. In a few more minutes, they should be ready to drive to where they would park the car with explosives. A timer would set off the car bomb. After parking the car bomb, they would meet Ahmed and help him carry out the attack with Sarin nerve gas.

Farid would drive the gray car packed with explosives, and Amari would follow in the blue getaway car. The target and timing for the explosion had been carefully chosen to inflict maximum casualties. The coordinated attacks on the target and the Jewish center would create chaos and enable the men to flee the city without being caught. But they were running late and would have to drive fast to get the car bomb in place and then meet Ahmed in time.

Right behind them in the garage, Ahmed, who was wearing a brown sports coat, finished putting Sarin nerve gas into a black car. He called to the men. "We have to go. *Now.* We're running late. The service will be over at the Jewish center if we don't hurry."

* * *

"There it is, the garage," Boulanger said, nodding ahead toward a small car repair shop on the right. "The one Omar told us about." Crammed in a narrow space between other shops at the bottom of a drab four-story building, it consisted of a roll-up garage door, which was closed, and a windowless door next to the roll-up door. Above the door was a crude sign in French announcing "Quick Car Repairs." Small, shabby shops lined the sidewalk, including some that were vacant. "It's the one Omar says is connected to Ahmed."

Boulanger circled the block and parked a half-block from the repair shop, on the opposite side of the street. "What do you want to do now," Boulanger said, glancing at Frank in the passenger seat and then up at the rearview mirror at De Luca in the back seat. "We watch? Or do we—"

"The door is opening," Frank said excitedly. The garage door was rolling up. It rolled open, revealing a heavy-set man who turned and disappeared inside.

"It's him!" Boulanger exclaimed. "The same man we followed from the apartments."

"Yeah, that's the fucker," De Luca said from the back seat. "The ones shooting at us."

Frank spoke quickly. "Alain, call in a SWAT unit. We can do surveillance until they get here, and then—"

The back car door swung open, and De Luca sprang out. "The hell with that. I'm getting the fuckers," he said, striding across the street while reaching under his coat.

Frank and Boulanger jumped out, hurried across the street, and caught up with De Luca on the sidewalk. As they walked, a small gray car, followed by a dark blue car, suddenly pulled out of the garage, turned right on the street, and sped away.

"Who was in the cars?" Frank asked. "Could you see?"

Boulanger replied that he couldn't tell. Then, a black car emerged from the garage and also sped off to the right.

Frank recognized the driver and yelled, "It's him! The one in the brown sport coat from the shootout!" Frank did a U-turn. "Come on," he said, running for Boulanger's car. In moments, they were speeding after the black car. It was far ahead in traffic, and they only caught glimpses of it. "Hurry, we're going to lose him. He's—Look! It turned left. Was that it? I couldn't tell for sure."

Hunched over the steering wheel, Boulanger shook his head. "I couldn't tell. Should we turn left ahead? Or go—"

"Left," De Luca ordered from the back seat as they reached the intersection. "Turn left! Here. Now!" Boulanger swung left, and they found themselves in heavy traffic with four lanes.

"Look!" Frank said. "The black car ahead on the right. That's it." A block ahead, a black car turned right at the next intersection and disappeared. Stuck in slow traffic, it felt like they were crawling toward the intersection. "Use your lights and siren to get to the intersection," Frank said urgently. "But turn them off before he can see us; otherwise, he'll run before we can catch up."

As he put a flashing emergency light on the dash, Boulanger said the car didn't have a siren. He maneuvered around cars and turned off the emergency light just before reaching the intersection. They turned right and spotted the black car almost two blocks ahead. In the heavy traffic ahead, it kept disappearing and reemerging for moments at a time. "We're going to lose him if we can't get closer," Frank said desperately.

He tried to think of something they could do. "The two cars that left ahead of him," Frank said, "the gray and blue cars. Can you radio units to look for them?"

Boulanger quickly radioed. It was a long shot without license numbers, but he gave the makes, models, and colors of the two cars and said they would likely be traveling together.

"Left!" Frank said. "He turned left." Boulanger turned on his emergency light again until they reached the turn. "I don't see it," Frank said, scanning traffic ahead. "Anyone see it?" The car was nowhere in sight. "Keep going straight," Frank said. "When we get to side streets, I'll watch to the right for the car, and De Luca can watch to the left but keep going straight unless we see that it turned. And—" Boulanger's radio squawked with an urgent request. Police headquarters wanted the location of the garage where they had first spotted the two cars and the time they had been last seen. While Boulanger responded, De Luca interrupted, his voice a heavy growl. "A SWAT unit. Send a SWAT unit to the garage, dammit." Boulanger added the SWAT request and urged them to hurry.

Amid heavy, noisy traffic, the three men frantically searched without success for the black car. Boulanger's police radio squawked with urgent but ultimately false sightings of the blue and gray cars traveling together that had left the garage just ahead of the black car. Finally, after several minutes of speeding in traffic, Boulanger slowed down and shook his head. "We lost it."

Frank was alarmed. "Something's about to happen," he declared anxiously. "They're moving to attack targets."

"I agree," Boulanger said, "but—" His radio squawked with an incoming transmission. The SWAT unit reported that the garage was empty, but they found bomb-making materials, including wiring, packaging, and residue of explosives. They had backed off and called in a bomb unit.

"Any papers or items that might show the targets of a bombing?" Boulanger asked hurriedly. The dispatcher didn't know. "What about the two cars traveling together?" Boulanger asked. "Anything?" A flurry of reported sightings, but all had proven negative.

Frank, Boulanger, and De Luca felt deflated. They had been on an adrenaline-pumping surveillance and chase, but everything had abruptly stopped. Boulanger started slowing. "No, keep going," Frank urged him. "The black car has got to be around here somewhere. Let's keep looking."

Across Paris, chaos erupted as a police car with flashing blue lights pursued Farid's bomb-laden gray car. Looking in his rearview mirror, Farid felt panic as the police car swerved in behind him, siren blaring. The police car crowded his rear bumper, its siren frantically wailing and whooping. But the officers had failed to notice the second car being sought, the blue car driven by Amari, which was a couple of car lengths behind them. Watching the police ahead, Amari reached under his seat and pulled out a handgun.

Up front, Farid slowed his car to a stop by the curb, and the police car pulled in behind him. Amari stopped behind the police. Two officers got out and approached Farid, one on each side of his car. Farid stepped out, with his left side toward the officers, a gun in his right hand, hidden from view. As the nearest officer approached the car's rear, Farid swiftly raised the gun and fired. The bullet struck the officer's vest, knocking him off balance. Farid fired again, hitting the officer in the head, and he dropped to the pavement. The other officer fired twice, striking Farid in the chest, and he crumbled to the ground.

Behind the police car, Amari had already opened his door and was halfway out with a gun when several police cars screeched to a halt, their sirens blaring. Amari fired wildly. In a frenzied exchange of gunfire, Amari was hit numerous times and killed instantly.

Hearing the urgent radio transmissions, Boulanger turned on his emergency light to rush to the scene. "Wait," Frank said. "Stop. The black car is the threat now. We've got to find it."

"Marsh is right," De Luca barked from the back seat. "We gotta find the fucker."

Boulanger's mouth tightened, but he nodded and kept driving so they could search for the black car. Frank knew how he felt. When an officer is down, every officer wants to rush to the scene, even when the shooting is over. Boulanger radioed the dispatcher. "Warn the officers that one or both cars will likely have explosives. And get a bomb unit to the scene." A few minutes later, they learned that a bomb unit had arrived.

Frank felt useless, but searching the area where they had last seen the black car was the only thing he could think of doing. Except for one thing. He looked at Boulanger. "Quick, tell them to search the two terrorists and their cell phones right away for anything indicating any targets they planned to attack. They need to do it *now*," Frank insisted. Boulanger made the urgent request.

Several long minutes later, Boulanger received a call, and didn't look happy as he listened. After the call, he looked at Frank and glanced over the seat at De Luca. He frowned and shook his head. "It's not good. The cell phones are locked and likely encrypted. It may take several hours or longer to unlock and examine them." De Luca uttered an obscenity. Frank slumped and rubbed the back of his neck. He looked at Boulanger and nodded. "Okay. All we can do is keep riding around and searching for the black car. It's got to be—" He stopped and stared unseeing, struck by a sudden thought. Puzzled, Boulanger and De Luca looked at Frank. Frank's face suddenly brightened. "Wait," Frank said excitedly, his eyes wide. "The maps."

"The maps?"

"The GPS maps in the cars. Tell them to check the two cars for GPS map displays. If they put in addresses, then the locations will still be on the display or in the map logs. Hurry."

Boulanger made the call. As they waited, Frank anxiously rubbed his chin. Tense minutes drug by. "Are they doing it?" Frank finally asked impatiently. "Find out." As Boulanger picked up his phone, it rang. He answered and looked excited as he listened. Ending the call, he said excitedly, "They found three locations on the car maps. They're sending units to check them, but one is close to us. Just three blocks away."

"Let's go!" Frank yelled.

Boulanger made a frantic U-turn and sped toward the location. Frank's heart was pounding. Would they be too late?

"There!" Frank exclaimed. "What's that?" A multi-story building in white stone rose on a corner, surrounded by a green lawn and a sidewalk leading to ornate double doors at the entrance. "It's the Franco-Jewish Center," Boulanger replied, reading the sign outside the building. "But a synagogue is on the other corner."

"That's got to be it," Frank exclaimed. "One of them is a target. Drop me off. I'm going to the center. De Luca, cover the synagogue. Alain, call it in and follow me." Alain Boulanger stopped the car in a screeching halt, and Frank jumped out, running toward the center.

Meanwhile, Ahmed was in a dilemma. The men driving the other two cars were supposed to drop one car off for a car bomb explosion and then join him in carrying out the Sarin nerve gas attack on the Jewish center. But they were late and had not answered his calls. Should he abort or go ahead without them? After hesitating, Ahmed picked up a computer bag containing canisters of Sarin nerve gas, pulled the strap over his shoulder, and set out for the entrance to the center.

Twelve-year-old Melanie Levy and her mother were walking toward the entrance at the same time. Melanie was excited to be part of the annual Holocaust Memorial service. She clutched Anne Frank's diary against her breast as if it could calm her nervousness about speaking in public. Melanie didn't need the book to read the passage; she had memorized it. She felt close to Anne Frank, and having the book was like having Anne with her. Melanie was also excited about her new white dress and hair bow.

She looked up at her mother, walking beside her. "Mama, do I look all right?"

Her mother glanced at Melanie's eager brown eyes and smiled. "Yes, Melanie," she said, taking her daughter's hand. "You look beautiful. And you'll do fine. I'm proud of you." Nervous about her speech, Melanie didn't pay attention to the man in the brown sports coat with a bulky computer bag strapped over his shoulder. But even at a distance, Frank spotted him immediately and knew something was off.

"Stop!" he yelled, gun in hand, as he ran toward Ahmed with Boulanger beside him. Ahmed saw them coming, and in a split second, he grabbed Melanie with one arm, pulled her against him, and fired at Boulanger. Uttering a cry, Boulanger fell to the ground, writhing in pain.

Ahmed swung his gun toward Frank and fired. Frank ducked, then rose, holding his gun with both hands. But he couldn't snap off a shot because Melanie was clutched against Ahmed's chest. Frank planted his feet, extended his arms, and began sighting as if calmly practicing on a firing range. But he felt anything but calm.

Ahmed was firing rapidly, and Frank felt something hit him. He ignored it, breathed, let part of it out, and squeezed the trigger. The gun bucked in his hands, and Ahmed dropped to the ground. Melanie ran screaming to her mother. Frank rushed to Boulanger. He was squirming on the ground with his hands pressed against a bloody thigh. Frank knelt and checked Boulanger's wound. "It didn't hit an artery," Frank said, relieved. Boulanger's eyes were fearful as he gasped for breath. "The bag," he said, nodding toward Ahmed's body. "The bag!"

Frank ran to Ahmed's sprawled figure. He knelt and carefully opened the bag. He stopped, stunned. It held canisters of Sarin nerve gas. Earsplitting sirens created a frantic clamor as French security forces roared in from several directions. Frank yelled and waved for onlookers to get back. His yells were drowned out by the whooping and wailing of the sirens, but people could see he was waving them away from danger. Frightened crowds scattered.

He backed away from the Sarin and went back to Boulanger. But as he helped Boulanger sit up, Frank felt a sharp pain in his left side, followed by a searing, burning sensation. Looking down, he saw his shirt stained with blood. He ripped it open and saw a bloody groove and torn flesh where a bullet had grazed him.

Later, Frank remembered the following events as a blur. Being knocked to the ground by French security forces, handcuffed until they confirmed his identity, and medics rushing Boulanger away on a stretcher. De Luca raging like a bull when he was briefly detained. The stinging in his side growing worse. Being treated and patched up in an emergency room, followed by endless debriefings all night by French officials while FBI headquarters bombarded him with calls, demanding every detail.

By the early morning hours, Frank was still at the French security offices and almost delirious with exhaustion. The adrenaline had long worn off. At last, the incessant demands for his attention ended. And then there were congratulations and backslaps. He was relieved the attacks had been stopped. It was a close thing. But he was too tired and mentally drained to join in the celebrations.

As he slumped in a chair, Frank's mind whirled with images, and he felt overflowing emotions. It had been a long journey and struggle to get to this point. He thought about everything and everyone along the way. He wiped an eye with his fingers and then the other one. "Sir, someone is waiting for you." Frank looked up, startled. He couldn't process what the official had said.

"What?" Frank mumbled wearily.

The official nodded toward the stairs. "Someone is waiting downstairs for you. Come. I will take you."

He led Frank downstairs, past security, and onto the sidewalk. When they emerged, Frank stopped and stood still. Dawn was breaking. Golden rays from a rising sun lit the tops of buildings with a necklace of dazzling gold. The light gray sky was turning cloudless blue. Frank raised his face to the sky and breathed deeply. He heard a car door open. Kathy was running toward him.

THE END

EPILOGUE

A week after stopping the terror attacks, Frank, Boulanger, and De Luca met at their Paris office for one last time. They were cleaning out their desks before going their separate ways. They worked silently, feeling the weight of the moment. Boulanger's cell phone rang, and before he could answer, Frank's rang and then DeLuca's. During their separate conversations, the men began nodding. When the calls ended, Frank spoke first. "Gabrielle Lemaire came out of her coma. She's going to make it," he said, beaming widely and relieved. They all had received similar messages and were all smiling, even DeLuca. Their eyebrows raised, Frank and Boulanger exchanged a knowing look. It was their first time seeing DeLuca smile, but they knew better than to break the spell by mentioning it.

The following morning, the three men arrived at the hospital and were escorted to Gabrielle's room. Boulanger limped slightly from his leg wound and used a cane. As they walked down the corridor to Gabrielle's room, nurses and aides smiled and greeted "Monsieur De Luca" like an old friend. Frank and Boulanger exchanged puzzled looks. Boulanger stopped and talked with a nurse as Frank and De Luca continued to the room. He rejoined the men just after they entered.

Gabrielle lay in her hospital bed, her eyes half-opened and weak. Boulanger patted her hand and spoke to her in French, and she managed a small smile. Frank introduced himself and held her hand. "A boat," she said weakly. "Truck and men." She paused to catch her breath, but before she could continue, Frank stopped her. "We know. We stopped them. Because of you," he said, nodding. "*You* did it." Gabrielle's eyes moistened. Frank felt a lump in his throat and couldn't speak anymore. Pressing his lips tight, he stepped back as De Luca came forward and took her hand in his big paws. After introducing himself, he held up a gold NYPD Detective shield for her to see. He placed the shield in Gabrielle's palm and wrapped her hand around it.

Boulanger leaned over to Frank and whispered. "The nurses said De Luca visited Gabrielle several times, holding her hand and talking to her while she was still in a coma." Now, as they watched, De Luca bent over and whispered in her ear. She smiled, and tears began rolling down the sides of her face. Minutes later, they drove away in silence. The air was too heavy for talk.

The following morning, De Luca arrived at the hospital with a framed picture of a little blond girl. After his brief visit, nurses noticed Gabrielle clutching the framed photo to her chest and smiling through tears. That night, she whispered, "Mary, my baby."

The next day, Frank drove De Luca to Charles DeGaulle Airport to catch his flight to New York and went inside with him. "Sir, it's time to board," said the airline attendant at the boarding gate. "The doors will be shutting in moments," she added, motioning toward the runway to the plane. NYPD detective Rizzo De Luca didn't move. Instead, he stood silently, staring past the boarding gate.

"Sir?" She motioned again to the big bear of a man but didn't get his attention.

Frank looked at De Luca beside him, wondering why he wasn't moving to board the flight. Then, with a grunt, De Luca turned and met Frank's eyes. Frank gave him a quizzical look.

"Well, Marsh," De Luca growled and paused. After a moment, he said, "I guess you'll do." De Luca extended his hand and nodded. "For a bureau fucker," he added.

Firmly gripping De Luca's hand, Frank nodded, "You too, Loco." Frank thought he saw a nearly imperceptible smile cross De Luca's lips, quickly followed by a scowl. De Luca picked up his bag and began walking toward the runway. He called out over his shoulder, "But don't let that go to your fucking head, Marsh."

Frank smiled and shook his head as he watched De Luca disappear.

SLANO, CROATIA

Twelve miles north of Dubrovnik, Croatia, the picturesque village of Slano lined the bay of the same name. Quaint cream-colored and pastel-yellow villas with red-tiled roofs decorated the shore and hills. White sailboats anchored placidly in the bay's glistening blue waters. Although yet to be widely discovered, Slano drew increasing numbers of tourists to its unspoiled beauty and tranquility.

On a sailboat in the bay, Kathy watched as Frank stood at the bow and threw out the anchor. She loved watching the fluid movements of his lean, athletic body and the rippling of his corded muscles. As the anchor line began rapidly uncoiling, he returned to the cockpit. He shifted the engine in reverse, backing the boat gently until he felt the anchor catch and set. Frank shut off the engine, and the boat lazed securely at anchor.

"Now," he said brightly, "I have something special for us." He took a bottle of Roederer Cristal Champagne from an ice chest and worked the top with both hands. The cork popped, and champagne foamed over the top. They looked at each other with expectant smiles. Frank filled glasses and handed one to Kathy.

Frank couldn't suppress his grin or happiness. He savored the moment. This is one of the high points of my life, Frank thought, a moment to be cherished. He knew they were a perfect match. They complemented each other's strengths and compensated for each other's weaknesses. They thought alike and saw and felt things others didn't.

While sipping champagne in the cockpit, Kathy sat with her back against his chest. Frank set down his glass and began massaging her neck and shoulders. "What do you think, baby," he said, "will this do?"

Kathy sighed and smiled. "It's perfect." She lifted one of his hands off of her shoulder and kissed it. The boat swayed gently on the calm bay in a lulling and calming embrace. The setting sun painted a pink and rose palette on the horizon. Frank kissed the back of Kathy's neck and shoulders and murmured softly in her ear. Soon, they went below and made love in the cabin. Gently and unhurriedly, taking time to savor each other. He loved the sensual feeling of caressing her smooth curves and the exciting white places her bikini had shielded from the sun.

Afterward, they lay against each other, drowsily talking. "Tell me more about you," Frank said. "About when you were growing up. I want to know more."

Kathy talked about how she had learned to ride a horse bareback. "After that," she said brightly with a charming smile, "it was easy peasy."

Frank grinned and shook his head. "'Easy peasy?'" he said, turning onto his side and propping his head on a hand while looking down at her. "How can you be so enchanting, Miss 'Easy Peasy?' And cute? And where did you learn to say 'easy peasy?' I haven't heard that expression since I was a kid."

"I don't believe it," Kathy said.

"I haven't," Frank maintained. "I haven't heard it since I was a kid."

"I don't believe it," she said with an even bigger smile. "I don't believe you were *ever* a kid. But if you were, I bet you were a cute one."

"Come here, you," Frank said, pulling her close, their lips meeting in a luscious, lingering kiss.

They spent the night on the boat, cuddled up in the cozy confines of the cabin. Frank snuggled against Kathy's back, with his arm wrapped around her and his hand cupping her breasts. Finally, they drifted off to sleep, the gentle rocking of the waves soothing their slumber. The next morning, they made breakfast together. The sun was shining, the sky was blue, and the sea was calm but with a steady breeze. They spent the day sailing and docked at the marina in the late afternoon. From the pier, they held hands and strolled to a popular seaside restaurant.

Kathy's white sun dress billowed gently in the breeze as they walked, pressing it against her thighs and shapely legs. The dress was radiant in the sunset, highlighting her honey-colored tan and golden hair. Frank loved looking at Kathy's trim figure and graceful movements, sparkling blue eyes, and the shimmering tones of her golden hair. She wore no makeup except lipstick, and he marveled at her natural, fresh-faced beauty. My enchanting princess, he thought. How can I be so lucky?

They dined alfresco on local seafood. A white linen tablecloth, a gentle warm breeze, a flickering candle in a globe on the table. Kathy's face glowed in the dancing candlelight. After dessert, Frank raised his wine glass, clinked it against hers, and looked into her eyes. "Kathy, as I've told you many times. I am in awe of your stunning beauty, brilliant mind, and wonderful heart." He paused and added, "You don't realize how special you are."

Kathy smiled. "Frank, are you just trying to get me into bed?" she said coyly.

He returned her smile. "I love you," he said softly. Her eyes brimming, Kathy reached out and held his hand on the table.

After dinner, they put a few things from the boat in the car and drove up the hill to the villa. Frank carried in the ice chest. As he set it down inside, his cell phone rang. Standing a few paces away, Kathy heard Frank's end of the conversation.

"Hello... What? ... Why?... When? ... Okay. But what about Kathy? She ... Good... Alright... Yes, sir." Ending the call, Frank looked at Kathy. He took a deep breath and blew it out. "I'm sorry," Frank said. "We have to go back to D.C. That was Bill Nelson, the assistant director. He said something urgent and important has just come up, and they want me to work it." He paused. "But he's trying to arrange for you and me to work it together," Frank added quickly. He raised an eyebrow, silently asking if it was okay with her.

Kathy cocked an eye and shook her head slowly. "Oh no," she said with a wry smile. "Here we go again."

ACKNOWLEDGMENTS

I am indebted to friends and family who generously helped by reviewing drafts, making suggestions, and helping with edits. A special thanks to my fellow authors Ace Atkins, Tom Dawson, Jessica Schexnayder, and Connie Rachal. They were generous with their time and talents. Thanks to Shelia and Chris Casselberry, Marsha and Greg Bursavich, Deborah Spillers Booksh, Carolyn and Jimmy Rudder, David (DD) Rachal, and my Iraq colleagues and friends Lou and Pam Nelli for sharing their thoughts and suggestions. Any faults and errors in this work are mine alone. As always, my wife Evelyn encouraged me and made writing possible.

Thank you to all the readers who enjoyed *Confessions of an Undercover Agent: Adventures, Close Calls, and the Toll of a Double Life* and the first book in this series, *Whirlwind: A Frank Marsh Novel*. Many have read *Confessions* twice, three times, and more. I am grateful that it continues to resonate with readers.

Whirlwind was published in 2018, and since then, readers have frequently asked when the next book would be out. I hope *Flashpoint* meets your expectations. And yes, I'm already working on the next book.

I love to read books that are so enjoyable that I slow down near the end because I don't want the pleasure to end. As a writer, I try to give readers that same joy.

ABOUT THE AUTHOR

Charlie Spillers is the author of *Confessions of an Undercover Agent: Adventures, Close Calls, and the Toll of a Double Life*, and *Whirlwind: A Frank Marsh Novel*. He is a former undercover agent, Mississippi Bureau of Narcotics Regional Commander, Baton Rouge Police Officer, career federal prosecutor, U.S. Department of Justice Attaché for Iraq, adjunct professor at the University of Mississippi, and combat Marine.

His gripping memoir, *Confessions of an Undercover Agent*, published by the University Press of Mississippi, describes his daring exploits and narrow escapes during a decade of undercover crime-fighting. Playing different roles, he infiltrated burglary and safecracking rings, drug trafficking groups, Dixie Mafia auto-theft rings, and Mafia-linked drug smuggling operations.

Transitioning into a distinguished career as a federal prosecutor, he tackled major drug trafficking organizations, violent street gangs, corruption, and white-collar crime. He volunteered for three tours in Iraq for the Department of Justice, serving as an attorney-advisor to the Iraq court that tried Saddam Hussein and other regime leaders.

During his final tour, Mr. Spillers served as the U.S. Department of Justice Attaché for Iraq. He examined chemical warfare samples in Belgium, collaborated with the British government on a war crimes case in the High Court of England and Wales, and worked on a notorious Hezbollah commander who orchestrated attacks against American and British forces in Iraq. His work related to Iraq was recognized by the FBI Director, the Italian Embassy, the British Ambassador, and Britain's Minister of State for the Armed Forces. These thrilling international experiences drive his Frank Marsh novels.

www.ingramcontent.com/pod-product-compliance
Lightning Source LLC
Chambersburg PA
CBHW050557190726
48283CB00007B/2174